THE
SILK
ROAD

MARK LEGGATT

The Silk Road
Mark Leggatt

Published by:
Fledgling Press Ltd,
1 Milton Road West,
Edinburgh,
EH15 1LA

www.fledglingpress.co.uk

ISBN 9781912280117

Printed and bound by:
MBM Print SCS Ltd, Glasgow

FSC
www.fsc.org

MIX
Paper from
responsible sources
FSC® C117931

To Kirsty B.
For stealing her name.

CHAPTER 1

A faint shadow on the stone showed where the crucifix had been. He turned his back to the bare altar and brought up his hand to his chest, then touched the butt of the pistol in the holster, next to his heart. The door to the church, like all the other doors in the village, lay wide open.

To his right, the stone staircase cut into the mountain that made up the east wall, twisting steeply up to the bell tower. The rough-hewn steps were bowed and smooth after a thousand years of worshippers, though they had long gone.

The bell tower would give the best vantage point. He peered over his shoulder to make sure the exit was clear. If he was trapped in the tower, he was a dead man. Keeping to the wall, he shoved his way past the crumbling remains of the wooden pews, then edged towards the door. He pulled the pistol from the holster and knelt just inside the doorway, then glanced down the street. It was clear, but he knew they were close.

He sat back and wiped the sweat from his forehead. His hands stung where the rocks had cut into his flesh during the climb. He took another look. The church was at the end of the street, the highest part of the village. To his left, the road wound past the open doors of the houses that had survived destruction, then dropped suddenly at the end, down into the valley, hidden by the bushes and stunted trees clinging to the mountainside. He wondered how many centuries it had been since the villagers had left. Scattered between the empty houses lay piles of rubble, shattered roof tiles and exposed, crumbling timbers, in a graveyard of buildings that had succumbed to the earthquakes. He checked the street again, then pinpointed the alley that led to the cliff on the south side where he had entered the village. The treacherous climb up the south face had been the only way to follow the suspects without being seen. One road to the top of the mountain and the same road down. He would have been spotted in minutes. And he'd be dead.

Halfway down the street, he saw faint tire tracks curving around a low, leaf-filled water trough. A gouge in the earth led to the edge of wide wooden doors. Above them, just below the pointed roof, a weathered beam jutted out, the remains of a hoist to a hay loft.

He turned away, and leaned back against the wall, feeling the dust stick to his sweat-soaked t-shirt. The stable doors seemed to be the only ones closed in the entire village. They must be in there. He wiped his wet hands on his jeans then pulled back the slide on the pistol and chambered a round. He stood, his leg muscles tight from the climb, then stepped out into the road.

The stable doors swung open. He ducked back into the doorway of the church and watched the two men each drag a wheeled suitcase down the street. One walked like a soldier, head high, and the other, a fat, squat guy, took quick steps to keep up. They turned and disappeared down an alley towards the village square. The suitcases left a track in the dust behind them. They looked heavy.

He stood for a moment, then edged out of the doorway, his gun raised, keeping his back against the wall of the church. He listened to the rumbling wheels of the suitcases become fainter. Mr. Pilgrim had told him there were two suspects. He had seen two men in the BMW as it climbed towards the village and two men had come from the stables. He glanced left and right, his heart thumping. They weren't here for a vacation. He ran over to the stable door and ducked inside, then brought up the pistol.

Out of the glare of the Tuscan sun, the sweat cooled on his skin. In the center of the stable stood the BMW, thick with dust and grime from the drive through the endless mountain tracks. He could hear the engine ticking as it cooled. He made to reach for the door handle, then noticed the cloth rags on the floor and the lines through the dust caked onto the windows and doors. They had wiped their fingerprints. He stepped back, lowering the pistol. If the men were leaving the car behind, how were they going to get out of the village with two heavy suitcases and one road down to the valley? Mr. Pilgrim had said the CIA were interested in the two men, but he had no idea why. Yeah, he thought, you and me both, buddy.

He ran into the sunlight and sprinted towards the church. There had to be another way down the mountain.

Dust from the church floor flew up as he ran to the foot of the bell tower. Plaster flaked off the wall when he stuck out a hand to steady himself up the steep, winding steps, and stopped at the top, just before he placed a foot on the rotting floorboards.

The bell had long gone, and shafts of sunlight shone through the wooden slats of the louvered windows. The wood was grey and twisted, swollen with winter rains, then baked dry in the summer.

I'm missing something, he thought. Why an Italian ghost town? He shuffled around the edge of the tower, the paper-dry wood creaking under his feet. The village commanded a view across the low, wide valley to the north, and the forested plain he had come through from the south. He peered through the slats towards the north, down to an expanse of green fields, and a river cutting through the valley hemmed in by steep hills. He watched the white flecks of the water tumbling across the rocks. The thick, hot air in the tower caught in his throat and he dried the wet butt of the pistol on his t-shirt.

Something doesn't add up, he thought. They had cleaned the car of prints. They weren't going to drive out of here. Why would they dump the car?

He gazed over the jumble of low rooftops. The two men were nowhere to be seen. Nor their suitcases. He turned towards the village square overlooking the valley, hidden from the road behind the houses, and bordered with a low wall at the edge of the drop down the north side of the mountain. In the center, below a broken wooden roof, lay a wide stone trough, filled with dry leaves, where the villagers had once washed their clothes. For a moment, he wondered how they had managed to get water up so high, then realized it must have been the hard way. He looked down the valley to the river. The only things up here are goats or tomatoes, he thought. No wonder they emigrated. Like so many before them, away from the feudal landowners and crushing poverty. Along the steep hills bordering the valley he saw more abandoned homes, some no more than a scatter of rocks down the hillside. One famine, one earthquake too many, and they had left in their thousands, down to the sea, and across the Atlantic to the promised land.

Shards of sunlight flashed on the river coursing through the valley. If villagers had carried water up the mountain, he knew there had to be a path down to the river. The east side of the village square was bordered by sheer rock. He peered down to the bottom of the bell tower, hard against the rocks on the west side, but the trees blocked his view. If there was a path, it had to be there, somewhere in the trees, and down through the thick forest to the valley.

The sound of a door creaking open made him twist his head towards the village square. He pulled out his phone and brought up the map, then traced the blue line of the river, before it ended abruptly. That's not right, he thought. Rivers don't suddenly stop. He expanded the screen and saw a shaded area to the west. He looked up, but the area on the map was hidden behind the forest on the west side of the hill. He switched to satellite view, and the whole area was blurred out on the screen. That's got to be military, he thought. Is that why they're here? To set up a spy station? On the map, he saw several arrow-straight tracks at each end disappear into the blurred area. He grinned when he realized it was an airport. He tried to look west, but it was hidden behind the forest.

Now it's making sense, he thought. That's why the CIA and Mr. Pilgrim are following these two goons. If they were spying on a CIA airport in the middle of no place, then they were gonna get their asses kicked all the way back to Rome. No wonder they needed an escape route. The CIA wouldn't be happy about their black ops flights being monitored. Italy made for a perfect stopping point to the Middle East. He expanded the map, trying to gauge the size. He realized it was a long runway. Too long for private jets full of terrorists with a bag on their heads being invited back for coffee and a chat. But long enough for a bomber. He peered down to the village square. If it was a secret site for stealth bombers, then Iran would be very interested. And the Russians.

From the corner of his eye, he saw the two men enter the village square, dragging their suitcases behind them. He looked at his phone. Mr. Pilgrim would be very interested. Then Langley could send some goons to clean up. They probably had a unit at the airport. He almost laughed out loud at the thought of phoning the CIA and telling them himself. That's one call he couldn't make. Somewhere in Langley, a team of technicians would be crouched around computer screens, dedicated to only one thing. Finding him. And if that ever happened, a world of shit would descend, and the only thing left would be his lifeless body. Treason and murder tended to shorten your life span, especially where the CIA were concerned. When you blow the whistle on a CIA black op to buy Afghan oil using the lives of US servicemen, then watch it unravel live on CNN while you stick a bullet in the Afghan Ambassador's head, they tend to get a bit pissy. They tend to dedicate a whole team to making sure your next breath is your last. Though if the desk-bound bastards in Langley knew where he was, they might not bother sending anyone. They'd probably napalm the whole goddam mountain just to make sure he was dead. Then they'd carpet-bomb Tuscany just to be absolutely sure. He could imagine them whooping with delight when they found the charred corpse of Connor Montrose. "Yeah," he muttered, "but not today, bitches."

The two men placed their suitcases against the stone water trough and stood before the low wall, looking down to the valley.

Montrose shook his head and laid his pistol on the window ledge. If they were going to set up a spy station, they should have used one of the houses, not the village square. Anything they set up there would stick out like a bulldog's balls.

A low rumble came from the West. He looked up then realized it was coming from the valley. The rumble echoed around the hills, then grew to the roar of aircraft engines.

In the village square, the fat guy pulled out a phone and jammed it to his ear.

Low in the valley, a USAF C-130 transport plane emerged, climbing slowly into the air, its engines roaring under full load.

The fat guy dropped his phone and pointed to the valley.

A cold shock stabbed through Montrose's spine when it dawned on him. They didn't care if they were seen. They didn't give a shit.

The fat guy laid his suitcase down and popped the locks, then lifted out two green cylinders from the foam packing. He laid them carefully on the ground and slotted them together before twisting off the end to reveal a red cap. The other man had his suitcase open; he lifted a black mechanism onto his shoulder and faced the valley. The fat guy stood behind him and fitted the cylinder onto the top of the mechanism.

"Holy shit," said Montrose. "That's a fucking missile."

"We have company."

The Director leaned over the operator's shoulder towards the video screen. The village street was empty. "Where?"

"One man. With a gun. He ran into the church."

The Director stood up and cleared his throat, ignoring the other board members gathered around the wide table. It was unfortunate to have an incident so soon into the plan. "Only one?"

"We're checking all the footage. There's no trace of anyone else."

"And our friends from the CIA?"

"We have another drone monitoring the approach road to the valley, and the village. They are still in convoy. About five minutes from arrival. They don't seem in a hurry."

The Director smiled. "No hurry? That will change." He heard the low voices of the other directors behind him. He knew he couldn't show any concern. "Lift the first drone higher. I want a view of the village square. But before you do, show the view from the valley drone."

The operator swapped the screens to show a line of SUVs negotiating the twisting roads through the wooded valley and the climb up to the village.

"Inform our two operatives about the man in the church. I'm sure it will focus their minds on the task in hand. That is all." He ignored the voices at the table, then placed his hands behind his back and strolled to the window, gazing out over the industrial estate, and across the forest canopy to the spires of Dresden. The British bombers must have seen the same sight, he thought, but at night, when the fires would consume the city. "Gentlemen, the operation will continue as planned."

CHAPTER 2

Montrose tried to shove the muzzle of the pistol between the narrow wooden slats covering the window in the bell tower but couldn't twist his hand to get a straight shot. Floorboards cracked as he ran towards the steps and threw himself down, thumping his shoulder into the wall to keep upright. He vaulted the broken pews and ran into the street. Between the houses and deserted alleys he could see the blue sky of the valley to the north and hear the C-130 as it rose into the sky. He scrambled over a pile of rubble and saw the edge of the village square. A house to the right was still standing and he ran through the twisted doorway, across the earth floor and jammed his gun out of the broken window frame.

The tall man stood still, the missile launcher on his shoulders. The C-130 climbed higher.

Montrose rested his hand on the wooden frame, blew out a breath then squeezed the trigger.

The tall man fell to his knees. The fat guy spun around holding a machine pistol and fired towards the house.

Bullets tore through the thin mud and plaster wall and Montrose threw himself to the floor. Above him, sunlight speared through ragged bullet holes and the swirling dust. Another burst blew over his head and he forced his face onto the floor. He scrambled through the door on his knees and crouched behind a low wall. The fat guy would be covering either side of the house, waiting for him to raise his head. Only an idiot would try to fire from the same position. The cloud of dust obscured him as he crawled back into the house. He peered out the window and saw the tall man lying motionless on the ground, a pool of blood spreading around him.

The fat guy was facing the valley. He widened his stance, then lifted the missile onto his shoulder.

Montrose snatched at the trigger, firing off four rounds and caught him in the leg and arm.

The fat guy toppled backwards and a searing jet of orange flame burst across the square as the missile launched into the air, streaking away from the valley and back over the roofs of the village.

Holding his pistol level, Montrose watched the C-130 as it rose into the sky. "You missed, asshole!"

The fat guy clutched his leg and rolled sideways behind the stone water trough. Montrose reckoned he wasn't going anywhere and ran back through the door and into the street, listening for an explosion far behind him. Dust stuck to the sweat on his face and he looked up into the sky and watched the missile continue south, then lift gracefully into the air and curve north in a wide arc, back towards the village. His mouth dropped open. "No!"

A thin stream of smoke traced its path high over his head, and down to the valley. He ran between the houses to the village square and saw the C-130 rising between the hills, before the nose lifted sharply and the engines screamed. A shower of flares erupted from the belly of the plane, their blinding lights piercing his vision, and clouds of silver chaff blew out from the wings, sunlight glinting on a million tiny strips of aluminum in a shimmering cloud as the plane weaved left and right.

The missile speared through the cloud of chaff and flares and exploded just below the starboard wing. The C-130 flipped left and seemed to hang in the air before a fireball erupted from its ruptured fuel tanks. It rolled over and began to fall from the sky, tumbling backwards towards the valley floor, then slammed into the ground. A mushroom cloud of black smoke spewed out across the valley then slowly lifted, drifting over the hilltops and revealing the burning wreckage strewn across the green fields.

The Director stood up, nodding slowly as he watched the screen. The whole valley floor seemed to be ablaze. "Turn back to the village."

The operator rotated a joystick and the view on the screen spun around and showed the village square. One man lay spread-eagled in a pool of blood. Another crouched below the water trough, ripping cloth from his shirt and bandaging his leg.

"Where is our visitor?"

The screen moved to show a man standing between the ruined houses, staring up into the sky.

"Can he see us?"

"It is unlikely, sir," replied the operator.

A hand slammed on the boardroom table behind them. "Kill him!"

The Director didn't turn around, but squeezed his lips tight, then relaxed and spoke slowly. "All in good time. Patience is what is required here."

"He nearly ruined the entire operation! If he captures our operative, then…"

The Director turned and walked towards them. "Then what? Do you think I have not planned for this eventuality? Every situation provides an opportunity. It is wisdom to know when to seize that opportunity, and when to let it slip." He faced the operator. "Is the drone armed?"

"Yes, Director."

"Good." He pointed to a man on the screen. "Don't let him out of your sight."

"Tracking enabled."

From the cover of a ruined house, Montrose saw the fat guy scramble from behind the water trough, weaving unsteadily on his injured leg, heading for the rocks and trees below the church. The smell of burning aircraft fuel drifted up towards the village. "You bastard!" He fired two rounds then took off after him. "Stop!" He fired off another round at the man's feet.

The fat guy stumbled and fell to the ground, clutching his leg.

"Don't move!" Montrose advanced with the gun pointing at the fat guy's head.

He held on tight to his wound and pushed himself slowly to his feet.

"On your knees!"

He smiled. "No."

Montrose stood before the man and thrust the gun against his head. "Get on your knees. Do it now."

The fat guy closed his eyes for a moment, then turned slowly to look down at the valley. "Go to hell."

"Listen to me, you want to go and meet your maker, that's fine by me."

The fat guy gave a sideways glance at Montrose's gun. "I'm impressed you got here so quickly."

Montrose saw blood spill out through the man's fingers and pool into the dust. He shifted his stance and pointed the gun at the man's chest. "What the hell you talking about?"

The fat guy thrust his chin towards the village. "Your friends from the CIA. I hope they give you a medal for shooting my partner." Then he flicked his eyes at the valley. "Or maybe not, eh?" He began to laugh, and using his free hand to shield his eyes, he looked up at the sky.

"Don't move." Montrose could hear car engines and the squeal of tires from the mountain road to the village. "The CIA?" If they find me here, he thought, I'm a dead man.

The fat guy shifted his weight and stepped nearer the trees. "Tell them I said hello. If you're still alive, which I seriously doubt."

"You stay right there or I'll empty this gun into your head."

"Only one of us is going to leave this mountain alive." He stopped, resting his wounded leg, and looked up to the sky. "You want to make a guess who that's going to be?"

*

"Get closer, I want to see his face." The Director leaned forward on the desk and dipped his head towards the screen.

The operator twisted the joystick. The view from the drone focused on the two men.

"So, who's our new friend?" said the Director.

The operator checked a laptop to his right. "Face recognition is running. Nearly complete."

"Is the weapon armed?"

"Yes, sir." The laptop screen flashed and a name appeared.

"Connor Montrose?" said the Director. "I've never heard of him."

The operator scrolled through the text. "Ex-CIA."

The Director heard chairs being pushed back from the boardroom table, and a voice behind him. "Ex-CIA? Is he a private contractor?"

The operator shook his head. "According to the files he's a wanted man."

The Director cleared his throat to stop his voice from shaking. "Wanted by whom?"

"The CIA, FBI, DGSE, the Germans and quite a few others. Everybody, it seems."

A voice boomed behind him. "This is unacceptable! This was not part of your plan, Director!"

The Director fixed his gaze on the man but spoke to the operator. "And where are the CIA?"

The operator flicked through the screens. "Nearly at the village. They're in a hurry now."

"Of course they are." He slowly turned, then lifted a hand and placed a finger on the screen. "Kill him."

CHAPTER 3

Blood spattered high up the sides of the church and the fat guy dropped to the ground, his chest a gaping, ragged hole. Behind him lay shattered rock where the high caliber round had burst through the man's body and slammed into the ground.

Montrose felt the spray of blood start to trickle down his face. He began to look up to the sky, then scrambled for the cover of the forest, his feet slipping on blood and dust. In front of him, leading into the trees, he could see a narrow furrow in the ground where generations of footsteps had worn away the rock. He sprinted for cover and ducked under the low branches.

The furrow continued for a few feet, then the ground became covered in lichen and leaf litter and he could barely pick it out. He scrambled his way down the mountainside, grabbing branches to steady his descent as he ran. He saw the path level out in front of him, then turn sharply and drop out of sight. Through the trees, he could see the path continue twenty feet below. Leaping to the side, he pushed branches from his face and slid down the crumbling earth, throwing his hands up just before he slammed into a tree. The breath was knocked out of his chest, and he tumbled forward, branches tearing at his face as he fell onto the path. In his mind, he could still see the fat guy's body explode in a cloud of blood and he knew the shot had come from above. That's why he was looking up, thought Montrose. An armed drone.

He knew if the drone was fitted with an infra-red camera, he would light up on the screen like a roman candle. He scrambled to his feet and kept low. The path weaved between the trees but the ground started to flatten and the foliage and bushes became thicker as he approached the valley. Below the path lay a steep slope of grass and low bushes that dropped down to an edge. He jumped down the slope, holding his arms out for balance. His feet shot out from under him and he slipped on his ass, heading straight for a tree. He brought up both legs and took the blow feet first, pushing himself to the side. Wrapping his arms around his head, he tumbled through the bushes until he dropped off a ledge and slammed into the path.

He lay on his back, the sky and tree tops swimming around his vision, then rolled onto his knees. He could hear the river. That was the way out. The air was thick with the stench of burning aircraft fuel. He got to his feet and could see fast-moving water through the trees. On the far side, burning wreckage lay scattered across the fields.

He stopped at the tree line and ripped out a low bush and gathered up some fallen branches, held to them to his chest and ran for the river.

"Stop!"

Montrose slid to a halt.

"Drop the foliage, old boy. You aren't Robin of Sherwood, you know."

He let the branches slip from his fingers. He turned to see a man emerge from the trees, holding a gun. Montrose glanced back at the water, then up at the sky.

"Now, just who might you be, my friend. And what's the hurry?" The man flicked his gun towards the wreckage across the river. "Something to do with a plane crash?"

Montrose held out his hands. The British accent had caught him by surprise. "Hey, fella, that's got nothing to do with me. I tried to stop them but…"

"An American, eh? I'm intrigued."

"I was following someone. One of the bastards that did that, I think he went…"

"Of course, you were, old boy," he smiled, "of course you were. Dressed as bloody Robin Hood."

"Listen, there's an armed drone up there, and the CIA are right behind me, so why don't we…?"

The Brit pointed his gun at Montrose's head. "I'm sure they are. And you're running through the forest with your arse on fire." He dropped the gun towards Montrose's jeans. "Lose the hardware. Slowly. Don't make me nervous."

Montrose pulled the pistol from his pocket with two fingers.

"Drop it."

He let it fall to the ground.

"Good lad. Kick it over here."

He pushed it over with the toe of his boot.

The man kept his gun on Montrose as he bent down and picked up the pistol. "Switch your phone off."

"Look nobody is going to…"

"It's not for you, it's for me. Now, listen very carefully." He brought out a pair of field glasses from his pocket. "I saw the two men at the edge of the village square with the missile. One with a machine pistol. And I heard the firefight." The Brit ejected the magazine from Montrose's gun, cleared the breech then sniffed the barrel. "One man with an automatic weapon and the other with a pistol, by the sound of it. So, I am assuming that you tried to stop the attack." He pulled back his arm and threw the magazine in a high arc towards the river. "Don't make me regret that assumption." He lifted his own gun and pointed it behind him.

Montrose saw the tailgate of a Range Rover sticking out from the trees.

"Get in the trunk."

He didn't move.

"If I had wanted to shoot you, I'd have done it by now." The Brit pointed his gun at Montrose's feet then flicked back the barrel and shoved it into his pocket. "Move." The Brit turned away, then looked over his shoulder as he made for the Range Rover. "And one piece of advice: Hold on tight."

Montrose lifted the corner of the blanket and glimpsed the sun from the top of the tailgate window before it was blacked out by a passing truck. He closed his eyes and pictured the road on a map with the sun above and worked out they were heading south. He felt the speed drop and looked again, but all he could see was sky. He rubbed his head where it had taken a hit on the way out of the valley. The Brit seemed to have taken every mountain track in

Tuscany before the road levelled and smoothed out, then picked up speed as it hit the autostrada.

The sound of emergency vehicles and screaming sirens had punctuated the whole journey. The Range Rover slowed again and moved down a fast incline, then came almost to a halt. Traffic fumes drifted into the trunk. Montrose checked his watch. It was too soon to have reached Rome, so they must be in Florence. And Mr. Pilgrim would be waiting, even though this wasn't the way he had planned to arrive. He felt the phone in his pocket but ignored the temptation to switch it on and check the map.

Car horns blasted around them and the Range Rover took off fast, throwing him sideways. When he lifted the blanket he could only see the rooftops of terraced buildings. The Range Rover came to a sudden halt and Montrose pictured a typical Italian scene; drivers gridlocked at a four-way, squeezing through, blasting their horns. He fumbled around for the interior emergency tailgate release. There was nothing. He lifted the blanket to look and realized it wasn't fitted on European trucks. He lay back again. The headrests made climbing over onto the rear seats impossible. He was trapped. He searched around for a toolkit to use as a weapon, but the trunk was bare. The Range Rover slowed once more, then turned a sharp left down a steep descent. The traffic noise drifted away and Montrose peeked out. Everything was dark. Here we go, he thought. MI5 reception committee. And I bet they won't be offering me a cup of tea.

CHAPTER 4

He heard the driver's door open and felt the suspension rise as the Brit got out. A moment later, the tailgate rose and Montrose lifted the blanket and looked out to a dimly lit underground garage. In front, several battered Fiats were parked in a line, each with a fading apartment number stenciled on the dusty concrete floor.

The Brit stepped back with Montrose's gun in his hand. He grinned and spun it around on his finger, then offered the pistol grip to Montrose. "Welcome to Florence, old boy. Sorry there wasn't much room for you in there, but you know, safety first and all that jazz."

Montrose took the gun. "Yeah." He swung his legs around and sat on the tailgate.

"And sorry about the roads too, I had to take a rather unorthodox route out of the mountains."

Montrose got to his feet and the Brit closed the tailgate.

"Well, Mr. Montrose, that was all rather exciting. Damn shame about that plane. Poor buggers. But right now, I need a drink. This way." He turned towards the far wall of the garage and gestured at the latticed door of a tiny elevator.

Montrose walked beside him. "How do you know my name?"

"I heard a little chatter on the grapevine. Seems everybody wants to talk to you. And not for a pleasant conversation, I think."

"Yeah, well, I'm not flavor of the month right now."

"Indeed. Your suitors seem to consist of the entire CIA, FBI, NSA and other acronyms that even I hadn't heard of. Just about everyone, it seems."

I don't need reminding, thought Montrose.

The Brit stood in front of the elevator door, grabbed the handle and hauled it back hard. The metal lattice squealed and rattled as it folded to the side.

Montrose looked into the cramped space, the deep dent in the floor and the cracked wood lining the sides. One fat guy, he thought, and this would be full.

The Brit stepped in. "This won't take long. Which is just as well, because I hate the bloody thing."

Montrose edged in alongside him.

The Brit squeezed past and grabbed the cage door handle, taking several attempts to slam it shut. "This stupid door will be the death of me."

"That's the door?" Montrose looked out through the metal lattice towards the underground car park. The Range Rover stood gleaming beside several tiny, battered Fiats.

"Going up!" The Brit jabbed a button and the elevator lurched to the side, then rattled upwards. "First floor, haberdashery and lingerie."

Through the lattice, Montrose watched the car park disappear below his feet. Grinding noises came from all sides as the lift housing scraped the elevator shaft.

"I'd take the stairs, but it means walking across the lobby. And I'm not in the mood for a conversation with the concierge. Stand behind me. He's a nosey bastard and I don't want him to see me taking strange men to my apartment."

Montrose shuffled past the Brit and stood back hard against the wall; he could feel it rolling against the elevator shaft. The lift scraped past the ground floor, and he saw a marble-lined lobby with a uniformed concierge at a desk. The Brit moved forward and raised a hand to the man as the elevator rattled upwards, past two more floors showing empty hallways. It slammed to a halt at the third floor.

The Brit grabbed the handle with both hands and hauled the door back. It stuck halfway open, and he gave the lattice metalwork a hefty kick and shoved it into the wall. He jumped out. "Someday that bloody thing is going to cut me in half."

Montrose stepped out and the Brit tugged the door shut. "Nineteenth century technology. Deadlier than the plague and lasts just as long." He turned and pointed down the corridor. "This way."

The walls of the corridor were painted in faded, classical frescos. "Beautiful, aren't they? Typical Florence. Over-the-top decoration at the slightest opportunity and painted in a heady cocktail of arsenic and lead. I'm surprised anybody makes it out of their teens in this country." The Brit marched down the hallway towards a door at the end.

Montrose's rubber-soled boots squeaked on the marble floor.

The Brit stopped and pulled out a blackened key.

The door opened onto a wide, sunlit salon. Montrose stood in the doorway, looking up to the high wooden beams of the roof and tall windows facing out onto a river.

The Brit checked the corridor then closed the door. "I have inquisitive neighbors. They think I'm a visiting art professor. Frankly, I couldn't tell Canaletto from cannelloni, but there we are." He weaved around various pieces of period furniture, wood gleaming and cloth and gilt faded and worn. He stood in front of an ancient bureau and opened the door to reveal a bar which seemed to be solely stocked with bottles of gin. The Brit held up a tall glass. "G&T?"

"Why not."

The Brit grabbed a handful of ice cubes from a refrigerated bucket, then cut through a lime and dropped a slice into each glass. "No lemons, I'm afraid, I haven't gone completely native."

"I don't give a shit as long as it's strong enough to kill a horse."

The Brit splashed some tonic into the glass and offered the drink to Montrose.

The cold gin hit home and he felt the rush of alcohol and the sharp tang of juniper in his throat.

The Brit stood before him, holding out a hand. "Linden's the name. George Linden."

Montrose took his hand. "MI5?"

Linden smiled. "Good Lord, no. They are purely internal to the sceptered isle and are generally concerned with running around after whatever flavor of religious or political fanatics are trying to blow up our civilians this week." He sipped his drink. "MI6 deal with anything outside our borders, Mr. Montrose."

"Understood. My name, how did you know?"

"Like, I said, a little bird told me." Linden smiled and tapped his nose.

"Listen, I don't want to get all formal here, but let's see some ID."

Linden laughed. "My dear boy, I'm not the mystery man here! But, if it makes you feel more at home, why not." Linden pulled out an ID card. "And you?"

"Not even a swimming certificate."

"Quite right too. One can't be too careful. And so, Mr. Montrose, to business." Linden pointed to the door. "That door is unlocked. I'm currently the only man in MI6 that knows you are in Florence. In fact, other than your own organization, I'll bet I'm the only man on the planet who knows you are in Italy, or that you were anywhere near the earlier unfortunate incident."

"Good. Your point?"

Linden sipped his drink. "The point I am making is that I want to find the bastards behind what happened today. And I'm prepared to take extraordinary steps, and extraordinary risks to make that happen. Which is why I returned your weapon."

Montrose said nothing.

"I pride myself on being a good judge of character. Let's hope that is not a conceit."

"So, what do you want from me?

"Well, I hope that we share the same objective."

"If you mean kill the assholes that were behind that attack and kick over any rocks to crush the vermin beneath, then we do."

"Yes, quite. You Americans certainly have a marvelous way with words."

Montrose took another drink. "Yeah, listen, I'm familiar with British insults, so if you…"

"No offense intended, old boy, I'm just a little less Hollywood in my stating of the obvious. Though I can quote Shakespeare that would keep you awake at night." He pointed to the door again. "Open, remember? I am not your jailer, Montrose. I want to find out who did this, and I will kill any bastard that gets in my way." Linden downed the remains of the gin. "And that includes the CIA."

Montrose fixed his eyes on Linden and took another drink. He let an ice cube drop onto his tongue, rolled it around his mouth then spat it back in the glass. "Just what do you mean by that?"

Linden walked to the window, looking out over the river as he talked. "I know very little of your history, Mr. Montrose, but I know who you are. What I don't know is why you were in that village today. I am assuming that you were aware of the impending attack, and that you tried to stop it."

"You got that right. Forget the CIA for a moment. I've got a question for you."

Linden rattled the ice in his glass. "Fire away, old boy."

"In the village, you saw me shoot the first guy, right?"

"From my vantage point, I saw him shot. Then when you appeared in somewhat of a hurry, I assumed it was you."

"Then how did you know I wasn't CIA? Or the second terrorist?"

Linden waved a hand in the air. "Elementary, my dear Montrose. I had a photograph of the two men that the CIA were following. And you are clearly not one of them. And since you were about to jump in the river dressed as Robin, Earl of Locksley, to flee the scene, I assumed you were not CIA either."

"So, what were you doing there?"

"Well, you may have been following those two men, but I was following the CIA. I was very interested to see why they had allocated a significant amount of resource at short notice to tracking two men. And I'm not stupid enough to drive behind a rather large CIA convoy up a dead-end road to the top of a mountain. I drove around to the north to see what was going on. When I heard the gunfire, I thought the CIA had arrived early to give a touch of the old *'shock and awe'*. But it wasn't the CIA, was it? It was you. I checked my tracker and the CIA hadn't arrived yet. And I knew they would be loaded up to the gunwales with automatic weapons. Much like the general population of the United States, to be fair, but I digress. All I saw was one of the two men with a machine pistol and heard someone taking pot-shots with a handgun. Not the full-on gunfight at the OK Corral I was expecting. Then you come rattling down the hill. Which brought me to a question. Why would you be running? Surely the CIA would have been delighted with your brave, if somewhat fruitless efforts?"

Montrose shook his head. "That's my business."

"I'm sure, and I don't expect you to tell me, but if it makes you feel better then get it off your chest. I'm all ears. I'm sure it'll do you the power of good."

Montrose grinned. "Not gonna happen."

"I understand. I have no idea what agency you are with, though if you dropped those two bastards in the village, then you're alright by me." He raised his empty glass.

"Sure. So why were you following the CIA?"

"Well, we knew they were up to something and they had cut us out the loop. We don't like it when that happens. And when it does, we know they're up to no good. And a question for you, Mr. Montrose. I assume you also followed those two men to the top of the mountain. Did you know what they intended?"

Montrose shook his head. "I had no idea. And neither did the CIA."

Linden looked out towards the river. "You think so?"

"What?"

Linden let out a bitter laugh. "Perhaps my cynicism is surprising, but given the history of the CIA, it really shouldn't be."

Montrose said nothing.

"And in the absence of a convincing rebuttal from your good self, I'm sure you understand exactly what I'm saying."

"Hey, listen fella…"

"Let me be absolutely clear. I believe we want the same thing. To find out who is responsible for that murderous atrocity in the valley and stop them. Including anyone who is assisting them. And I mean anyone. That includes the CIA." He placed his glass down on a table. "This is not a safe house, Mr. Montrose. It is not known to MI6 and therefore not known to the CIA. This is my personal bolthole. I'm working off the grid on this. Contact with London is at a minimum. We have too many CIA moles in MI6 and whatever Langley are up to, they are keeping their cards close to their chest. MI6 need to know what is going on and not through secondhand reports from Langley. We have our own informant. They told us an attack was imminent and that the CIA would stop it. That's all. But the CIA didn't stop it, did they? My job is to find out…" He waved a hand in the air, "Why didn't they stop the attack?"

"What the hell are you talking about? We just lost a plane!"

"I'm sure you can work it out for yourself, Mr. Montrose, you're not stupid."

"Listen, you are way off the mark on…"

Linden fastened a button on his suit and straightened his tie. "I have to go. As I mentioned, this is not a jail. There is a spare key in the table by the door. If I'm going to find out the truth, I'm going to need all the help I can get. But if I feel that my trust is unfounded, then I will disappear faster than snow in the Sahara." He walked over to a desk by the window and pulled open a drawer, then held up a cell phone. "This has my number on it. It has never been used. If you need me or you want to share information, then call me. Right now, I have to make some form of report back to London. I will not be mentioning the fact that I've made your acquaintance." He turned towards the door. "I don't expect you to be here when I get back, but I really think we should keep in touch." He stood in the open doorway. "We can help each other, Mr. Montrose." He closed the door behind him.

Montrose lifted the cell phone and switched it on. The ice in his glass chinked as he thumped it down on the table then strode over to the door. Only one number had come up in the address book. He switched the phone off then took the spare key from the table and pulled the door open. The corridor was empty.

He locked the door behind him and ran to the end of the corridor then turned down a polished staircase. He emerged into the lobby where the concierge stood up. Montrose held up a hand. "Buongiorno, fella." He ignored the stream of questions targeted at him and headed for the street.

Shielding his eyes from the sun he backed against the wall, away from the stream of pedestrians, and checked the street.

28

He took out the cell phone, switched it on and checked the single number in the address book, repeating it to himself several times, then headed down the street. To the right he passed an arcade of shops with an exit onto the street at the far end, bordering the river. He stopped and doubled back, then weaved through the shoppers milling around. Aromas of cheese and cured ham surrounded him. An old woman stepped in front of him, dragging a tattered shopping bag on wheels. He brushed past her and palmed the cell phone into her shopping bag, then headed for the sunlight.

He turned right and stood behind a newsstand, watching for any tails to leave the arcade. He glanced to his right and saw the Ponte Vecchio and the three wide arches stretched across the River Arno, below the haphazard jumble of three levels of medieval apartments built across the bridge. At the end, he spotted the tower.

Mr. Pilgrim would be waiting.

CHAPTER 5

The members of the board sat around the wide table, some perfectly still, others tapping ornate pens on old-fashioned paper blotters. A technician disconnected the monitoring equipment and bundled it on to a trolley.

The Director stood at the window, gazing across the forest canopy, his eyes fixed on the spires of Dresden. He knew they would all be looking at him. Waiting for his words.

He thought of the small workshop on the edge of the city, below street level, where his mother, an itinerant Dutch worker who had survived the bombings had met his father, a visiting US Army liaison officer. While the Director was still in her womb, his father had found a way to repatriate her to the Netherlands, then back to the US. He had grown up in the countryside around Harvard, but he never failed to be amused and fascinated by his place of conception. His love for history had led him to uncover the hidden horrors of the forests bordering Dresden, and when his internet business had expanded and required an international base away from the prying eyes of US regulations, he could think of no better place. The retreating communists of East Germany had left a vacuum of land ownership and disputed titles, but money talked, and he built his nondescript headquarters on the remnants of a Soviet Army transport base, and leased the land to his own foreign registered haulage firms, hidden behind a web of shell companies. Then, he could hide in plain sight.

The technician left with the last of his equipment and closed the door.

The Director turned to face the room. "Now, we may begin."

A fat man with a Dutch accent leaned over the table. "Who is he? This Montrose?"

Closing his eyes for a moment, the Director calmed himself. He would save his ire for later. "According to our files, he's ex-CIA. He was a whistleblower. And in his desire for revenge, he seems to have left a path of dead bodies across Europe. He is wanted for treason. But then, one man's traitor is another man's hero."

"I will come straight to the point, Director. I need proof that Connor Montrose is not a loose cannon and will not jeopardize this operation or threaten our investment."

The Director nodded. "Good. I want all your questions out in the open." The Director stood behind his own chair at the head of the table, his hands resting on its back. He had studied enough generals in his life to know how to enforce command and instill subordination. They would be allowed to ask questions. If they were not satisfied with the answers, then he would take a different course. An unmarked grave and an empty seat at the table could both be easily filled. "If you see this man as a threat or a risk to the successful conclusion of this very lucrative endeavor, then express that risk. What is it that you fear will happen?" The whole table turned towards the big man.

"It's obvious," he spluttered.

"Then you will have no difficulty sharing it."

He slammed a hand on the table. "Montrose is ex-CIA. He could go straight to them. Tell them everything."

The Director closed his eyes for a moment. "Tell them everything, you say. I appreciate your candor, but tell me, what exactly is *everything*?" The man stood open-mouthed and was about to speak when the Director continued. "You see, gentlemen, this is how I, and by extension, we, will control this endeavor. By clearly identifying risk and mitigating against it." He faced the man. "Please continue."

The big man sat back in his chair. "Montrose could go straight to the CIA and tell them everything he knows. He could have talked to the two men in the village. He witnessed them fire the missile. And what the hell was he doing there anyway?"

The Director began to walk slowly round the table. "We don't know exactly what he was doing there. But I think it is a fair assumption that he had become aware of the information that was leaked to the CIA regarding the two operatives. That, I suspect, is why he was there. And we can also assume that Montrose, like the CIA, did not know the contents of the suitcases, or the men's intent. Otherwise the CIA would have been waiting for them in the village. Or indeed, would have stopped them long before. Therefore, we have the CIA to blame for Montrose's intrusion on this endeavor, but as you all know, despite this local difficulty, it came to a successful conclusion."

"But… Montrose could tell them what he saw. And that he was there."

The Director shrugged. "You have the briefing notes in front of you. According to a CIA communiqué sent earlier this year, Montrose is suspected of being a psychopathic terrorist, and lately, a treasonous whistleblower. I think that unless Connor Montrose has a death wish, the CIA would be the last people he would talk to."

"But…"

"But let's say that he does. What would he say?"

"He could… He could tell them where he got the information on the attack."

"Perhaps, but remember, Montrose didn't know about the attack. We saw he tried to stop it. If he knew it was taking place he would have acted sooner. And what do we care where he got his information from?" The Director pointed around the table. "*We* are the original source of the information. We are the reason the CIA followed the two operatives to the village. The reason that the CIA knew, and by extension, Montrose, is because we told them." The Director stood up. "Montrose poses no present risk."

At the end of the table, an elderly man leaned his cane against his chair and bent over to flick through the pages in front of him. "Perhaps, Director, but it is clear that Montrose is a loose cannon. Impetuous and unpredictable. Those words are written right here. And judging by the spelling, this is a British report." He sat back, his bony hand grasping the stick, his knuckles showing through parchment-like skin. "He is out of control. A whistleblower. The kind that likes to talk. And he has a price on his head. He is a wanted man, and not only by the CIA. As far as I can see, he is wanted by every security agency in the West. Even the Iranians have been looking for him, but it seems they are content for the CIA to kill him when they get the chance. Montrose may not be running to the CIA, but we can be very sure that they will be searching high and low for Montrose, and if they find him, what else can he tell them? How can we be sure? You say that the information that led him to the village must have come from the CIA. Can we be one hundred percent sure?" He placed his hands flat on the papers. "My question is, why let him live? However small the chance, why take it?"

The Director said nothing, but stood for a moment, looking out over the forest, both hands clasped together as if in prayer.

"Director," said the old man, "you are a student of military history. This is not part of the operational plan. Kill him now."

Turning towards them, the Director walked slowly to his chair, then placed both hands on top, bowed his head and closed his eyes. He was an expert in military history, not a mere student. If he had thought that the board member's comments were in anyway a slight, then he would be dead within the hour. He opened his eyes, looking at each one of them in turn. "Do you take the time to study military history, gentlemen? You should. The logic and method of business is very much akin to that of war. Everything we have done, or are about to do, has in essence been done before. I remind you of the words of the philosopher, Jorge Agustín Nicolás Ruiz de Santayana y Borrás." He rolled the words off his tongue. *"Those who do not learn history are doomed to repeat it."*

He began a slow walk around the table, his hands clasped behind his back. "Study the great generals. Rommel, Zhukov, even back to Saladin. And not only their results, but their methods and approach to the fight. These are the men upon which our global history rests. We often need to go back generations to find the true leaders in global conflict, not that bumbling oaf Schwarzkopf. But not just the winners. Study Napoleon at Waterloo, or Von Paulus at Stalingrad. Learn their history, their decisions, their faults, and see you do not repeat them. Because the one thing that crops up time and time again is lost opportunity. In the words of the great Sun Tzu, in *The Art of War, 'in the midst of chaos, there is also opportunity'*. Napoleon should have committed his cavalry much earlier and dealt with the British infantry and artillery while he had the chance. That indecision destroyed an empire. Von Paulus should have ignored Hitler and retreated to his supply lines but spurning the opportunity cost him an entire army and defeat in the East. The skill of the great general is to see the opportunity and to seize it, no matter what it takes. And that, gentlemen, is what I intend to do. You see Montrose as a threat." He shook his head. "But you fail to see the opportunity. Ex-CIA? A wanted man? Suspected of terrorism? Gentlemen, I always plan for both fortune and misfortune. Connor Montrose is a gift from the god of war."

Director Napier stood before his office door, fumbling for his keys. He turned as two Marines in full dress uniform marched towards them down the narrow corridor. Napier pushed Faber to the side and let them through. "This is supposed to be a low-key CIA facility. Why do we have Marines running around like they're going to a cocktail party in West Point?"

"They're straight from the relief guard at the Embassy in Rome, sir," said Faber. "There are others on the way.

There was no time to get changed when orders came in from Langley to go to full operational mode."

Napier unlocked the door to his office. "Where is he? The technician?"

Faber followed him in and closed the door. "He should be here any moment, sir. He's one of my men. He knows to keep this tight."

There was a knock on the door. "Enter," said Napier.

A young soldier in fatigues entered the room.

Faber nodded to the soldier and gestured towards his boss. "Mr. Napier?" said the soldier.

"Yeah, you know who I am. Talk to me."

The technician held a sheaf of documents close to his chest. "It's Russian, sir."

"You sure?"

"No doubt. We examined the missile casing that was left at the village. The instructions in Cyrillic code had been removed, but not when you look at it under x-ray. Everything matches. We double-checked with the labs in Langley. We even spectrum analyzed the paint on the missile launcher. It fits the Khrunichev missile plant just outside Moscow."

Napier stared down at the floor. "That is all."

The technician stood for a moment then held out the documents. "You should read this, sir. I printed it off instead of sending it through the system. No one in the CIA has seen this except me."

Faber reached out and took the documents, and the soldier marched out of the door.

"Tell me," said Napier.

Faber flicked through the pages. "This is from our men at the scene. Confirmed USAF C-130 transport plane. Death toll is confirmed as five crew and ten medical staff heading for our NATO base in Turkey. The plane was loaded with medical aid and food for refugees. But they don't think that was the target."

"Yeah?"

"The Turkey aid flight was delayed by an hour. The flight ready to take off was a C-130 carrying over two hundred Rangers on their way back home from a combat zone."

"That was the target?"

"They're not sure. But it seems more likely. If they knew."

"If they knew?" Napier sat on his desk. "The soldiers and their families will have it all over Facebook. They can track civilian radar on the internet. It's not hard to find the movement of troops these days. So, who fired the missile?"

"Two men found dead at the scene. Gunshot wounds. Fingerprints establish that they fired the missile. They were the men we were tracking."

"But our team got there too late, yet they still end up dead."

"This report says that the two men had wiped down their car so they didn't plan on using it to escape. Our team found another way out of the village, a track leading off the mountain, down into the valley. We found a car well hidden, probably a means of escape."

"But they didn't escape. They ended up dead. So, who pulled the trigger?"

Faber turned over one of the documents. "Connor Montrose."

"Who?"

"It doesn't say. They tracked him by fingerprints in blood left at the scene. They checked the prints on the system and his name came up a 100% match. The technician tried to access his records, but it was blocked."

"You told me your guy had pretty high authority."

"He does. I made sure of it. Still a blank." He nodded to the laptop on Napier's desk. "Want me to try?"

"Later. What I want to know is how a C-130 that's just back from a combat zone, that has all the latest technology to combat missile attacks, that has pilots who get shot at on a daily basis, still manages to be taken out of the sky on the first shot?"

Faber rifled through the report. "The CIA team were on the road to the village and saw the missile pass straight over them, heading away from the valley. Then it changed direction back towards the plane. Eye witnesses at the airport says that the plane deployed all the flares and chaff, and we can be pretty sure they used all the latest jamming techniques. But the missile went straight through all the defenses. Which means it isn't heat-seeking, or someone just got very lucky, or very clever. But we've never seen this before. This is something new."

"If that's true, then there's no plane safe in the sky."

The phone rang on the desk and Faber grabbed it. "Director Napier's office." He listened for a moment, then held out the receiver. "It's Langley, sir."

"Speakerphone."

Faber hit a button and the voice came through the speaker.

"This is Director Campbell from Langley. You are aware of who I am?"

"Yes, sir," said Napier.

"A technician tried to access the online record of Connor Montrose. Why?"

"He has been identified as being present at the scene of the attack, sir. Two men dead, but no sign of Montrose."

"Napier, you may take it from me, that Montrose is a traitor to this country and a terrorist. I want you to find him, and I want no evidence left that Connor Montrose ever existed. Do not apprehend him, just shoot him on sight. Do I make myself clear?"

"Director Campbell, he may be crucial in finding out where…"

"You're not listening to me, Mr. Napier. Montrose is not part of your investigation. I have direct experience of Montrose, and you do not. I want you to find him, right now, and I want you to execute him as a traitor. Do not let him talk to anyone. Is that clear?"

Napier looked sideways at Faber, who held out his hands. "That is clear, Director Campbell."

"I have received an update on the progress of your team," said Campbell.

Napier turned to face Faber, who threw out his hands.

"When you have dealt with Montrose, Mr. Napier, the focus of your investigation is that a new type of Russian surface-to-air missile has just shot down an American service plane in the heart of NATO. I will take care of the political fallout, but you will find who carried out the attack. The Press have already been briefed that initial investigations indicate there was a technical issue with a plane on a NATO exercise in Italy. All the witnesses are service personnel at the airbase and will do what they are told. Now, listen to me. You may use any method, you will have access to every resource, and you may use my personal authority to find out who did this, but Montrose must be dealt with immediately. Get to work, Napier. Fast. We will be watching your progress with great interest. I expect updates every hour." The call ended.

Faber shook his head. "What the hell was that all about?"

"I have no idea, though I do know that Campbell is the biggest shit-weasel in Langley. If he wants Montrose dead, it's probably to cover his ass. And I want to know why."

"But we shoot him, no?"

"Shoot him in the legs. Then tape his mouth and bring him to me. I want to know what he was doing in that village. After that, Campbell can have his corpse."

CHAPTER 6

Dirty flecks of grey water burst around the wide stone supports below the arches. Montrose looked up to the three stories of medieval buildings that stretched across the bridge, some hanging over the water. A stone tower stood thirty feet above the roof on the south side of the bridge, its windows open wide. Montrose wondered if Pilgrim was watching, then ducked into a line of arches bordering the river and leading to the bridge. Cameras lined the route, fixed to buildings and old iron street lamps. He kept his eye on one as he approached, but it didn't move and he stopped at the corner to the bridge. He knew he was walking into a bottleneck. "Why here?" he muttered. "This is a crazy place for a safe house."

Crowds stood jammed together at the end of the bridge and he shoved his way past tightly-packed groups of teenagers with bulging daypacks, milling back and forth across the street, then backed into a doorway opposite the bridge.

One way in and one way out, he thought, or so it looks.

Check the secondary exit. Pilgrim said a courtyard. It should be right here. At least I'll know if I've got a tail. If I take them anywhere near the tower, the game is over.

To his right he spotted the entrance to a courtyard in between a cigar shop and a gelato vendor. He weaved past students, avoiding the ice creams in their hands, and into a wide space filled with tables crammed with tourists. He scanned every table but they all seemed to be full of families. At the far end of the courtyard was a small café and he kept his eye on his reflection in its window as he moved between the tables. Everyone ignored him. Next to the café was a door and he opened it to reveal an unlit corridor, lined with refuse sacks and vegetable boxes. He pulled the door behind him, lifted a rotten apple from one of the boxes and placed it on the door handle, then shuffled along the corridor, his back scraping the wall. In front he saw a sliver of light at the foot of another door. Pilgrim had told him to give it a hard kick. He grabbed the handle and booted the door. It sprang open and he stepped into a garage, stinking of old oil and gas. In front of him stood the modified SUV, facing a battered metal shutter to the street.

Over his shoulder, the door to the courtyard remained closed. Okay, he thought, if it all goes to shit then this is my way out. He tugged the garage door closed then stepped sideways, back down the corridor. The apple was still on the handle. He knocked it to the floor and pulled the door open. No one looked up.

Pushing past the tables, he stopped at the entrance to the courtyard. Twenty feet in front of him was the narrow entrance to the bridge and the high-end jewelry shops that lined each side. Above them lay a row of cramped medieval apartments, fronted with stained, warped wood that seemed squashed under the weight of the gallery above, which stretched all the way to the tower, then over the roofs of Florence.

No one looked his way. He stepped out and crossed the road, standing in front of a shop window, watching his reflection. Behind him, tourists moved slowly past. He glanced right. The door was so narrow it seemed to be part of the window frame. Without looking, he ran his finger up the door frame and found a small hinged panel. He slipped his fingers underneath, felt the keypad, then ran his finger across the buttons. Three along, and four down, he thought, then tapped in the code. The door clicked and he stepped sideways, pushing the door open with his shoulder. He nudged the door closed and stood in the darkness, feeling his breath bounce off the wall in front of his face.

His eyes began to adjust and a chink of light came from below the door, but there was nothing from outside, save the chatter of tourists. Holding his hands out to the side, he felt his way down the corridor. The sour smell of the river drifted past his face and his foot banged against a wooden step. His outstretched hand found the smooth rungs, and he started to climb, ascending only a few feet before his knuckles smacked into the roof. He placed his head against the roof and pushed. The hatch creaked open and light flooded into the stairwell.

Clambering upwards, he peered out of a porthole-sized window, crossed with iron bars. The river flowed directly below, slow and dark. In front of him, an iron-studded door to the apartments above was padlocked shut, beside a staircase of narrow, warped steps. The wood groaned under his weight and he pulled himself up fast then stood in front of the iron door. Behind and to his right were more porthole windows and he looked out to the rear of the bridge, along to the tower, where the window lay open.

Okay, he thought, look like you know what you're doing. He pushed down the door handle and stepped into a bright, narrow corridor.

Both walls were lined with portraits. He began to walk. Voices came from behind him as a group of tourists emerged into the corridor, led by a guide. Just make it to the tower, he thought.

The faces on the wall seemed to watch him, a weird mix of oil paintings, hundreds of years old, and stark black and white photographs. In the middle of the corridor stood three wide windows, and he looked out across the Florence skyline then focused on the corner where the corridor turned left at the tower.

The cameras in the ceiling didn't move. He stopped at the corner and stood before a door. He was about to try the handle when the door clicked and opened an inch. They've seen me, he thought.

He pushed it open and stepped into a waiting elevator, ignoring the staircase to the side. He watched the door to the corridor swing shut and heard it lock. The elevator door closed and the car moved swiftly upwards for a few seconds then opened into a sunlit wood-paneled room.

Mr. Pilgrim sat up in his wheelchair and slowly lifted a hand. "Welcome."

"Yeah."

A young woman in a bright sari came into the room. The hazelnut skin of her face creased into a frown when she saw Montrose and her dark eyes seemed to bore into his soul as she walked towards him. "Do you have your phone?" she said.

"Yeah." He pulled it from his jeans.

She took the phone from him, turned and tossed it out the window into the river below, then pulled a small metal rod from the folds of her sari and ran it over his body. "Lift your arms."

He stuck his hands into the air.

"Okay," she said to Pilgrim.

"I have a gun," said Montrose.

"I know." She smacked the detector against his pocket. "It was either that or you are very pleased to see me."

Montrose looked at a laptop on a desk showing a CIA login screen. Knowing Mr. Pilgrim, he guessed that the chick wasn't on Langley's payroll. "Okay, what do we know?"

"Wait." The young woman checked a monitor on the side of Pilgrim's wheelchair. "Okay," she said, "you can talk." She turned and left the room.

Montrose watched her go, then faced Pilgrim. "Glad to see your nurse is taking care of you."

Her voice came through the doorway. "I am not a bloody nurse!"

"That is Priti," said Mr. Pilgrim.

Priti entered the room again, a gun in her hand.

"Okay, I get it, you're not the nurse," said Montrose.

"Give me your gun and take this."

He handed over his Glock. "Missing a magazine, I'm afraid."

She shook her head. "Then what use is it? Or you?" She held out a pistol and two magazines. "Nine millimeter Beretta. Thirteen round magazine. No safety catch. It is unloaded."

Mr. Pilgrim shifted in his wheelchair.

Montrose could see where the strapping bulged beneath his shirt. "How is it?"

Pilgrim shrugged. "Painful and complex. If it wasn't for this current situation, I would be in a delightful Swiss hospital. But, no matter. Tell me what you know."

"Well, I didn't know about the village. That was a surprise. I thought I was only supposed to tail those guys."

"So did I."

"That shit went down so fast, I couldn't…"

"I know. I have the CIA reports."

Montrose loaded a magazine and shoved the Beretta into his jeans. "I saw that missile go straight over my head away from the valley, then turn 180° in the air and come straight back. It went through the chaff and flares as if they didn't exist. That's like no missile we know."

"I understand," said Pilgrim.

"Yeah, I'm sure you're gonna hear all about it," Montrose drawled, glancing down at the laptop screen. "But, here's the news. The British don't think the CIA are entirely blameless."

"The British?"

"What the hell have they got to do with it?" said Priti.

"There's an MI6 guy called George Linden. He stopped me in the valley when I ran out of the village, down the hillside. He saved my skin. If the CIA had caught me, they'd have ripped me apart. Then he brought me here to Florence."

"He brought you?" said Priti.

"I had no choice. It was at gunpoint. He wasn't taking any chances."

"Is he aware…?"

"Of course not. He took me to his place."

"Where is he now?" she said.

"I have no idea. He left to make a report and I came here. I made sure I wasn't followed."

"You had better…"

Pilgrim's eyes closed and he gritted his teeth.

Priti pushed past Montrose and peered at the monitor. "Do I give you a shot?"

Pilgrim let out a slow breath. "Give me a moment, it will pass. I need to keep a clear head."

She turned to Montrose. Her face tightened, "You better not have been followed. This is Italy. They have a tradition here of defenestration."

"Of what?"

She jerked a thumb towards the river. "Throwing people out of the window."

"Yeah, about that. Why are we on a bridge with only two exits?"

She tapped her head. "Think. Don't see the bridge. See the corridor. Built by Duke Cosimo de Medici nearly five hundred years ago for his personal security. He could get from his palace to his offices without going through the filthy streets and risking assassination. The whole corridor is lined with priceless art and covered by guards and cameras, and thanks to the European Union it must have wheelchair access. I can get Mr. Pilgrim a quarter of a mile away in thirty seconds. What's good enough for Cosimo de Medici, a man who spent his entire life avoiding being killed by his own people, is good enough for me."

Pilgrim looked up and his eyes came into focus. "Tell me what happened."

"I followed them to the top of the hill. I had to leave the car and climb up the rock or they would have spotted me. I got into the village and found their BMW which they'd wiped clean, and then I knew they were going to take another way out of the village. But why would they do that? Then I saw them pulling suitcases towards the village square. From the church tower, I could see they had a view of the whole valley floor, and I worked out from the blurred map that there was a clandestine airport further up the valley. I thought they were going to set up a monitoring station. Next thing I know, I hear a plane and they're pulling out a missile from a suitcase. Did you know there was an airport there?"

"No, that airfield disappeared from the maps in 1945, but we have since discovered the Italians only recently reopened it for a staging post for flights to the Middle East, presumably at the request of Langley. These two men in the village, did you kill them?"

"I dropped one and hit the other just as he fired the missile. He fell backwards and next thing I know there's a freaking missile going over my head." He looked out across the river. "I thought I'd done it. I really thought... Then it looped and came straight back, heading for the valley."

"And the plane?"

"They tried. There was nothing they could do. They fired everything they had at the missile. The sky was lit up like the fourth of July, but it was no good."

Pilgrim looked down.

"How many?" said Montrose.

"I'm sorry?"

"How many people?"

"Fifteen," said Pilgrim. "Crew and medics heading for Turkey on an aid flight. But behind them was a C-130 full of troops heading back to the US."

"You think that was the target?" said Priti.

"That flight was delayed. It's possible. Tell me about the Brit."

She typed quickly on the keyboard. "George Linden. MI6 operative for twelve years, currently on holiday in Italy. Ex-Guards officer. Impoverished aristocracy. Spotless record, fluent in Italian and Russian." She turned the laptop so Montrose could see a face on the screen.

"Yeah, that's him."

"And he is skeptical of the CIA's motives, you say?"

"He said that London isn't being kept in the loop. They want to know why."

"I'm sure they do," said Pilgrim. "He was in the village?"

"No, he was at the foot of the hill. That was the escape route. That's why they left the car at the village, they had another one waiting at the bottom of the hill, on the north side."

"But they had the element of surprise. Why wouldn't they escape the way they came? Why go to all that trouble?"

"Because the CIA were right behind them, they…"

"Yes, but did they know that? Did they seem in a hurry at the village?"

"No, they seemed to be waiting…"

"So, either they knew the CIA were behind them, or they did not. Or they didn't care."

"Oh, they knew. Or the guy who fired the missile knew. Once the shit hit the fan we could hear the cars tearing up the road. And he knew it was the CIA."

Pilgrim slowly shook his head. "But they were not martyrs. They planned to escape. And you say that the Brit is suspicious of the CIA's motives. Well, that's understandable."

"He gave me a phone."

Priti gave him a look. "Where is it?"

"Relax, I ditched it."

"You remember the number?"

"Yeah."

Priti brought up a screen on the laptop and turned it towards Montrose. "Type it in here."

Montrose leaned forward and punched in the number.

"You have missed calls," she said. "And there is a message."

A British voice came over the speaker.

"Mr. Montrose, I understand your reluctance to answer the phone, but I really think we need to keep in touch. The situation is escalating beyond my control. There is only so much I can do, and I must rely upon your help. This is no time to draw partisan lines. We both want the same thing. Now, listen carefully. I have been informed by a very reliable but discreet source that there is another missile for sale. I am desperately trying to find out where the sale will take place, and if I do, I shall pass on the information immediately. I have absolutely no doubt that MI6 have been compromised and will be used as a distraction. Ignore any distraction, Mr. Montrose, remember who is giving you this information. And also remember, we both have the same goal. I will be in touch very soon. Keep this phone switched on."

"Where did the call originate?" said Pilgrim.

"Somewhere between here and Rome," she replied.

"So, he's on the way to Rome?" said Montrose. "That's about three hours from here. Maybe that's where he's getting his information."

"Perhaps Rome should be your next destination," said Pilgrim.

"Yeah, and he won't see me coming. I want to know where he's getting his information."

"I think you underestimate him," said Pilgrim. "He gave you a phone. He will assume that you will use some method to work out his location. Otherwise his phone would not have shown his location so easily. If I was a cynic, which I am, I'd almost be tempted to say he is leading you to Rome. For his own ends, although perhaps he truly does believe you have a common purpose." Pilgrim pushed himself up. "Rome is our next port of call. Let's see what the eternal city holds."

Priti lifted the monitor and clipped it to the side of the wheelchair, then lifted the cables out of the way. "I'll drive."

"And let's be clear on our objective," said Pilgrim. "We must stop the sale of the second missile at all costs. Or find and destroy it, or direct the CIA to do so."

"Where the hell are they going to sell a missile? Down the market in Rome?"

Priti shook her head. "eBay," she said. "Think of eBay, but for terrorists. Bloody hell!" She slammed shut the lid of the laptop.

"What is it?" said Pilgrim.

"Someone is tracking us. When I accessed the call someone started to track my IP."

"How long have we got?"

"I have no idea. I can't tell without logging on. And if I do, I'll just make it easier for them. I could log on and change my IP but I don't know how close they are."

"Are you sure they can find us?"

"It will take time, though it's possible. I don't know who I'm up against."

Pilgrim stared out towards the river. "If they have enough men they can swamp the area. We go now."

Priti pulled out a phone from her sari and thrust it towards Montrose. "Take this. It has Level 5 encryption. You go first, you are the decoy." She grabbed the handles of Pilgrim's wheelchair and pushed him over to the elevator. "The safe house in Rome will be ready." She turned to Montrose. "But not for you. I will route the number MI6 gave you to your new phone."

"Won't they track me?"

"I will send it through a thousand onion routers," she said and bundled the laptop into a metal suitcase. "Many security layers, it would take weeks."

He held the phone in his hand, checking for the power button. "Are your numbers…?"

She snatched it from him. "Not here. Switch it on in Rome. You will leave first and go down to the east side of the river. They are looking for you, not us. You know the location of the transport?"

"Yeah, I've checked the garage behind the café."

"Then you're an idiot, but at least you're an honest idiot. *You* use that transport, since you have compromised it. We will use the backup." She pulled a pistol from her sari. "I will drive us out of here. Bengali-style."

"And God help anyone who tries to stop her," said Pilgrim.

She jabbed a finger into Montrose's chest. "Go the wrong way. Head north then double back across the bridge. It will give us more time. There are cameras there that will pick you up if they are smart."

"How long do you need?"

"Four minutes. Then we will be far enough away from here. If you have to use the phone in an emergency, my codename is Broadsword." She pointed to Pilgrim. "He is

52

Danny Boy. You must assume that all communications are being monitored. Don't make it easy for them."

Montrose pressed a button on his watch and saw the stopwatch hand move smoothly around the dial. "What about me?"

"You are Green Day."

"What, like the band?"

"Yes. I picked it for you. My favorite album is *American Idiot*. Go!"

"What if they have closed the bridge on both ends?"

"That's your problem, not mine. We are not going down to the end of the bridge. This is the Vasari corridor, remember? If it's good enough for psychopathic Renaissance despots to escape, then it'll do for me." She hit the button for the elevator. "You take the stairs. And Connor?"

"Yeah?"

"Don't fuck up."

The doors pinged open and she shoved Mr. Pilgrim into the elevator.

He ran down the stairs and kicked open the door into the corridor, then turned the corner and nearly walked straight into a guard.

"Chee fretta? Cosa stai facendo qui?"

"Yeah, sorry, I got lost."

The guard moved into the middle of the corridor and spoke slowly. "You... got lost? In a corridor?" He reached for his radio.

CHAPTER 7

Montrose grabbed the radio from the guard's hand and threw it behind him. "Fetch!"

The guard began to turn then stopped, pushing back his shoulders and widening his stance.

"Listen to me," said Montrose. "You work in an art gallery and eat too much pizza. I'm on the run from the world and his fucking dog, so get out of my way." He shoved the guard to the side and ran. A turning to his left appeared and he ducked in, just managing to stop before he fell over a balcony. Thirty feet below, the church of St Felicia opened up in front of him. He checked his stopwatch. She'd said four minutes then Pilgrim was clear. He knew the guard would be looking for some backup.

He leant over the balcony and saw a narrow ledge to one side, leading to the top of an arched doorway. He climbed over, his fingers slipping on dust, and edged along the wall, holding onto the ornate stonework, then lowered his feet to the top of the stone arch. He stood for a moment, and looked down. A gaggle of tourists stood in a doorway and began to lift up their cell phones.

The guard appeared on the balcony, shouting back down the corridor.

The ancient flagstones looked unforgiving. Drop and roll, he thought. Don't fuck around. Like I've got a choice.

He pushed his hands away from the wall and turned in the air, tucking his arms around his head and bringing up his knees just as his feet slammed into the flagstones. His shoulder crashed onto the floor of the church and he rolled onto his face. He lay stunned for a moment then flexed his arms. It hurt like hell but nothing was broken. Ignoring the shouts and camera flashes, he scrambled to his feet and faced the altar, then turned and headed for the door.

The stopwatch said two minutes to go. Pain from his shoulder stabbed through him as he lowered his arm. From the shade of the doorway he saw a cramped piazza, with high buildings on either side and tourists spilling out from pizzerias and panini shops. At the far end was a street leading off to the left and right. He looked down. The brim of a wide black hat tilted up, with thick, aromatic smoke curling around its edges. The wizened, grey face of a priest regarded him coldly, the cigarillo dangling from his lips.

"Padre, you gotta get some carpets. That floor is a fucking nightmare."

A shout came from inside the church behind him and he took off for the road, around the corner, then turned back towards the bridge. Cameras, he thought, slow down. Above him he saw the corridor and the tower. The window was still open. He stepped onto the bridge and tried to keep to the side, but tourists crowded the entrances to the line of shops on either side. The only way was straight down the middle, and no cover. And if his pursuers were already on the bridge, he knew it didn't matter.

A gap opened up between the buildings and he saw the murky waters of the Arno. It's a long way down, he thought. But if there is someone waiting for me at the end of the bridge, that's exactly where I'm going.

He picked up the pace and made it to the end, then glanced left and right. And saw them. They were moving too fast and too straight to be tourists. He crossed the road and broke into a run when he entered the courtyard, weaving past the tables. He grabbed the handle of the wooden door, slammed it behind him and ran past the boxes, throwing them over his shoulder. He booted his way into the garage, shut the door and threw the bolt.

Running past the SUV, he unlocked and pulled up the metal shutter to the street. The sunlight flooded in and he saw a Kawasaki trail bike at the other side of the SUV with a helmet hanging from the handlebars. He heard a metallic squeak and saw the garage door handle drop slowly then stop.

He swung his leg across the bike and kicked over the motor. The rear wheel spun as he stabbed it into gear, dropped the clutch and took off down the street.

Napier slid behind the polished marble table and faced the restaurant. The long salon was empty of customers, but filled with tables covered in bright white tablecloths and gleaming cutlery. He looked up to the ornate chandeliers and tapestry-covered walls. From the far end of the room a waiter walked towards them. Sunlight sparkled on the crystal glasses. "How long have we got?"

Faber slid into the booth and placed his phone on the table. "They open for lunch in thirty minutes."

"Good, because I think that's how long it's going to take the waiter to get here. Where's Montrose?"

"We left him in Florence. There are teams combing the city, but he slipped the net."

"Shit."

Faber's phone buzzed and began to slide across the marble table. He flattened it with his hand and checked the screen. "It's Campbell."

"It's asshole hour. Right on time."

"Want me to take it?"

"No. I want to know why…" The doors behind the waiter flew open, and three men marched down the center of the room. The waiter stepped aside to stop himself from being mown down. Napier shook his head. "They don't do subtle, do they?"

Two of the men grabbed chairs from nearby tables and placed them in front of Napier's booth. The other stood to the side, his jacket open.

Faber leaned over. "I said two men only. Lose the goon."

The Russian dropped onto the chair. "That one is here to stop me killing you." He grabbed a glass from the table and poured himself some water, his knuckles white as he held the bottle, then gulped it down.

Napier thought the glass would shatter in his hand. "Oh, a bit upset, are we?" He placed both hands on the table and leaned over. "There is a valley north west of here, covered in the body parts of fifteen American servicemen and women. And if their plane had not taken off first, then the bodies of over a hundred combat troops would be lying there. But that doesn't matter, because poor Ivan is a bit upset. What fucking planet are you on?"

The Russian took another drink. The bodyguard shifted his stance.

Napier pointed a finger at the bodyguard. "You start to get brave, big boy, and you'll be leaving here in a fucking box."

Spittle flecked at the edges of the Russian's mouth. "I'll tell you what planet we are on. The planet where our latest technology is stolen from us and ends up in the hands of terrorists. And who do they target?" He slammed down the glass. "The fucking Americans! What a surprise!" He jabbed a finger at Napier. "You're behind this. I can smell it. We didn't even know those missiles were missing. Because if we had, you'd be the first place we'd come looking."

Napier leaned back in the booth. "Seriously? Your latest technology is missing, and that's the best you can come up with? Let me tell you what I think. You *lose* a missile, then suddenly it takes down an American plane, then, er, what happens next?" He looked up and shrugged. "Oh, yeah. Its market value increases tenfold." He stared straight into the Russian's eyes. "I'll bet you've got the Iranians and Chinese and all those fucking goofballs in North Korea jerking themselves into a frenzy over getting their hands on a portable missile that can bypass all the latest systems and take down a plane flown by a combat veteran pilot. Congratulations. You must be fucking delighted. Sanctions are biting, yeah? Nobody wants to do business with you, yeah? So, you come up with this shit. And you think we..."

"You disgust me. If you think this is about money... You..."

Napier threw his hands in the air. "Well, remind me, how much did the price of your Buk Missile system go up after you shot down Malaysian Airlines MH17 in 2014 and murdered nearly three hundred people? And you tell us it was the Ukrainians? The whole world knew you were lying. And still do."

The man standing behind the Russian growled and placed his hand inside his jacket.

Napier stood up and jabbed a finger at him. "You start playing the tough guy, asshole, I swear I'll fucking shoot you first!"

"Enough!" The Russian jerked a thumb behind him. The man seated beside him rose slowly, not taking his eyes from Napier, then followed the other man out of the salon. The Russian closed his eyes and slowly rotated his neck until there was an audible click. "This is getting us nowhere. Now is the time for cool heads and cold hearts. We have known each other too long. The Ukraine is a sensitive topic, but you know that. It's why you said it."

"Dimitri, your militias blew MH17 out of the sky. All those civilians. That's what happened. And you still deny it."

"You set us up! You made sure that plane flew over a war zone that was covered by anti-aircraft batteries. You sent them to their deaths!"

"Oh, man, that's internet conspiracy bullshit. The plane left from a NATO country. And we stand together, because when one is attacked…"

"Do not make me laugh! NATO? Your own little private army! Tell me, when was the last time you invoked Article 5 of NATO? I'll tell you, because like most Americans, your grasp of history is laughable. It was 9/11. And who did you attack in revenge for the destruction of the Twin Towers? Eh? Afghanistan. A bunch of mud huts and opium growers. And tell me what was the nationality of the attackers?

Saudi Arabian. Did you attack them? No. You've had half of Europe's armies chasing local gangsters across Afghan mountains. It was a farce. You didn't destroy Al Qaeda! You didn't even find them. Tell me, the Madrid atrocities, the Paris attacks, the London bombings and murders, did you invoke Article 5? When Argentina invaded the British territory of the Falkland Islands, back in the 80s, did you fly to the rescue of your fellow NATO member? No. You tried to persuade them to give up the island, so you could curry favor with the fascist junta of Galtieri. Your NATO allies, they know what kind of friend you are, and they will come to the same conclusion as us. That you set this up to fire NATO into action, and…"

Napier's and Faber's phones buzzed together in quick succession.

A high-pitched beep came from Dimitri's pocket. They sat in silence for a moment.

Napier read out the message on the screen. "New missile for sale. The Silk Road." He looked up but the Russians were already running for the door.

The Director stood with his hands on the back of the chair and looked at each person in turn around the boardroom table. "I have good news. The second missile is ready for sale and has already attracted a great deal of attention."

"I'm glad to hear it," said the fat man. "It is, as you say according to plan. Except one thing. Is he dead yet?"

The Director smiled. "I think you have something of an obsession with Montrose, but I appreciate an eye for detail, that is no bad thing. I will come to Montrose in a moment. First, to the price. I'm told that Moscow and Washington are testing the waters. They may be under the foolish assumption that they will be able to bargain."

A thin, reedy English voice came from the far end of the table. "And you are sure we should involve no one else? We could treble the price if the Saudis or Chinese knew about this."

"Patience, they will find out, then the feeding frenzy will really begin. First, we let the dog see the bone. As lucrative as the second missile may be, it is not part of the final deal. The Russians would pay dearly for the return of the missile, and they will try, but the CIA will win this auction quite easily, and at the right price. Remember, gentlemen, this is the *hors d'oeuvres*."

"Director, I am aware of the need for secrecy, though I'm sure I speak for the other members around this table when I say…"

"My friend, if you need support, then you are unable to stand on your own." The fat man began to protest, but the Director waved a hand. "The best method is a need to know basis. That is all the knowledge that is required at the moment."

The fat man's lips tightened, and his Dutch accent became clipped and guttural. "Then perhaps we can move on to Montrose and whether he is dead?"

"Gentlemen, remember what I said about opportunity? Carpe Diem!" He watched as puzzled faces turned to each other and allowed himself a wry smile. "Tell me, what would happen if we had video evidence of a known CIA operative in possession of a missile?" They stared at him. "I'm sure you can appreciate that would be very beneficial, no?"

The Englishman spoke slowly, "You mean... Montrose? He no longer works for the CIA. They want to shoot him on sight."

"Indeed, they do, but that is of no consequence. The fact that he was once a career CIA man is all that matters."

"He was just a technology specialist. A geek. And he was to be killed in Florence. You told the CIA..."

"That was then, this is now. We must adapt our tactics to extract the maximum from our forces. With Montrose, we only have to win once."

"And the risk, Director? How do we express that risk?"

The Director placed his hands behind his back and clenched them into fists. "The risk is that he is shot by the CIA before he is any use to us. But, if he tells them all he knows, then he will tell them nothing new. After all, they were the source of his information."

"But Florence..."

"Forget Florence." He relaxed his hands and let them fall to his side. "Are there any further questions?" There was silence. "Then we shall move on. The delivery logistics have been prepared."

"And the payment? Will they track it?"

"They will try, of course. But our Swiss friends have prepared and isolated an entire technology platform and can replicate it within a day. The account will be open for ten seconds and then disappear forever." He stepped back from the table and walked towards the window. "Now, the video of the first attack will soon be ready for release. I hear the drone had quite a spectacular view. The second missile is now on its way to the collection point. We will inform the CIA and Moscow at our convenience. In the meantime,

Mr. Montrose is to perform one last act before his untimely death."

The fat man spluttered as he spoke. "We cannot… what if he…?"

"Fails?" The Director strode towards the table and placed both hands down, leaning over at the fat man. "And what would you do?"

"What? What would I…?"

"Too late. If you fail to plan, you are planning to fail. You become reactive, not proactive, and then you are dancing to someone else's tune. We will do this our way. We are the pipers. The others will follow."

CHAPTER 8

He let the Kawasaki's engine idle and stretched both arms above his head. This is a little unexpected, he thought. All the time he had been speeding down the autostrada, the engine screaming as he weaved between traffic, he had pictured his destination as a nondescript hotel, one star, maybe two, in a forgotten part of suburban Rome that the tourists shunned. Or a dingy apartment in a 60s tower block overlooking an industrial estate on the outskirts of town. But not this.

He stamped on the gear lever of the Kawasaki and edged forward, pulling in behind a stretch limousine when it turned through the high gates. Beyond lay a tree-lined drive, leading to a six-story mansion fronted by huge Corinthian pillars that reminded him of the White House. Looking up, he heard the chopper before he saw it. The Sikorsky flew low over his head and descended onto the middle of a manicured lawn. While the rotors wound down, several golf carts pulled out from the wide steps at the front of the hotel and trundled across the grass to the chopper. At the end of the drive, Montrose pulled into the side of the steps, killed the engine and flicked out the stand. A uniformed concierge hurried over. Montrose slowly lifted his leg off the seat, his hips and knees aching from the ride, and flexed fingers that had been wrapped around the handlebar grips for three hours. He pulled out his phone. The concierge stood before him gesturing away from the front of the hotel.

"Non puoi parcheggiare qui!"

Montrose held up the phone. "I have a reservation. And I bet you do too. Badoom-tish! You do valet parking?"

The concierge shrugged, "Si, signore, but…"

Montrose pulled the helmet from his head and held it out to the concierge. "Safety first. Good luck." He headed for the steps. Halfway up, he could feel the joints in his knees grinding together and he stopped then turned towards the chopper.

Shit, he thought, I'm getting old. Next time find a Harley. Or my own helicopter. I reckon Mr. Pilgrim has got the cash.

A valet opened the door of the Sikorsky and held out a hand. A black-haired woman in a bright red trouser suit that clung to her generous curves like a second skin reached out and took his hand, then adjusted her sunglasses and stepped down. Her high heels sunk deep into the grass. Montrose watched her bend forward, peering down over her breasts with amusement, and some difficulty, then step out of the heels, stand barefoot for a moment, then ignore the golf carts and walk across the grass in a way that threatened to set off car alarms. A valet pulled her heels free from the turf and hurried behind her. The other valets loaded her luggage onto the carts and followed her in procession, every one of them with their eyes fixed on her ass.

Montrose looked up at two more uniformed staff flanking the door. They watched in horror as he wiped his shades on his t-shirt, where they left a grimy smear. "Hi, guys. Where's reception?"

They both said nothing for several seconds before one swept a hand behind him. "Straight ahead, signore."

"Cool. And more importantly, where's the bar?"

"To the right. You can't miss it."

Montrose replaced his sunglasses and strolled into a cavernous lobby leading to a hall so high it reminded him of a cathedral. At the far wall, he saw the marble reception desk set below long, high windows where the altar would have been. All around him, potted palm trees, garish furniture and gilt-lined tables crowded every pillar. It was a church of wealth and appalling taste. Americans would love it, he thought. And the Russians.

Through open doors to his right, he saw a bar lined with bottles and chrome beer taps. A sudden thirst hit him and he tried to swallow but his tongue stuck to the roof of his mouth, and he could taste bitter dust from the autostrada and exhaust fumes.

A white-jacketed barman stood slowly polishing a glass. His greased hair shone like the steel buttons on his coat and he held the glass up to the sunlight streaming in from windows overlooking the lawn, then turned towards the door.

Montrose could see him watching through the glass as he approached. He made to sit on a bar stool, then reckoned that sitting down was something he wanted to avoid for a few days. The barman held the beer glass up to him and Montrose nodded. Yeah, he thought, I look like a beer drinker. He watched the barman pull the beer from a chrome tap then slide it towards him.

The bubbles burst on his lip and the beer seemed to

evaporate in his mouth, but the alcohol washed away the grime and soothed his throat. He had finished three quarters of the glass by the time he set it back on the bar.

"You came on the motorbike?" said the barman.

"Yeah."

The barman smiled. "I have a Moto Guzzi 1982 Le Mans." He held his thumb and finger in the air. *"Classico."*

"Oh yeah," replied Montrose, trying to remember what a Moto Guzzi Le Mans looked like.

The barman took a cloth from under the bar, sprayed it with some water and tapped his cheeks, then folded it expertly and placed it on the bar beside the empty beer glass.

Montrose nodded and quickly wiped his face, and saw the stains on the cloth. "Thanks, man."

The barman pushed another beer towards him and picked up the cloth.

"I'm going to enjoy this one." He closed his eyes and lifted the glass, but a hint of heavy, sweet musk made one thought stab through his mind. He placed the glass on the bar before it slipped from his fingers.

Kirsty.

The scent played a movie in his head. Her red hair falling across his face. Her hand around his throat. And the red and green dragon tattooed on her perfect ass. He felt her breath on his neck.

"The swallow flies low over Vladivostok." She flicked her tongue against his earlobe.

He looked up to the mirror behind the bar and saw her reflection, making a little kiss with her lips.

"I was going to grab your arse," she said, "but I didn't want that thing going off in your pocket."

He took a long drink of the beer. "It's not loaded."

"I wasn't talking about the gun."

He turned around and couldn't help staring down at her bright red trouser suit. "You are…"

"Rocking a fat suit." She slapped the padding on her ass. "A little booty works wonders."

"Well, you look…"

"Hot and chubby. Literally." She drained his beer. "Maybe you like that in a girl? Well, tough." She placed the empty glass on the bar. "How's Mr. Pilgrim?"

"In a wheelchair."

"Will he walk again?"

"I don't know, he has to heal inside. That bullet he took made a mess. He was pretty ripped up. He should be flat out in a hospital bed."

"He took it for us, Connor. That time in London, if he hadn't… it could have been me, or you."

"I know. We owe him."

"Yeah. Is he here? In Rome?"

"Somewhere."

"I know where the safe house is. I know my way around this city."

"So do I." His mind flashed back to where he found the body of the secretary, and the office near the Coliseum. He shuddered at the thought of the blood. He felt Kirsty squeeze his hand.

"That was before my time," she said. "Were you in love with her?"

Montrose shook his head. "The one that was killed in Rome? No. I never knew her. She was killed simply to set me up."

She leaned in and rested her head against his for a moment.

"Ah, the one you loved, it was Paris, wasn't it? Maybe you'll find her again. Mr Pilgrim is good at finding people. He found you in Morocco."

He shrugged. "Another life. Some people don't want to be found. I was an innocent then."

"In some ways, Connor, you still are. But I like that."

He looked down at his hands. "I won't give up. I'll find out who killed her."

"Your sister?"

"Yeah. One day…"

She whispered in his ear. "And I'll help you. So will Pilgrim. I know he will."

Montrose nodded. "He's a good man at collecting lost souls. He found you, no?"

She kissed him. "Not all those who wander are lost."

"Yeah."

"We need to go." She smiled at the barman and spoke in a cut glass Long Island accent. "Put the beer on room 502, *prego*. And send up some sandwiches and San Pellegrino." She gave the barman a wink that made his mouth drop open, then turned away and took Montrose's arm. "Let's go, Connor. I have to get out of this suit. I'm sweating like a nun in a sex shop."

"You just made his day."

She raised an eyebrow. "If you weren't here, he'd be making dinner tonight. But I'll make do with you." Once clear of the bar, her lilting Welsh accent returned. "I'm so hungry I could eat a scabby horse. I can't eat a thing in this suit or I'll bloody burst." They entered the lobby and she gently pulled him to a stop. "You know, let's not be seen together, just in case."

"Kirsty…"

"Do what you're told, there's a good boy. Room 502, the elevator is over there, stay ten feet behind me. And don't stare at my arse."

The door to 502 was ajar. Kirsty stood in the middle of the room unzipping the fat suit and wrestling her arms and shoulders out of the tight cloth. She lifted both arms free and pushed it past her belly, then hopped on one leg trying to shove the suit down over her knee. She giggled and fell to the floor, looking up as Montrose closed the door. "Get me out of this thing." She lay on her back and lifted her legs in the air.

Montrose grabbed the thick material around her ankles and gave it a tug, but it had no effect other than to drag her across the floor.

She burst out laughing. "You're going to get carpet burns on my backside!" She reached back and held onto the bed and he dragged it from her legs. "Thank God, I was melting in that bloody thing." Her skin was damp with sweat, and she pulled off the black wig. Her red hair fell across her shoulders. She stretched out her arms and let her head drop back. "Oh, that feels so good."

"Is Pilgrim paying for this?"

"No, I am. I just cleaned out a pedophile politician in London. He was laundering money for the Russian mob. There are plenty of those bastards if you know where to look. And I do. He shouldn't have kept all his eggs in one bank account he thought he had hidden offshore."

"Does he know?"

"Oh, yeah. I even took his pension fund."

"But what if he…?"

"Who's he going to tell? MI5? They'd have him by the balls if they knew he was taking money from the Russians."

"And what about them?"

She nodded towards the red trouser suit lying on the floor. "They'll be looking for her."

"It might not be all his money, what if the Russians…"

Kirsty opened up her suitcase and pulled out a laptop. "Then I'll kill him." She peeled off her damp underwear. "He's the kind of guy who buys little boys and girls. Robbing him is just the start. I've told him if he stays away from kids, he might get his money back."

"Kirsty…"

"But there's no chance of that. I want to see him suffer and fall. His expensive aristocratic wife is about to find out she won't be staying in the Ritz any more. And once I get back, I'll take care of him personally."

"Right now, we need to…"

"Connor, this is business. London is pleasure. It can wait." She stood close to him and sniffed. "You need a shower. C'mon, scrub my back and tell me the latest. Then you can pump me for information."

"Kirsty, I can't believe you just said that."

She leaned forward and kissed him on the chin. "Pretend you're in a Bond movie. You know what happens next."

Napier stood at the window and let the blast from the aircon cool his neck and shoulders. The sweat chilled on his neck. Faber closed a door behind him. He didn't turn around, but peered down into the busy street. "So, what's new? Any good news to brighten up this tsunami of shit?"

"Not much. The guys in the village were known to us. Ex-Syrian militants. They were supposed to be retired. We gave them money to drop out or disappear. Looks like they changed their minds."

"Or somebody changed it for them with a big pay check. Suicide?"

"No, the guys were professional. One shot with a 9mm round, probably. Forensics think the other was shot from above with a .50 round, judging by the meat counter display that was left of him. Might have been from a high point across the valley."

"So, who's the paymaster?"

"Maybe the…" A sharp knock came from the door. Faber pulled it open and the technician stood holding a piece of paper.

"I didn't send it through the system."

"Good man." Faber took the paper. "That's all." The technician turned away smartly and Faber closed the door.

"Well?"

Faber scanned the handwritten note. "We have an address on The Silk Road, and the auction time."

Napier stepped forward. "And the opening bid price?"

"One billion dollars."

"Holy shit."

The phone rang on Napier's desk. He walked over, blew out a breath then pressed the speakerphone button. "Director Campbell, this is Na…"

"I know," said Campbell, "can you hear me?"

"Loud and clear."

"Good, because I am not sure you heard me before. I told you to kill Montrose."

Napier glowered at the phone. "When we find him, we will. Right now…"

"Where is he?"

"He slipped the net in Florence."

"I count that as a failure," said Campbell.

Napier pressed his fingertips to his mouth for a moment, then spoke slowly. "Who told us he was in Florence?"

"Don't overthink this, Napier, just find him. I don't want questions, I want results."

"Mr. Campbell, he is the only one alive who was in the village when the missile was fired…"

"You're not listening. Kill him. With another missile on the market he is too much of a threat. Save your powers of deduction for tracing the two men killed in the village. Are we clear?"

Napier closed his eyes. "It's not…" The cell phone buzzed in his pocket. He pulled it out, but didn't recognize the number. He hit the answer button. "Yeah?" He listened for a moment, then held the phone away from his ear. "Dimitri, listen to me, just calm down, I'm going to make this call more secure. Hold the line." He pressed the mute button. "It's the Russians. They're not happy. About the missile or the price."

Campbell's voice came over the speaker phone. "I am unconcerned at Moscow's dilemma."

"We have an address on the Silk Road," said Napier. "One billion dollars."

There was a pause from the speakerphone. "We will have the money waiting," said Campbell. "But if they have an auction, why state the price?"

"I believe it's a minimum bid, Sir," said Faber. "It's a closed auction between certain parties. We don't know who the other parties are but we can expect the Russians."

"Bid two billion," said Campbell.

Faber looked over at Napier.

"How do we pay?" asked Campbell.

"They give out a bank account to transfer the funds. Usually open for about thirty seconds, then it disappears."

"Understood. Get the Russians on."

Napier hit the mute button, then the cell phone speaker. "Dimitri, the line is secure."

"Hey, no hurry, yeah? One of our stolen missiles is up for sale and you tell me you're making the line more secure? Bullshit. I assume you were connecting this call to your superiors in Langley who are trying to track the call. Well, I'm in Rome, if that's any help. But it's good I'm being broadcast, because at least I'm talking to the organ grinder and not his fucking monkey."

"Get to the point."

"You know who I am. You know what authority I have. So, you and the other monkeys on the line listen to me very carefully. You will not bid for the missile. We will bid, and we will win and we will recover our missile. If you try to undermine us in any way, then you will leave us in no doubt that you are behind these attacks."

"Hey, hold on Dimitri, that's just Moscow bullshit, you..."

"Listen to me! You will address me as Colonel Saitsev and you will treat me with the respect that my rank deserves. The time for nice chat is over. The next call may be from the president of Russia. Do you want to take that call? Or your president? Or your friends in Langley who are listening? If they are, they can tell you about the two men at the top of the hill in the village when the attack took place."

Napier said nothing and threw out his hands.

"You have nothing to say, Napier? We have our informants. We have our intelligence. I'll leave you to guess who they are. But these two men, these Syrian terrorists who were trained by the CIA, who attacked our troops in Syria with American weapons, a whole regiment of them, all funded by Uncle Sam. Did they do one last job for you? The only two who survived?"

"Look, Dimitri, who's yanking your string? Who's feeding you this line of…"

"That's pitiful. You know, the way I see it is, you lost control of your own terrorists. Maybe it's payback time for abandoning them in Syria. They all died, you know, when your president did what he was told and stopped funding or sharing intelligence. You left them there and abandoned them to their fate. They were attacked from all sides. You do know that, don't you? Hundreds died because you walked out on them. I tell you, I never want to be your ally."

"Dimitri, I have no time for this conspiracy shit."

"We can see what is coming our way, and we can see where it is coming from. And we will not stand by and watch it happen. Russia is ready to take whatever action is necessary to expose your lies. So, you listen to me. We will win the auction. We will recover that missile. If there is any other outcome then you leave us no choice. We will expose your hypocrisy to the world."

Napier said nothing.

"Our army has been given mobilization orders. Your move, Napier. But I will give you one last piece of advice. Do not play Russian Roulette with us. There are no empty chambers in this gun."

The call ended. They stood in silence.

Campbell's voice came over the speaker phone. "Listen carefully, Napier. Ignore those Russian thugs. You will win that auction. You will recover the missile. I will take care of the intelligence leak. Expect some guests. But if the Russians win that auction and another US plane falls from the sky, I will have you back in Washington within hours and you can explain it to the President himself. Focus, Napier. The next attack will not happen if you recover the missile. The Russians are bluffing."

"Mr. Campbell, we can't be sure... Look, there's no way they could have found out from us about the two men at the village. I hand-picked my team. And he doesn't know about Montrose."

"I don't care who you picked. And if he knows about the two Syrians then do not make such an amateurish assumption that he does not know about Montrose. If they have found out that the only man left alive in that village is an ex-member of the CIA, then they have all the evidence they need for the conspiracy theory and false flag attack by the US on its own troops. The world's press will have a field day, and the Russians will have won. This must be prevented at all costs. You will win the missile. Use any means necessary. And kill Montrose."

CHAPTER 9

The phone buzzed in his pocket. Montrose hauled his t-shirt down over his head. "It's Priti."

Kirsty shrugged off the bathrobe. "So, you've met the Quartermaster? What does she say?"

"It says *'ask her.'* What the hell does that mean?"

"It means she doesn't trust you yet. And she knows exactly where you are." She unlocked her phone and tossed it to Montrose. "Check the messages," she said, and pulled a pair of panties from a suitcase then sat on the edge of the bed.

"It's a message from the MI6 contact, Linden. My God."

"What?"

"There's another missile for sale. The Silk Road. And she has the asking price. One billion dollars."

Kirsty stood up from the bed. "Who the fuck is it? Austin Powers?" She grabbed her laptop and opened it up on a desk. "Time to go work, Connor. Get your knickers on. I'll establish comms to Mr. Pilgrim and Priti."

"Where is he?"

"No idea. Best not to know, eh?" She sat at the desk and began typing on the laptop, then took a sheet of hotel letter paper from the desk and folded it over the laptop camera.

"You could just put some clothes on," said Montrose.

"Mr. Pilgrim wouldn't mind, but I'm so very shy." She hit the keyboard. "He's not responding, though there's no alarm signal. They should be online any moment." Her screen beeped. "Message from Pilgrim. Your MI6 contact left a message with the information on the phone he gave you. Pilgrim wants you to find out anything you can about the missile for sale and then we'll talk."

"The Silk Road," said Montrose, "can you access it?"

"Sure, if I'm looking for three tons of methamphetamine or a bus full of underage Russian prostitutes. But not the part of the Silk Road that Austin Powers is using. That's like finding a needle in a galaxy of haystacks. It's the most secure internet on the planet. You can find it, but only if it tells you where to look. It's invitation only."

"Seriously? I know there's a dark web, but…"

"This is the internet your mother warned you about. Not the one with the boobies. This is eBay and Amazon for criminals and fraudsters and sex traffickers. Though hidden away in the corner is the place where the big boys play. If you're invited, and you have enough money, you can buy anything. Chemical weapons, government assassinations or plutonium. Where do you think North Korea got all that shit to build their missiles?" She stared down at the keyboard. "I'll tell you who's got access."

"Pilgrim?"

"No. MI6, your new bestie."

"Kirsty, I've got serious doubts…"

"You and me both, mate. Let's see how much your new friend really likes you. Get him on the phone."

"You want me to call him?"

"Well, we could just sit here half-naked, but one thing would lead to another, and I think you need a rest from what happened in the shower. Besides you're not getting any younger, so let's get some work done, yeah?"

"Okay, I'll call him." He lifted the phone.

"Not yet, Priti will send you a number. You call that and it will be routed to him. That way, he'll never find out where you are, super spy."

"Okay, I'm ready."

"In fact, he'll never find out where you are if I do the talking. Remember, half the world is looking for you to put a bullet up your arse. Nobody knows me. Let's see what Mr. Linden of MI6 has got to say for himself when he's not patronizing a Yank." She checked the screen, whispering to herself as she typed. "This is Connor Montrose, super spy..."

"Kirsty..."

She began to roll her vowels in a Scottish accent. "Welcome to my world of guns and girls..."

"Can you just..."

"And foxy Welsh chicks in fancy hotels with remarkably spacious showers for hochmagandy..."

"Kirsty, can't we maybe...?"

"D'ye mind? I'm trying to channel Sean Connery and all I'm getting is Fat Bastard from Austin Powers."

"Why do you need a Scottish accent?"

"Connor, I'm Welsh. Wales is a country of three million people. Assume that half are female. The percentage of Welsh women that are likely to be chasing a missile around

79

Europe is going to be quite narrow. But in there, somewhere, will be a Welsh chick that is very technically savvy and who appears on most security and police databases, even if they don't know her name. That's too close."

"I got you. Why don't I do the talking?"

"Because I want to wind him up and see what makes him tick."

The phone buzzed in his hand.

"Hit it."

He pressed the link and switched it to speaker.

The call was answered immediately. "Montrose? Hello?"

Kirsty held a finger to her lips, then leaned over to the phone. "This is the Connor Montrose residence, how can I help you?"

"Who is this?"

"Miss Jean Brodie."

"Montrose?"

"I'm here. Keep talking."

"Who's your friend?"

"Technical support," said Kirsty, "all calls come through me. The last time you two had a nice wee chat, someone was tracking the number. So, what do you want?"

There was a pause on the line. "This is for Montrose, not for you."

"Linden, Miss… Brodie is on the team."

"Well, I'm glad to have a Brit onboard. I hope, Miss Brodie, like me, you are keen to do your bit for your country."

Kirsty grinned at Montrose. "Oh aye, and what country is that?"

"Well, Britain of course, unless…"

"That's not a country. That's a state. Basic geography, bawbag."

"Oh, I see, a Cybernat, eh? I wonder which side you're on, then?"

"Less of your cheek, posh boy, now piss or get off the pot."

"Well, I'm sure Mr. Montrose got my message about a second missile being for sale. Correct?"

"Yeah."

"I'm expecting more information very shortly. GCHQ are accessing the Silk Road to get as much information as they can." Linden cleared his throat. "That's my news. Anything you'd like to contribute?"

"Yeah," said Montrose. "The phone number you gave me had the goons descending on my tail as soon as I called. What's going on?"

There was a pause then Linden spoke. "I'm sorry to hear that, Montrose. I take it, since we are talking, that you managed to evade them and resolve that situation. But you may have just saved my life. I shall cut this call and find a new number." The line dropped.

Kirsty shook her head. "I don't trust him."

"Neither do I, though he's all we've got."

She stood up and grabbed a t-shirt from the suitcase. "What's bugging me is GCHQ hacking into the Silk Road. Sure, they've got access to all the usual criminal areas, that's where they do business. But without the links to that site where the missile is for sale, that single transaction, then they have no chance of finding out the price. Someone is feeding Linden information. The CIA?"

"I doubt they would be chatting to the Brits about this. That's why Linden and MI6 are on the case in the first place, because the CIA were up to something and they weren't sharing."

"I know the security on the Silk Road. Sure, if you are looking for drugs, moneylending, credit card numbers, you can find a way in. But at the top end, the underground banks, the arms sales, the people trafficking, the trade in refugees and children, the security is so tight that even governments cannot break in, though they don't have to."

"What do you mean?"

"Because they are the best customers."

"C'mon. We're talking the intelligence services here."

"Exactly, that's where they get their intelligence. They pretend to be customers and make bids, find out about the deals, and use all the information to their own advantage. You know when it's all going to kick off in an African or Middle East country when the orders start coming in. Especially if you're the one that's doing the selling."

"Kirsty, there's no way the CIA…"

"Oh, get real, Connor. How do you think the Syrian rebels got all those arms? From Santa? The CIA learned their lesson from the Iran-Contra scandal. The Silk Road is the best thing to happen to them in years. They can arm rebels at the drop of a hat anywhere in the world, and there's no scrutiny by the Washington Post or any budgetary committees. All they have to do is buy it on the Silk Road and it will be delivered to wherever they want. There are container ships in Jo'burg, London and Rotterdam, ready to be delivered anywhere in the world. Business is business." The laptop beeped and her head snapped back to the screen. "It's our friend from MI6. Looks like he's still alive." She hit the keyboard and the phone buzzed. "Is that London calling?"

"No time for fun, Jock. We were too late. The missile has

been sold. And whoever the buyer was, it wasn't Ivan in Moscow. I can hear some of the SIGINT chatter, and you take it from me they're going ballistic."

"So, who was it then?"

"We have absolutely no idea. I have to go, but I can tell you MI6 are getting closer. The geeks in GCHQ tell me that the deal had a delivery time. Two hours."

Kirsty threw out her hands. "How did they get…?"

"Listen, Jock, I don't know how they do what they do, I just get the info. And they tell me that if that missile has a delivery time of two hours, then it's here. In Rome."

"How can they possibly know that?" said Kirsty.

"Because I'm in Rome and I see what's happening. Our cousins in the CIA have all got their shades on and are running around in blacked-out SUVs with police escorts. All the SIGINT chatter is coming from here. The first missile attack was only a few hours north of here. It seems that whoever stole the two missiles held them in a central Italian location."

Kirsty nodded to Montrose. "That makes sense. Did they say anything else? GCHQ?"

"No, but if someone finds out what they are doing, this could come to an end very quickly."

Kirsty leaned forward, closing her eyes and held her head in both hands. "Listen, if they have been able to access the delivery time, have they found out the delivery address?"

"All I can say is that they are working on it. Though I get the feeling that's not going to last. If Downing Street find out, they're going to shut us down. They'll do what Washington tells them. If I get any more I will pass it on, but this could be the end of the line. Understand?"

"I got you," said Montrose.

"I have to go. I'll be offline while I sort out some new communications. The numbers will stay the same though I will have to keep them moving. And Miss Brodie?

"Aye?" relied Kirsty.

"We're on the same team for this operation. Lives will certainly depend on it. I want you to consider your allegiances to the people of our island."

"Yeah, *alba gu brath*, bawbag." The call dropped. Kirsty closed the laptop. "Get some clothes on."

The Director looked down at his phone and tried to stop himself from smiling. "Two billion dollars."

The fat Dutchman slapped the table. Others began to punch into calculators.

"The money has been transferred into a Swiss account and will be transferred again immediately. The original account has already disappeared. The funds will be divided evenly and deposited in the escrow account and then transferred to your nominated accounts."

"And there will be no trace?"

"The Swiss banking industry are very accommodating when you can afford their services. There will be no trace of the bank, the transfer method, the country or the continent where it originated. Nothing."

The Dutchman drank greedily from his glass of water, spilling some onto his tie. "I can't believe the Russians are so easily fooled. They are the masters of this game."

This time the Director couldn't help but laugh.

The Dutchman looked up, the water dribbling from his fleshy lips. "Did they really try to outbid the Americans?"

"No," replied the Director. "They were very far behind. They must have thought that Uncle Sam was going to let them win. How very naïve."

"But they will know?"

"Not for certain. The Russians think they have the monopoly on being the most immoral, duplicitous and ruthless government in the northern hemisphere. In reality, they lost that title many years ago. But Washington is content to entertain their fantasy."

"Will the Russians discover it?"

"The CIA have an entire mountain hollowed out in Colorado, dedicated to their cyber criminality. There is absolutely no way that the Russians will find any evidence that the CIA bought that missile." He lifted a glass of water and took a sip. "So, I'm going to give it to them."

Every face at the table looked up at him. He turned and walked to the window and waved a hand towards the landscape. "You know, it was around eighty years ago that the Russians swept across this plain heading for Berlin. The endless columns of tanks and trucks full of men, charging unopposed through the fields. Are we so sure it won't happen again?" He pointed to the east. "Through that forest they came, down the road and found the ruins of Rhiandorf."

He turned back to the table. "Then they bulldozed and flattened the entire site and laid two feet of concrete for their tanks. If you look down to where the trucks are parked, you'll see it still survives. 'Hard standing,' gentlemen. Vital for military transport in the spring when winter has left the roads a sea of mud. And the roads from here point to all corners of Europe and to Asia Minor. In East Germany this was an important military hub. The Russian army knew the logistical importance of this site. And if the Russians come back to Germany, then they'll be coming though those trees and heading straight here."

Several of the men shifted in their seats.

The Director returned to the table. "Relax, my friends. Even the next terrorist outrage will not get the fat Russian bear moving again. Today's Moscow is only interested in making money. Anything that threatens the pockets of the people in charge of Russia is off the table. And that includes war. It's a very expensive business. Especially when the Americans could freeze their bank accounts in every country outside Russia. And they have many, many accounts outside Russia. Europe and America could strangle the Russian economy within a week if they ever chose to do so. And the Russians know it. I am unconcerned with the bellicose Russian threatening hellfire. It will never happen." The Director sat back in his chair. "And there is one thing of which we can always be sure. Greed will win the day."

CHAPTER 10

"C'mon, Connor, get your knickers on." Kirsty pulled a thin woolen sweater over her head.

"Hey, I'm ready to go. I'm not the one wandering around half-naked."

"I didn't hear you complaining earlier." She peered down at the laptop. "Mr. Pilgrim is online."

"Good, we need to talk."

Pilgrim's face appeared on the screen. "My dear Kirsty, it's always a pleasure to see you."

"Likewise, Mr. P." She jerked a thumb to the side. "Trouble is here too. I rescued him from all the lonely MILFs at the bar."

Pilgrim gave a slight smile as Montrose sat behind her on the bed. "I take it that Linden from MI6 was in touch?"

"Yeah," said Kirsty, "Priti patched him through. She'll have the whole recording. He got straight to the point. Starting price was $1 billion. Then he cut the call due to security and called back. By that time, the missile had been sold."

Pilgrim nodded slowly. "It sounds to me like they already had customers."

"He said it wasn't the Russians. That they were going crazy."

"I'll check that for myself," said Pilgrim.

"I don't trust him," said Kirsty. "He says he's getting this information from GCHQ, so either the Brits just became the best hackers ever, or he's talking bollocks."

"Both are possible," replied Pilgrim. "It depends on his motive. But we have no other choice than to use his information, it's better than any I can find. The CIA really do have this sewn up tight."

"He's expecting more info from them," said Montrose. "They are trying to locate the delivery. And you know, what he's not saying directly is that he thinks it was the CIA who bought the missile."

"And your reasoning?" asked Pilgrim.

"He said that if Downing Street find out what GCHQ are doing, they will shut it down. Downing Street would only do that to protect the CIA, either because the CIA didn't buy the missile and are keeping this whole operation to themselves, or they did buy it, and Whitehall will do what Washington says and back off. But that makes no sense."

"Why?"

"Because you can take it from me that the British intelligence services are the sneakiest bastards on the face of this planet. They'd tell Washington whatever Washington wanted to hear and keep right on doing what they do. Linden is sharing some of the best results I've ever heard. GCHQ would not want this to get out. So, either Linden is a fantasist, or the British really are panicking that the CIA have gone rogue for some unknown reason, and are trying to false flag and blame Russia by blowing one of their own planes out of the sky. That is madness."

"Well, I can't disagree with you on the last point. But let me step back a bit. You said they are trying to determine the delivery point?"

"Yeah, and he thinks it's right here in Rome. Why here?"

"All the major players are here. Italy is a strategic location for the Middle East and home to a number of NATO and US bases. We have about twelve thousand troops here. And the Russians have a pretty big diplomatic operation in Rome. Let's just say information is easier to come by in Italy."

"Yeah, I'm sure," said Montrose. "I've been down that road. But what if Linden comes back with a delivery point?"

"Well," said Pilgrim, "I think it would be very interesting to see who collects the delivery."

Kirsty pointed to the hotel telephone on the desk. "Connor, get on the blower to reception. I want a limo. Right now."

"You think they'll have one waiting? We could…"

"Connor, they have gold-plated taps in the crapper and a frickin' helipad. They'll have a limo. And don't get a stretch limo. I don't want to look like a dick."

The technician stood in the open doorway as Napier and Faber approached. "I received your orders, sir. Director Campbell is online."

Napier looked up to the screen on the wall and saw Campbell sitting alone at a desk, staring at his cell phone. "Can he see us?"

"No, sir," said the technician, "you have to activate the call at this end." He pointed to a button on the speakerphone. "The sound is muted too."

"Got it," said Faber. "That will be all."

The technician closed the door behind him.

Napier held out the printed report to Faber. "Shred it."

"We should tell him, sir."

"He'll know. When someone raids a Russian missile base and steals the latest SAM missile, it gets out. I just wish it had got out before and we didn't have to go asking our men in Moscow to go looking for it. That makes me suspicious. And in the meantime, the missiles are out of Russia and halfway across Europe and we only find out when a C-130 drops out of the sky."

"You don't think it was the Russians, sir, and this is just a cover-up?"

"I don't know what to think. But you saw Dimitri. You saw his fear. He nearly had a coronary. I've never seen him that angry. Whatever is going on, he didn't know."

Faber straightened his tie. "Then we're no closer to knowing who stole them."

"It's whoever got those two bastards in the village to take down a plane. But this isn't terrorism. They may want it to look like that, but this is different. They could have taken down an Airbus A380 with nearly nine hundred people heading to New York. Yet they chose a military target." He pointed to the screen on the wall. "I want to hear what he says." He hit the mute button. "Director Campbell?"

Campbell's head lifted from the phone. "Director Napier. I hope you have some good news for me."

"Good and bad." He watched Campbell straighten in the chair. "Good news first, we won the auction."

Campbell didn't move. "And?"

"I don't think it's the only missile out there. Someone raided a Russian SAM missile store. We know where it was because of the spectrum analysis and chromatography of the paint on the missile parts we recovered. What we don't know is how many missiles were stolen."

Campbell checked the screen on his phone. "My report tells of a raid and that two missiles were stolen. You are telling me that this is incorrect, yet you cannot counter this figure with an exact number?"

"No, I can't. But I saw the look on Saitsev's face. There are more out there, I'm sure of it."

"I'm not interested in your concerns or assumptions. Have you recovered the missile?"

"We are awaiting collection instructions. We'll get it. Though that's not my concern. If there are more out there, what the hell happens next? We keep buying them? It's only going to take one plane down over a European capital to set this continent alight."

"I'm not interested in your concerns, Napier, we need that…"

"Or the next one might be a flight to New York, so you know, you might want to be fucking concerned!"

Campbell blinked. "Lose the emotion, Napier. I don't have to remind you of my seniority, but if you would like me to demonstrate by having you marched from your office and have someone more competent put in charge, I shall do so in an instant."

Napier glowered at the screen.

"I want you to retrieve that missile, and I want it on a fast jet within the hour. There is a team waiting for you at the Ciampino airport outside Rome. Refueling planes have already taken off from RAF Mildenhall in England to provide cover across the Atlantic."

Napier said nothing.

"I suggest you start moving, Napier. The sooner we get that missile to the USA, the sooner we can counteract its capabilities and our Air Force, including the President's plane, will be safe in the skies. We look after Americans first, Europeans second. Remember that. I am capable of making tough decisions. If I think you are not, you know what will happen. You have my full authority, and that of the President of the United States to do what is necessary. I suggest you use it."

Kirsty had her laptop open by the time Montrose had settled into the soft leather seats, and the chauffeur had closed the door. "Okay, this is Rome. The eternal city. Pick a destination."

"Well, we've no idea where the hell we are going, just head for town."

The chauffeur settled into his seat. "Signore, signora, where would you like to go?"

"The Colosseum," said Montrose.

"Interesting choice," said Kirsty. "Why there?"

He leaned forward, his face turning white as he remembered the blood, the body of the young woman, and the brains of the old man scattered across the floor.

"Connor? You okay?"

He rubbed his face and sat back. "Yeah. Another time. Another life." He leaned forward to the chauffeur. "Signore, I changed my mind, can we go to the Forum?"

"*Certamente.*" The car pulled away. "The wifi password is 'Mercedes.'"

"You read my mind," said Kirsty. She pulled her phone

from her bag and handed an earpiece to Montrose. "Mr. P is online. He can hear you."

Montrose shoved in the earpiece. "Pilgrim?"

"Loud and clear," he replied.

"We're mobile and heading for town. We're going central to give us the best chance of responding."

"Understood," said Pilgrim. "Priti will inform you if she receives the delivery point."

"Yeah. Let's hope we get there first and see what the hell is going on. I have no idea what our chances are."

"Understood. We can only do what we can."

"Listen, if we do get there first…"

"I expect no heroics," said Pilgrim. "If we have an opportunity to recover the missile, we should take it. We do not know for certain who bought the missile, only that it may not have been the Russians. Though we can take nothing for granted."

"I hear you. But if we do, we want to give it to the CIA, yeah? We want them to take it apart and see how it works, so we can stop another attack."

"Indeed," said Pilgrim. "I can ensure that it reaches safe hands."

"I'm sure you can," said Montrose, "but if I handed it over…" he looked over at Kirsty.

"I'm listening," said Pilgrim.

"If I handed it over, then they would see I'm not a terrorist. Or a traitor. They would know, yeah?"

Pilgrim paused before replying. "I'm sure it would go some way to rehabilitating your reputation, but I fear it will take much more than such commendable action to reverse your current situation. However, I am not averse to such a scenario. Therefore, if it emerges as a possibility, I am willing to consider it, if it does not threaten the operational security of the team."

"That was a yes," said Kirsty, "as long as you don't put the rest of us in the shit."

"Quite succinctly put, my dear," said Pilgrim. "Let us see what opportunity we have before we make any plans. We have to rely on GCHQ cracking the information, and Linden…" Pilgrim paused.

"What is it?" said Kirsty.

"You have a text message coming through," said Pilgrim.

Montrose lifted the phone and it buzzed in his hand. He brought up the message and held it out to Kirsty. "It's a code. There's directions down some steps. It says the street is near the Via Arenlua."

"Oh, shit. That's on the other side of town. We're never going to… Signore!" She leaned over to the chauffeur. "Can you find us the nearest scooter hire?"

"Scooter, signora?"

"Yeah, we've got to be somewhere very soon, and no matter how fast you can drive, this is Rome. The fastest way is scooter."

"You sure?" said Montrose.

"Oh yeah, it's big business for tourists who like a near-death experience and Italian hospital food."

"Maybe we should…"

"Connor, shut up for a moment, I have to send an email. I need to know more about that address."

"There is one not too far," said the chauffeur, tapping on the satnav screen. "It's right here. But in this traffic…"

"Where exactly?" said Montrose.

He pointed down the street. "Second on the left and fourth on the right."

"Okay, we'll walk. Or run!" Kirsty pulled the earpiece from Montrose's ear and grabbed the door handle. "Let's go."

"The cars are ready, sir."

Napier nodded, pulled his jacket from the back of the chair and headed for the open door. "Any news of the location?"

"Nothing yet, sir."

"It's going to come to my phone?"

"It's all set up."

"Okay, let's move. We'll formulate the plan once we have the location."

"Italian police will monitor and clear roads as necessary. We have a blue light passage through town with a police helicopter and traffic light control if required."

"So much for covert ops. We should just broadcast it on TV."

"It's the traffic in Rome, sir, it's crazy."

"Understood. Get the cars rolling. Head for town." Napier looked down at his phone. "They promised an address. What the hell are they waiting for?"

CHAPTER 11

Kirsty straddled the scooter and held up her phone. "It's about a mile from here and the traffic is solid. Don't lose me. And wear your helmet. It's the only traffic law the Italians obey. Ready?"

Montrose threaded the Velcro loop under his chin and hauled the helmet down hard. "What's the plan?"

"The plan is to follow me and do what you're told. You might know Naples, but I know Rome. This is urbex heaven. Urban Explorers, remember?"

"Yeah, though if it's the same as the last time, the missiles are going to be in suitcases. How are we going to get them on a scooter?"

"Duh! How the hell do I know? I'm making this shit up as I go along. You said they're on wheels, right?"

"Yeah, normal wheeled suitcases."

"Well, Connor, that pickup address is part of an excavation of ancient Rome. It's closed off to the public. But this is Europe. Everything has to have around five disabled and fire exits. And it's right in the middle of Rome. It's a tourist spot.

That excavation has more than one exit, you can bet your life on it. Whoever picked it knows what they are doing. They would need a hundred policemen to find us down there, and if we're on the streets with a couple of suitcases they haven't got a chance. The entire bloody city is full of bloody tourists dragging bloody suitcases. And we have to get there first, so let's go!" She wound the throttle open and darted through the traffic.

Montrose followed her, trying to keep his balance and wrestling the narrow handlebars between cars.

Kirsty turned right and down a narrow street, the scooter's engine screaming as she weaved around pedestrians. They heard her coming and stepped aside.

Montrose held up a hand to signal a right turn then thought better of it and headed down the street, holding on tightly to the handlebars. In front, he could see no cars, but pedestrians parted in waves as Kirsty stabbed the horn. People moved to the side without looking behind. This was Italy. Two scooters racing down a street full of pedestrians was par for the course.

She stopped at the end and turned into the traffic. Montrose watched her force her way to the middle of the road and join a line of scooters screaming along the white line in both directions. He spun his scooter around a car and shoved his way into the line. Other riders started shouting but he ignored them and twisted the throttle. He edged up to the rear of the scooter in front, an old lady in a voluminous black dress, with plastic shopping bags hanging from both the handlebars and her arms. Up front, he could just see Kirsty about half a block ahead. He waited for a gap and tried to sweep past the old lady, then pulled back in when another scooter tried

97

the same coming from the opposite direction. In his mirror, he caught a flash of red and glanced back to see an elegantly dressed young lady in sunglasses, bright red lips pursed tight, edging her scooter alongside. "Back off!" he shouted and accelerated up to the old lady, narrowly avoiding hitting her rear wheel. In the distance, he saw Kirsty stick out an arm and point to a side street. Montrose looked around, trying to keep an eye on the oncoming traffic, the old lady's shopping bag swinging out in front of her, and the girl right behind him. He stood up on the footplate and saw a gap in front then twisted the throttle and pulled alongside the old lady.

She saw him coming and moved out to block him. He pulled in just in time. "Son of a bitch!" He grabbed another handful of throttle, shot forward and booted her shopping bag. The contents spilled out across the street and she slammed on her brakes.

Montrose swerved in front and glanced in the mirror to see the old lady holding up a torn shopping bag and giving him the finger.

He stood up and saw Kirsty waiting by the side street. The traffic slowed to a halt, and he accelerated past the cars. As a car in front pulled away, he slammed on the brakes and turned in to the side street, seeing her move away from the curb. He wound open the throttle and held on tight as they careered down the white line.

Kirsty pointed right and slowed, then headed down a narrow alley.

He felt the skin cool on the back of his neck as high walls shaded them from the sun.

She stopped and wheeled her scooter around a corner into a small square, bathed in sunlight. On each side, high walls were studded with small windows, each one with a washing line strung from it, where clothes hung like pennants.

Montrose followed and hauled his scooter onto its stand, beside her. Beyond the washing lines, he saw the intricately carved doorway of a church and above, a bell tower that rose several stories into the air. He tried to look up, but the sun was directly behind the spire and blinded him.

"Leave the scooters here," said Kirsty. "We'll know where they are if we need to get out fast."

"Where's the place?"

"Around the corner." She pointed to a high building at the rear of the church. "That's a government department, and below is an archaeological exhibition. The whole thing was built over old Roman roads, homes and streets. No one gave a shit in those days. And they're still there. You can walk down them."

"We go in with the tourists?"

"No, the directions are to a small side door, away from the main exhibition, though part of the same network. A lot of it is still being dug out, but it's pretty big."

"Where did you get all this from?"

"The email I sent from the limo, it was to my urbex pals in London. They've sent me back all the maps I need. They know all about it. A lot of the streets were filled in with rubble in the 18th century to support the building above."

"Wait, if we've got these maps…"

"Yeah, I know, whoever gets the address might have them too. It's not a secret, if you know where to look and who to ask. Anybody who studies Roman archaeology or urban exploring knows about places like this. Rome is full of these underground sites; it's an urbex mecca. Places like this can go back nearly three thousand years. There's a lot of old stuff under our feet." She pointed to the ground. "It's like a warren. We can do this. If that door is blocked, I have routes leading to the crypt of the church and to twenty other exits."

"Okay, how do we get in?"

"We were given a code. Check out that street. There's only one door that takes a code and it's that fire exit with the metal doors. Those are the directions. Down the steps and through a door. End of the street turn left. Remember it's a street from ancient Rome. Best of luck. I'll be right here."

"And I've got to carry out two suitcases?"

"I'm your lookout." She handed him a Bluetooth earpiece. "Connect this up. We're not the only ones searching for the missiles, remember. I see them coming, I'll let you know. Don't be a hero. I've got plans for you later, but I'm not talking dinner. Let's just say nudity is involved."

He patted the gun in his pocket. "Okay, though what if…?"

"I've got lots of ways to get you out. Remember, I've got the map. And not the official one. And put this in your pocket." She pulled a cheap plastic leprechaun from her pocket and twisted its neck.

Montrose heard it click. "For luck?"

"No, you idiot, it's a tracker. Then I can see where you are on the map. Your phone might not work down there, but that little bastard gives off a signal that could shatter a window at fifty yards."

"I hear you. Though if they are already down there I'll be out of that place like a rat with its ass on fire."

"And I'll be here to beat out the flames, just bloody go!"

They ran towards the door. The side street was too narrow

for cars and the government building stretched five stories high into the sunshine. A metal keypad was set into the wall beside a grey metal door.

"The code is FC9000," said Kirsty.

"Got it." He punched in the code. Nothing happened. He pulled the handle and the door sprang open and he jumped back.

"Good luck," she said. "Down the steps, end of the street, turn left."

He ducked in and raised his gun. There was no sound. To his right were steel steps. He moved down them as quietly as he could and walked into a low corridor with pipes above his head. In front was another grey metal door. He pushed down the handle and it swung open into darkness. He brought up the torch on his phone.

The floor was thick with dust, and cables and pipes ran just over his head. The ground felt uneven beneath his feet and he kicked at the dust and saw the cobblestones. Yeah, he thought, this is it. Ancient Rome.

The metal door swung closed behind him.

Napier jumped as the phone rang in his lap. He checked the number. *Campbell.* "Fucking shit-weasel." He leaned forward and tapped the driver on the shoulder. "Wait outside."

Faber lowered the window and spoke to the driver. He pointed to the line of Range Rover SUVs in front. "Make sure they do a full weapons check. I want everyone locked and loaded in thirty seconds."

Napier waited until Faber had raised the window then hit

the speaker button on the phone. He sat back in the reek of expensive leather and gun oil. "Director Campbell," he said. "We are ready to go."

"Have you cleared a route to the airport?"

"Yes, and we will use the police helicopter if there are any major traffic jams. I'm expecting the pickup location any moment."

"Good, then we look forward to hearing of your success," said Campbell.

Napier watched the men closing the doors of the SUVs. A police car in front waited with its blue lights flashing. "What about the others?"

"The others, Napier?"

"The others, Director Campbell. I have no doubt there are more than two missing. I've seen the latest raw intelligence report. There is no confirmation that there were only two missiles stolen. I understand the immediate priority, and we will recover this missile, but what next? I think the president should know we have a very great deal to be concerned about."

There was a pause on the line. "But I do not."

Faber's mouth dropped open.

Napier stared down at the phone. "Could you repeat that, Director Campbell. From where I'm sitting this makes very little sense."

"Exactly, Napier, from where you are sitting. I think you are getting caught up in the drama of the events. The raw intelligence did not confirm there were only two missiles stolen. Similarly, it did not confirm there were *more* than two missiles stolen. The ludicrous story that someone broke into one of the most secure missile bases in Russia and stole a large number of missiles is absolutely laughable. The Russians have fooled you, Napier. But not me. I have no doubt that Moscow has planned this to show the effectiveness of the missile, and hugely increase its market value. The Chinese, the Iranians, everyone will be lining up as a customer."

"No, there's more to this…"

"Napier, despite your vast experience in operational matters, you are woefully lacking in strategy. Why on earth would the Russians allow the missile to be bought by the CIA? They could have bid five billion dollars. That's nickels and dimes for an oligarch. No. They let us buy the missile because they know that when another goes on sale, we would make sure that one way or another, we will have developed a counter measure against it. They must be enjoying the panic they have created. But the Russians always play the long game, Napier. This is not about these missiles. This is about the next generation. They sell missiles to Syria and Iran and we counter the threat. Then they sell an upgraded version, and again, we counter the threat. The Russians will have customers for life. After all, they're just following the USA's lead. We have already created our own market for the Patriot missile system. We've sold it to over twenty friendly countries, and each upgrade brings the USA billions in profit and tax dollars."

Napier spoke through gritted teeth. "They shot down a USAF C-130. Our servicemen and women died."

"I understand. We will retaliate in our own time. We don't dance to Moscow's tune."

"Campbell. Listen to me. I saw the look on Dimitri Saitsev's face. There are…"

"I think you've been reading too many spy thrillers. Just do what you're…."

A message flashed up on the phone's screen. "The location. It's coming through. Old Government building. Next to the Jewish quarter, near the via Arenlua."

Faber hammered on the window and the driver spun around. "Go!"

"Get that missile," said Campbell. "Don't let the president down."

Napier cut the call. "If he's as crazy as you then he can go fuck himself." He grabbed a mic from the radio between the seats and thumbed the button. "All stations, listen up. I want the area around Via Arenlua sealed off." He let the button go and turned to Faber. "How many cops we got?"

"Two hundred, twenty cars and two helicopters. More if we need them."

"Get all the cop cars rolling and the choppers in the air. I want that missile. And I want to take it back to the USA and shove it straight up that shiny-faced bastard's ass."

CHAPTER 12

"Kirsty?" There was no reply. He checked his phone, but the signal was gone.

Keep moving, he thought, the steel door had cut the signal. Just get this done. He took off down the ancient road. Above him, low hanging cables brushed his head, and dust played in the torch beam.

Steel brackets holding the cables stretched across the roof, and he saw a video camera set into the wall. He leaned in close. There was no power light on the camera. It seemed to be dead. Yeah, he thought, I'll bet they're all switched off. The last thing they are going to want is evidence. Fine by me.

He picked up the pace. Dark doorways opened up along the wall in the torch beam. He ducked his head and began to run. The walls on the other side changed from smooth sandstone blocks to small, crumbling bricks. Damn it, he thought, I'm in ancient Rome. The torch found the wall at the far end and the cobbled path stopped dead, against an eighteenth-century foundation of thick blocks of stone. He saw a warped wooden door set into the wall. He pushed it and brought up the torch, entering warily. At the far side of what appeared to be an abandoned storeroom, the beam flashed onto a pile of rubble that reached to the roof, then down and played across the dull metal of two aluminum suitcases.

He checked the signal. One bar. "Kirsty?"

"Yeah?"

"I've got them."

"Then get the hell out of there."

He shoved his phone between his teeth, grabbed the handles and hefted the cases up, pushing one in front of the other through the door and onto the ancient road. The walls were too narrow and cobbles too uneven to drag them along on either side, so he grabbed the handles and lifted them into the air, holding one in front and one behind him, then ducked his head and ran. The torch light bounced off the cobbles and the steel door came up quick. He let the first suitcase drop and grabbed the handle.

It didn't move. He leaned down with all his weight and pulled hard.

It was locked. He dropped the other suitcase and took the wet phone from his mouth and shone the torch around the frame. There was no keyhole. There was no number pad.

"Kirsty?"

There was no answer. He hauled at the door, but it didn't move. He booted the door. "Kirsty!" He checked the signal on his phone. No bars. He felt sweat begin to gather at the back of his neck. He grabbed the suitcases and ran back down the corridor. "Kirsty!"

There was a crackle on the line, then her voice. "I hear you. Where the hell are you going?"

"The door's locked. The door to the steps. It was open

before. There's no lock I can see. It won't move. It's fucking locked!"

"Shit."

"Kirsty, this could be a trap. You better move."

"Understood. Go back to the room, there's another way out."

He got to the end of the road and threw the suitcases through the door. They slid to a halt at the foot of the pile of rubble that stretched across the room and rose up in a steep slope to the roof.

"Connor, I've got a cop car at the end of street and a chopper in the sky. I've got to move, but I'll talk you out, okay?"

"Understood." He heard her revving the scooter engine.

"I'm heading for the Jewish quarter. Are you back in the room?"

"Yeah."

"There's a blockage at the far end."

"I see it."

"At the top is a long, flat stone. Behind it is a gap. Crawl through and into the next room."

"Got it." Rubble slipped under his feet and dust kicked up around him when he began to climb. He saw the flat stone and pulled it hard. It slid down the rubble and landed beside the suitcases. He scrambled back down, picked up the first suitcase and ran up the slope again, shoving it through the gap. Then he returned for the other and shoved it against the first, pushing it deeper into the opening. He held on tight to his phone and used his elbows and knees to propel himself along, pushing rubble away from his face, his chest flat on sharp rocks. He shoved hard on the suitcase which slid easily and he heard the first suitcase drop down the other side, clattering onto stone. Launching himself forward, the second suitcase fell away and Montrose dropped head first down another pile of rubble.

He brought up his phone. Before him the cobbles of a Roman alley stretched into darkness, with shadowy doorways on either side. "Kirsty?" He checked the phone. The call had dropped. He hit redial and she answered immediately, the sound of a screaming scooter engine in the background.

"Connor, where are you?"

"Other side of the rubble. I've got both suitcases."

"Good. Move forward. Look out for a brothel sign. Left hand side."

"What?"

"Two people fucking. It's a clue. Although, to be accurate, it's a sign."

He peered into the darkness. "What about the alley?"

"It's a dead end."

"What kind of sign?"

"Jesus, Connor, I'm reading the description on a phone from an internet blog and riding a scooter. It's been written by a guy who obviously didn't have a girlfriend judging by the length of time he's taking to describe exactly what the sign looks like, but it's detail you don't need to know. Just imagine a menu for a brothel, in pictures, on the wall. With people."

"I hear ya." He kicked a suitcase forward and dragged the other, shining the torch down each doorway. Then he saw the faded sign, and he could just make out the various couples. It didn't leave anything to the imagination. "I got it."

"You sure?"

"Oh, yeah." He booted the suitcases into the doorway and

brought up the torch. Another pile of rubble stretched to the roof. "I'm in. But it's blocked."

"That's part of the eighteenth-century foundations. The urbex guys have cut a path through the top, just like the other room. Go to the top and find the biggest stone and pull it down."

"I see it." He scrambled up the rocks and hauled at the stone. It slid to his feet. He lifted the torch. "Shit."

"What?"

"It's not like the other room. I can maybe squeeze through, but there's no way I'm going to get two suitcases through."

"No way?"

"I'd have to dig it out. We haven't got time for that. It would take me an hour."

"Okay, wait there, let me check."

He felt his pulse thumping in his neck.

"Connor, you have to…" The call dropped.

The sound of hammering on the steel door sent a shock through his spine and the phone fell from his hands. He grabbed it from the earth and stood up. They're locked out, he thought. It's the one I came through. They have to get through that to get to me. He looked up at the narrow passageway over the rubble. He made to hit the redial when he saw a thin red beam flicker across the doorway and he clasped the phone to his chest to shut out the light.

The hammering on the steel door became louder.

His eyes were transfixed on the red beam as it bounced across the doorway. Focus, he thought. That beam's not close or it wouldn't be moving all over the place. But how far? Fifty yards? A hundred? He pulled the gun from his jeans and couldn't stop a nervous laugh. He's got a laser beam. I'll bet he's got infra-red sights too. All I've got is a pistol. Someone came prepared, and it's not me.

Montrose shoved the gun in his pocket and scrambled for the slope, then stopped. Do it, he thought, you won't get another chance.

Sliding down the rocks, he grabbed the first suitcase and popped the locks. It sprang open to reveal a green missile section and red warhead, held tight by hard foam. Shoving the gun in his pocket, he pulled out the plastic green leprechaun and tucked it between the foam and the suitcase, then pulled out the warhead and scrambled up the slope, pushing the warhead in front of him. He pushed the warhead into the gap between the rocks and roof and wriggled behind it, dust choking him. The warhead slipped from his grasp and tumbled into darkness. He froze and heard it clatter to the floor, then pulled himself through the gap and slid headfirst down the stones and came to rest at the bottom, the cold metal of the warhead against his face.

He brought up the torch and blinked at a spider dangling inches in front of him. His eye was drawn up the silvery thread, to the metallic glint of a tripwire.

He stared open-mouthed for a moment, then tried to slowly edge back up the slope. Rocks rolled down past his head and settled just in front of the wire. The spider swung in the air, moving in the downdraught created by his rapid breathing.

Montrose rolled back and sat on his ass, then shone the torch around. The tripwire ran from a pin in the wall to the dull green plastic cover of a mine, half-covered by rubble. He let his legs slide down behind him, holding back the rocks, then gently brought them forward and got to his feet. He bent

110

down and picked up the warhead. The phone buzzed in his pocket and the warhead slipped in his hands, but he pulled it close to his chest. He shoved a hand in his pocket and answered the call.

"Are you through? The tracker…"

"I'm through. And about one hundred years older, but I'm through. Kirsty, there's some crazy… Listen, I've got the warhead and there's someone trying to get in from the street, and I've got a guy down here with a gun and he's on my tail."

"Okay, go straight ahead. There's an access ladder at the end. It goes directly up to the road. I'm waiting."

Clasping the warhead to his chest, he lifted a boot to step over the tripwire, then froze as a red beam played around the floor at his feet and slowly lifted to his chest. It refracted off the warhead and lit up the rubble and dust around him in a starburst of red light.

"Put it down," said a voice. "Slowly."

The beam of a flashlight dazzled him. He tried to look down, but he couldn't see the trip wire.

"If you're thinking of a suicide mission," said the voice, "then forget it. Sure, you'll kill me, but you set that missile off and you'll destroy the whole building. Think of the hundreds of innocent people above us. You don't want to do that. Put it down." The flashlight beam dropped to the warhead, then along to the tripwire. "You see, I will help you. Be careful."

In the corner of his eye he saw a red beam flickering behind him, and heard someone scrambling over the rocks from the other room.

"You see, there is no escape. Put it down, and I will let you live. "

Kirsty's voice whispered through his earpiece. "No

fucking chance. Now, do exactly as I say, because I'm using full metal jacket ammunition and I don't want to get two for the price of one, or that bloody warhead. I'm aiming in the dark at a shadow behind a flashlight. Ready?"

He heard her let out a slow breath.

"Bend over, Connor."

He stepped over the tripwire, then bent over, lowering the warhead to the floor. A crack flew past his ears and blood sprayed across the flashlight beam. A man tumbled forward at his feet.

"Run!"

Dodging around the bloody corpse, he sprinted into the darkness, holding the warhead to his chest. A torch beam lit up in the distance and he saw the figure of Kirsty at the bottom of a ladder, leading up through the roof. "Go!" he shouted, and she climbed out of sight.

Holding the warhead hard against him with one hand, Montrose reached up to grab a rung when the stone wall splintered around him. He twisted to the side and the warhead slipped from his grasp and tumbled to the floor. A red beam flashed across his legs and the rungs on the ladder sparked into flame in front of him, sending hot shards of metal into his face. He lunged up and fixed a boot on the rung and pushed himself up towards the light. He felt a searing heat as a round grazed his leg and for a moment he thought of the warhead, then clambered upwards, desperately grabbing each rung, and hauled himself out and onto the street.

Kirsty pushed him to the side and pointed her pistol down the hole. "C'mon, you bastard, walk right into it."

"No," said Montrose, "the warhead!" He could hear the chopper overhead.

Kirsty lifted her weapon and shoved a metal plate over the hole.

"I couldn't…"

The scooter stood waiting on the curb. "Get on the back. The cops are everywhere."

The motor strained under the weight, but she twisted the throttle and set off fast down a narrow alley, then made a sharp turn into a dingy courtyard, then out again into a wider street lined with pedestrians and market stalls. She edged slowly past the people and at the end of the road he could see a busy street and a police car. Two policemen in crisp white shirts stood by the trunk, smoking and examining the crowd through their sunglasses. Kirsty pulled into the side and took the helmet from the catch by the seat.

"Put yours on. I don't want to get stopped by some flatfoot. Shooting him would totally ruin his shirt."

Napier leaned against the SUV, his eyes closed. He heard the thump of the explosion and waited for them to clear the sandbags, but he knew it was a waste of time.

Faber came running to the top of the stairs. "Empty. Nothing. There is a tunnel. The men are checking everything, though according to the maps we've been sent, we'll be down there for hours."

Napier shook his head, and looked down as the phone buzzed in his hand.

The Director pointed to the TV mounted on the wall of the boardroom. A face filled the screen.

"Is that him?" asked the old man.

The Director smiled. "It is indeed our dear friend, Mr. Montrose, exploring ancient Rome."

"And the missile?"

The Director nodded to the technician and the screen capture moved to a video. The image was in shades of grey, but high definition. "Infrared cameras," said the Director. "He had no idea."

Another camera showed Montrose walking over the cobbles and through a door. Another camera picked him up as he lifted the two suitcases and headed out of the room and back towards the street. The first camera picked him up again, hurrying down the cobbles, and stopping before the metal door.

"That's all we need," said the Director and the screen went blank.

"You are sure?" said the old man. "You are sure it is him?"

The Director pointed to the screen. The picture changed to the original screen capture of Montrose, then moved to split screen, showing alongside a CIA ID card with Montrose's face. There were murmurs of approval from around the room.

The old man sipped from a glass of water. "There is no doubt. I wonder what the CIA will have to say?"

"Well, I think we will find out soon enough. I left the Silk Road account open just long enough for them to send a message. And of course, when they discovered there was no missile, they contacted me immediately."

The fat Dutchman sat upright. "They contacted you?"

"They did, and I replied with a phone number connected to an IP address and sent through over a thousand routers across the globe." He took out a cell phone from his pocket. "And here it is." He handed it to the technician, who connected it up to a laptop. "All I have to do is switch it on."

The Dutchman stared at the phone. "They are going to call? Here?"

"They have been trying for some time, but I wanted to wait until we had completed work on our fascinating video. I'm sure you all want to listen?" He smiled. "Relax, gentlemen, this call number and location are absolutely untraceable and we will be using voice masking. Are we ready?" He permitted himself a thin smile at the shocked faces around the table, then nodded to the technician who pressed a key on the laptop.

A low hiss came from the speakers and the Director lifted the handset and held a finger to his lips. "You will hear my natural voice, but all that they will hear is a metallic composite rendition, with no inflection. It is, like this phone, untraceable." He pressed the button on the handset. "Speak."

There was a silence for a moment then an American accent came over the line. "This is … the customer."

"Talk to me."

"You have set us up. There was no missile. Do you realize what we will do if you do not deliver that missile?"

"There was a missile. Two suitcases. And you collected it."

"We collected nothing. The door was locked when we got there and the room was empty. So, you listen to me, I want…"

"That is not true. The door was open. Your agent entered. He collected the suitcases." The Director pointed to the technician who pressed the enter key on the keyboard. He spoke slowly into the handset. "You have mail." He turned and gazed out of the window.

"What do you mean…?"

"Mr. Napier, your voice has been recognized. I have sent you a video. Watch it immediately."

There was no response.

"Mr. Napier, did you think you could collect the missile and then demand your money back? That is no way to do business. I shall remember that."

"That man… Montrose," said Napier. "He is not a CIA agent."

"Mr. Napier, I have no more time for your games. Your agent picked up the suitcases. You were the only party that was informed of the location. The deal is complete." He cut the call and handed the cell phone to the technician, then looked up at the table. "How did you enjoy your chat with the CIA, gentlemen? Isn't technology a wonderful thing?"

The technician gathered up his equipment and hurried from the room.

"What about Montrose?" said the old man. "I hope very much for all our sakes that this time you have succeeded in killing him. Anything other than that would be failure."

The Director felt his hands trembling and pushed his palms together. In a moment he recovered his composure. The old man would not see the end of the day. His next glass of water would be his last. It would be a pleasure to watch his heart stop. "No, I am unconcerned with Mr. Montrose."

"The risk has not gone away. And it grows all the time. The task to kill him has been a failure."

The Director gripped the back of his chair. "The risk remains the same. That has not changed. The likelihood may have increased, but not the impact. However, the mitigation against the risk has changed to our advantage, and utilizes the resources of all the Western intelligence agencies, and that of the mighty Russians. They are all about to expend a considerable amount of time and energy looking for Mr. Montrose, and I have no intention of getting in their way. I think Mr. Montrose's life expectancy can be measured in hours, perhaps minutes."

The old man opened his mouth but the Director held up a hand. "You see, after that phone call the CIA will be absolutely focused in preventing Mr. Montrose from committing another dreadful atrocity. They will shoot him on sight. And I, frankly, wish them well."

"They think he has the missile? You're sure?"

"Why would they think otherwise? They can see it with their own eyes. Let them chase around Europe in search of the elusive Montrose. I will do nothing to impede them. As Napoleon said, never interrupt your enemy when he is making a mistake."

"And the missile?"

"On the way to the final location, unhindered by the CIA or any of their little helpers. Each suitcase will be taking a different path. I have chosen a location with an uninterrupted view of the flight path over Rome."

The old man tapped a fingernail on the table.

"You have a concern?" said the Director.

"Yes," said the old man, and took a sip from his glass. "You quoted Napoleon. Let us hope that this is not your Waterloo."

CHAPTER 13

"This is going to hurt," said Kirsty, "and I'm going to enjoy it."

"I thought it was a good idea," replied Montrose.

"It was a good idea, but you scared the crap out of me." She dabbed his leg wound with disinfectant, then smeared on a pungent pink cream. "That'll keep it clean. No need for a bandage."

Priti stood in front of the high open windows looking out over the Spanish Steps. "What has he done now?"

"He placed his tracker in one of the suitcases. I thought he was still trapped and about to get his ass shot off. Just as well I went down to check."

"Bad luck," said Priti.

"Any sign of the tracker?" said Kirsty.

Priti shook her head.

Pilgrim entered the room in his powered wheelchair. "Ah, Montrose. I'm getting a report that there are quite a number of CIA operatives searching for you. Any reason why?"

"Well, according to my record, I'm a psychopathic terrorist and traitor to my country, but you know," he shrugged, "no more than usual."

"Perhaps your MI6 friend has been talking."

Montrose walked to the window. He looked over to the steps, crowded with tourists. The sound of someone murdering a Beatles song on a cheap guitar floated into the room. "It has to be Linden. If they link me to the attack in the village, I'm screwed. There is no other way they could know I was involved."

"Perhaps. I shall endeavor to find out more. In the meantime, I'd stay away from the window."

Montrose turned away. "Yeah, for the rest of my life." He felt someone squeezing his hand.

Kirsty laid her head against his chest and smiled. "You're a fucking jinx." She pulled her hand away and patted his butt. "But you've got me to look after you. Well, maybe for the next few days. Then you're on your own, big boy."

"I have checked for the tracker everywhere," said Priti. "I can see nothing. They would have to be far underground to block the signal, or be entirely cased in metal."

"What about the trunk of a car?" asked Montrose.

"No, I have used them in a trunk before, and under a car. They work well. The metal suitcase may affect the signal, though perhaps it is a combination of all three."

"It's not likely," said Kirsty. "That would mean the suitcase is in the trunk of a car and in a deep underground car park. That might weaken the signal, but not stop it completely. The trunk would have to be lined with material specifically designed for that purpose. Do you think they discovered it?"

"It's possible," said Montrose.

Pilgrim looked up from his phone. "There's nothing we can do in the meantime. Yet my sources tell me two important things." He nodded towards Montrose. "The CIA are desperately searching for Montrose, and they do not have the missile."

"Yeah," said Montrose. "The guy that Kirsty dropped didn't sound like a homeboy."

"European?" asked Pilgrim. "Perhaps East or West?"

Montrose shook his head. "I honestly don't know."

Pilgrim returned to examining his phone. "We cannot discount the possibility that the Russians have recovered the missile, but it does not explain the CIA activity in the search for Montrose. Unless they think you are working for the Russians."

"Oh, yeah, that would be the cherry on the cake."

"But I think that is unlikely. I have reports of CIA agents being sent out to airports across central Italy. Whoever has the missile, the CIA suspect that they may use it." Pilgrim maneuvered his wheelchair to look out of the window at the sky over Rome. "But I cannot believe the threat comes directly from Russia, and I suspect neither do the CIA. Even for a false flag operation, they would never attack a civilian airport in the middle of Rome. That would be, quite simply, an act of war. It has to be a terrorist attack that the CIA are expecting." He looked back at Montrose. "Therefore, I am convinced that neither the CIA nor the Russians have the missile."

"Okay, then who does? The guys in the village were Middle Eastern. Who are they working for? Moscow could be using these guys at arm's length. And Langley are not so innocent. You know that."

"Perhaps, but Langley is not the most likely of options. At the moment, we can only assume that someone is about to commit an act of terror, the like of which has not been seen for many years."

Kirsty stood by Pilgrim's wheelchair and gazed out the window. "If it is terrorists, they are the best organized team I've ever heard of, and they've got to be getting that from someone. They have resources. Washington or Moscow." She turned back to Pilgrim. "Let me call the Englishman. We need to know what he knows. Or what he'll tell us."

Pilgrim nodded. "If we can do so safely, it may be our only chance. Priti?"

"I'll monitor everything," said Priti, and pulled a cell phone from her sari. "They gave themselves away last time, so I know what to look out for. Unless they try something different." She held up a hand. "I won't warn you. I'll just cut the call."

"Understood."

She held out the phone. "Use this, it's connected to my laptop."

"I'll take that," said Kirsty. "Because I've got a sexier accent and I'm going to wind him up." She dialed the number and pressed loudspeaker, then placed the phone on the table.

Linden answered immediately. "Hello? Montrose?"

"No, it's his attractive assistant, Miss Brodie," replied Kirsty. "How's life, Sassenach?"

"Ah, our resident grumpy Jock. You still...?"

"Enough of the pleasantries, mate, where's the fucking missile?"

"You may well ask, and I'm assuming that you did not recover it. And since you're asking, I take it you have no idea who did. That's disappointing, considering the lengths I have gone to and the risks I have taken to supply you with information. Perhaps I should…"

"Oh, stop whining, posh boy, I'm not your nanny. We were set up. Only good luck and good shooting got us out. Let me say that anything you care to share with us from now on will be taken with a pinch of salt. Which is a polite way of saying I think you're talking shite."

Linden laughed. "Take it or leave it, Jock. I couldn't give a toss if I've hurt your feelings. If you can't do the job I'll find someone else. Anyway, I'm not sure you have the temperament for this job, so why don't you let me speak to your boss?"

Pilgrim rapped his fingers on the armrest of the wheelchair then tapped his wristwatch.

Kirsty nodded. "Good try, bawbag. You are speaking to him, he's right beside me."

"How touching."

Montrose leaned forward to the phone. "You don't have it, and we don't have it, so who does? Give me your best guess, Linden, because it's out there and we have to know what the hell is going to happen next."

There was a pause on the line. "I have no idea. Though I can tell you the CIA don't have it, judging by the noise they are creating. What happened at the pickup?"

"We'll talk about that later. Have you got nothing we can go on?"

Priti held up a hand and stared at the screen.

"Call me an old cynic, but …"

"C'mon, Linden," said Kirsty, "you can do better than that."

"Listen Jock, you're not so naïve. I'll bet you're well past your first kiss. I'm sure you've been around the block a few times, so you don't need me to tell you how the Yanks play their games."

Kirsty looked up at Montrose and drew her finger across her throat.

"Linden," said Montrose, "remember, I was there when that plane got blown out the sky. I heard the CIA coming and they weren't taking their time. And the guy who fired the missile knew that they would be too late."

"Yes, and if you remember, I was there too. And the reason I was there was because of the CIA. You know, Mr. Montrose, maybe you've been playing me all along. Because all I'm getting from MI6 is a lot of noise about one person. And that's you. We have just moved to threat level Critical. And you know what that means. I think you..."

Priti punched the keyboard. "Too close. I had no choice."

Pilgrim nodded. "I understand. Mr. Linden was more than helpful."

"What security level?" said Kirsty.

Montrose looked down at the phone. "Imminent attack expected. They think that the missile is going to be used very soon."

Kirsty ran to the window and looked up into the sky. To the east, a faint contrail traced the path of a jet as it descended over Rome. "How far is it to the airport?"

"There are two major airports," said Priti. "Leonardo da Vinci to the west, near the Mediterranean coast, about thirty minutes from here. Their flights come in over the sea. The other is Ciampino to the south-east of the city. There are other smaller airports in the metro area, but I'm not sure where."

"They've got us by the balls," said Kirsty. "It would take…"

Priti's laptop beeped. "The tracker!"

"The phone?" said Kirsty.

"No, the suitcase. I can see it." On the screen a red dot flashed on a map of Rome. Priti zoomed in. "Colosseum Metro station. They've been underground."

Pilgrim looked up from his phone. "The entire Rome police have been mobilized on a terror threat. It's being broadcast on television as we speak, though they're giving no details."

Montrose stared down at Priti's screen. "They'll never make it to the airport. They must know that."

"We are making assumptions on the capability of this missile," said Pilgrim. "We know from the attack at the village that it uses line of sight. However, we do not know the maximum distance at which it operates. I suspect that a flight path over Rome is sufficient. From my experience, a portable device will have a shorter range, but we can't be sure of the power of this new variant. All it may need is a few miles."

"You can't just fire from the street," said Montrose, "all the buildings are in the way. And everyone in Europe is switched on to terror attacks. You stand on the sidewalk and stick a missile on your shoulder, people are going to notice. And it only takes one brave guy to knock them to the ground."

"Or one woman," said Kirsty. "But this isn't central New York, all flat land and skyscrapers." She pointed to the map on the screen. "The seven hills of Rome."

"The what?"

Priti expanded the map. "Rome is famously built on seven hills. Each one would provide a line of sight. They don't have to be anywhere near an airport. Just in sight of a flight path."

"What we know," said Pilgrim, "is that they came out of the metro instead of continuing to an airport. So, your hypothesis fits. If they are going to launch an attack then a vantage point is where they are headed. What was the name of that metro station?"

"The Coliseum."

"What if it's just a high building?" asked Montrose.

"Perhaps, but that involves a tricky escape. And a modern, high building is less likely in central Rome. They have preserved the integrity of the architecture to some degree."

"Okay, so where's the nearest hill?"

Pilgrim closed his eyes. "That would be…"

"Look here," said Priti, and switched to 3D Google maps. "What is that?"

"Most likely the Palatine," said Pilgrim, "the nearest of the hills to the center of Rome. May I see?" Priti carried the laptop towards him. "Can you superimpose a map of the flight paths over Rome on top?"

They gathered around his wheelchair and Montrose watched the red dot moving along the map. "That's the suitcase?"

"Well, it's the tracker," said Kirsty, "we've got to hope it's still with the suitcase."

"The Palatine is closed to traffic," said Pilgrim. "I know it from my youth in Rome. They will approach on foot." Blue lines appeared on the map, showing the flight paths over Rome.

Kirsty pointed to one of the lines, where the symbol of a plane tracked slowly to the south east. "That's heading for Ciampino airport. It's a few miles south east at most."

"That's close enough," said Pilgrim, "and the suitcase

is heading towards the Palatine Hill. It'll take around ten minutes to walk to the top. We have no choice. We have to call it in. We'll never get there in time. The CIA and the Italian police can stop them." He looked down at his phone. "News has just gone out to the police. The airports around Rome have been closed. That flight will be the last to land."

"Thank God," said Kirsty.

"No," said Montrose. "This is too easy."

Pilgrim sat up in his wheelchair. "Explain."

"They know they can shut down airports any time. These bastards aren't stupid. If we know all the flights are cancelled, so do they." He pointed to the screen. "So why are they still heading to the top of the hill?"

"That," said Pilgrim, "is what I want to know. By the time they reach the top, the skies will be clear. We may be wrong in assuming it is an attack, but I can think of no other reason. It may be that they are playing the long game. They know that the security services will scour the city. Perhaps they intend to wait it out amongst the ruins of ancient Rome. But, right now the immediate threat has gone. It gives us a little breathing space." He looked closely at Montrose and then Kirsty. "Get to the top of the hill. Recover the missile. I will make sure that it is returned to Washington to discover its secrets."

"Yeah, or maybe this time I'll get the chance to hand it over personally. Then they'll see I'm not a traitor."

"What about the men?" asked Kirsty.

"Identify them if you can, but I'm not concerned with their welfare."

"Me neither," she said, "so I'll just shoot them, if that's okay with everyone. What's the fastest way to get there?"

"Scooter," said Priti. "There's a shop around the corner. Use the fake ID. I'll take the SUV and meet you to collect the suitcases."

Montrose checked his weapon. "Let's go. But, you know, something is bugging me. Something doesn't fit."

"I understand," said Pilgrim. "If we see an immediate threat, we will inform you. And if there is, then I will also inform the security services and you must disengage immediately. Is that clear?"

Kirsty nodded.

"Understood," said Montrose.

Pilgrim pushed himself upright, wincing in pain. Priti hurried over, but he waved her away. "I'm not going to allow two terrorists with a surface-to-air missile to establish themselves at a firing position above a major European city. If you cannot stop them and recover the missile in fifteen minutes, then I'm going to call in the security services." He looked at his watch. "Go."

Faber cut the call. "It's done. The skies will be clear in ten minutes."

"What did you tell them?" Napier looked down at the street.

"Imminent threat of attack."

"And if nothing happens, I'm dead meat. This will cost the economy millions. If this thing blows over then it'll lead right back to me. Maybe the panic is what they want. Maybe they'll lie low for a few weeks, then do it all again."

Faber said nothing.

"Shit, that's what I get paid for. Are the choppers down too?"

Faber nodded.

"It's a cheap target anyway. But we need an eye in the sky."

"I'll send out for information on drones and high-altitude recce aircraft. I have no idea if we have any in the area."

"Yeah, if the Italians see a Reaper drone in the sky, that's not going to go down too well. Every two-hundred-pound virgin jammed behind his computer is going to have an orgasm when they see it on YouTube. But it might come to that. Find out where they are."

"What about the Italian Air Force? They have Typhoon Eurofighters at Ciampino airport. The military base is right next door. And we have F-22 Raptors about twenty minutes away."

Napier turned towards him. "If you could have a gold medal for a SAM strike, what would it be?"

"A USAF stealth aircraft. Like a Raptor, or the B-2 bomber."

"Right. Since there's no way in hell there's gonna be a B-2 over Rome in daylight, they'd settle for a Raptor or maybe a Typhoon Eurofighter." He shrugged. "Do it anyway. Get the fast jets in the air. That's what they get paid for. Tell them to circle Rome, maybe ten, no, make it twenty miles out. If they are a target, they'll be over the countryside. Those guys have got ejector seats."

Faber picked up the phone. "And Montrose?"

"No change. As far as I'm concerned, the first man to drop him dead can marry my daughter. Is his photo out there?"

"Every cop has it on their phones. If we need to, we can send it to every cell phone in Rome."

"Yeah. Let's keep that one for last. I don't care if a fucking meter maid beats him to death on the street, I just want him dead."

The phone rang. Campbell appeared on the screen.

"Deep breaths," said Napier and hit the speakerphone. "Director Campbell."

"Napier, I told you to find Montrose and the next thing I see is him on video, stealing the missile under your very nose. Give me a good reason why I should not have you charged with negligence and hauled back to Langley to explain yourself before the Senate Intelligence Committee."

"One good reason?" Napier tilted his head back. "Just one?" He saw his face in the bottom corner of the screen, showing what Campbell could see on his monitor. He walked forward until his face filled the space. "How about you don't have the authority?"

Campbell blinked. "You appear to have lost your mind, Napier, I have..."

"I don't give a shit what you have. But what I have is a situation where I have a known terrorist on the run, armed with a surface-to-air missile. A terrorist you initially refused to let me deal with directly when I had the initiative, including preventing my staff from accessing information, then gave conflicting advice as to the priorities supposedly held by Langley. If you want to bring me back to Langley, then I suggest you scuttle off to your desk jockey friends, get your little bit of paper signed and send me the airline ticket. Then we can meet the Director of the CIA and go toe to toe in front of his desk. I'd like that. Because I'd hand you your ass on a plate. Meanwhile, I've just closed the airspace over Rome and two of the busiest airports in Europe. So, if you've got anything useful to contribute, you go right ahead, otherwise stay out of my fucking way."

Campbell leaned forward slowly. "I warned you before, lose the emotion, Napier. You see, your turf may be running around the streets after the Russians, but mine is Washington and Government. I'd squash you like a bug, and you know it."

Napier was silent.

"I could ruin your career before you stepped off the plane. You wouldn't even make it to the gatehouse at Langley. So, you listen carefully, because you are on very thin ice. The Russians have set this up and you are walking straight into their trap. There is a Russian delegation flying in from Moscow. He might want to talk to you, or he might go straight to our Ambassador in Rome. I may recommend you keep your hot head out of things. You're clearly not up to the task."

"What do you mean they are…?"

"Shut up. The Russians have got you like a puppet on a string. If they have the same information as us, and there's no reason why they shouldn't, then they have a video of an ex-CIA agent wanted for treason, multiple first-degree murder and terrorism, collecting one of the stolen missiles in Rome. It's all they need to prosecute the case in The Hague, on the grounds that the USA are perpetrating a false flag operation resulting in the deaths of their own troops. And you are walking straight into it. Tell me, Napier, what if the next attack is on a NATO plane? Or a civilian carrier? Because that's what the Russians are waiting for. And it could destroy NATO in a matter of minutes. That's something that the Russians have been planning and dreaming about for nearly

130

seventy years. And you, Napier, are in the eye of the storm." Campbell pointed a finger at the screen. "You do what you are damn well told, or step aside right now."

Napier stared at the floor. "Back up a bit."

"What?"

"Back up. You said flying into Rome? The Russians?"

"Pay attention, Napier. They will fly into the Italian Air Force base at Ciampino, then…"

Napier turned to Faber and jerked a thumb behind his head towards the screen. "Switch that asshole off and get me NATO Air Traffic Control. Now!"

CHAPTER 14

"Hold on tight," shouted Kirsty, "you're all over the bloody place."

Montrose wrapped his arms around her and stuck his chin on her shoulder as she weaved between the traffic. "How come you get to drive?"

"I was first on. Tough luck."

"All they had left was a bicycle with a flat tire. Not much of a choice."

"You can bloody walk if you don't stop moaning."

In the distance he could see the Colosseum. "The Palatine Hill is on the right."

She swung the scooter across two lanes of traffic, beeping her horn to scatter pedestrians. The scooter slid sideways on the cobbles and a tourist guide dressed as a Roman soldier stood in the middle of the wide pavement, holding up his hand to stop them. Kirsty drove straight down the center and high-fived him as she passed. She headed along a passage lined with ancient, broken columns, and pedestrians stepped to the side as they heard her coming. At the end, she followed the signs for the footpath and turned between the trees, bordered by a high hedge. The throttle was wide open, but they began to slow with the gradient. She grabbed the brake hard and stopped at the top.

"We need the highest point," she said. "Look." She pointed to a sign indicating the best photo spots. "That's got to be it." She swung the scooter right, bouncing along a dusty path, then left through a copse of pine trees. The ground opened up flat and Kirsty stopped before a group of ruined buildings.

Montrose stepped off and looked east. Trees obscured the sky. "We need to go higher, and away from those trees."

"Over there," said Kirsty, pointing to a path running through a crumbling brick wall. "Follow the signs. And connect to Priti."

Montrose pulled the helmet from his head and punched a number on his cell phone.

Kirsty shoved in her Bluetooth earpiece. "Priti?"

"Loud and clear. I'm on my way."

"We're here," said Kirsty. "We'll start looking." She began to walk towards the gap in the wall. "Connor?"

"Yeah, I know. If the skies are clear then there's no target to attack, so why would they be up here? If they've got the means to set up deliveries underground, then what the hell are they doing? A meeting, or a swap?"

"Whatever. As long as we can just kill them all and get those suitcases, I'll be a happy bunny."

"Kirsty, there might be another way."

"I thought you Yanks liked guns and shooting? You seem to be…."

"Holy shit."

She followed his gaze towards the wall, as a man walked past dragging a metal suitcase. "You reckon that's him?"

Montrose patted the weapon in his pocket. "I think all my Spidey-senses just went crazy."

"That's good enough for me." She took the weapon from her jeans and loaded a round, then held it low. "Let's go."

"Slowly, there's no threat. Let's find out why he's here."

"Priti, are the skies clear?"

The voice of Mr. Pilgrim came over the line. "The skies are clear. I have the internet flight tracker on my screen."

"We've spotted him," said Kirsty. "Big ugly fucker with a metal suitcase at the top of the hill."

"All traffic has been grounded," said Pilgrim. "The last plane has landed without incident. Priti?"

"I'll be at the bottom of the hill in five minutes."

"Thank you," replied Pilgrim. "Now let me be clear, we still have a very serious situation. If there is no safe opportunity to recover the suitcases, then we will withdraw and I will inform the authorities. Are we clear?"

"Clear," said Montrose.

"Oh, if you insist," said Kirsty.

The sonic boom of a supersonic fighter cracked over their heads. Montrose looked around, but could see nothing. "Pilgrim, where's that fighter?"

There was a pause before he answered. "I don't have it on my flight tracker."

"Doesn't matter," said Kirsty, listening to the fading roar of the jet engine, "he'll be fifty miles away by now."

"And that doesn't make sense," said Montrose, "Fighter jets don't take off on a schedule. They can't be the target."

"Unless you had a spotter at an airbase. You wouldn't have

to be that close. Everybody knows when a fighter plane takes off."

Montrose began to walk towards the gap in the brick wall. "Pilgrim? Do you think they could take down a fighter jet?"

"Since they were able to bypass all existing defenses in the first attack, then we can't be sure. But they have lost the element of surprise. Whoever is controlling those jets knows of the threat. They may be using them to draw fire, though I think that is unlikely."

"Yeah," said Montrose, "but what a prize that would be. What about the flight tracker? Anything showing?"

"I'm working on it."

Kirsty began to run and Montrose followed close behind. She stopped at the gap in the wall and looked around. "There he is."

The man was dragging the suitcase down a gravel path surrounding an area of grass.

"Let's just walk. We're tourists." He shoved the gun in his pocket.

Kirsty took his hand. "Do you think they could shoot down a fighter jet?"

"No, I don't see it. Not from the ground. They go too high, too fast." Their feet crunched on the tracks made in the gravel by the suitcase. Ahead, the man stopped and pulled out his phone.

"What's he waiting for?" said Kirsty.

"Maybe the other suitcase and its owner." He pointed to a raised area in the center of the grass. "There. Looks like a pitcher's mound. I'll bet that's the top of the hill. Easiest place to meet."

"No, he's ignoring it." She pulled out her phone and

checked the map. "This isn't the top of the hill." She pointed to the far end of the grass, at a white stone building, bordered by low trees. She held up the map to Montrose and pointed to the camera symbol on the map. "Just past those trees. About twenty feet. That's the high point."

The man walked towards the trees.

"Okay, get ready to run," said Montrose. "As soon as he's out of sight."

"I'm ready. So, here's the plan. We walk up and shoot the fucker then grab the suitcase."

"Yeah, I'm with you, but we're missing something."

"You mean his bestie with the other suitcase? What if they packed it all in one?"

"No chance."

"Okay, softly, softly catchee monkey, then shoot monkey and his mate. Yeah?"

"If he's here."

"Well, he's bugger-all use on his own. Unless he's got a really good pitching arm. Let's get closer, just in case."

The man disappeared between the trees.

"Go!" Kirsty sprinted forward, kicking up dust from the gravel. She stopped at the trees and Montrose stood behind her, looking over her head.

The first man stood in front of the ancient foundations of a house, bricks jutting from the ground and covered in thick grass. In the center stood a tree on a raised mound of earth. Behind him was a white building and the remains of Roman arches. He turned towards the arches and a second man emerged, dragging another metal suitcase.

"Oh, shit. Game on," said Kirsty.

"Yeah, but we're still missing something."

Kirsty adjusted the grip on her pistol. "What? A nine-piece orchestra and dancing girls?"

"No, a target. The skies are empty."

"Fuck it, shoot them anyway."

"We need to get closer," said Montrose, looking down at the pistol. "I'd be lucky if I hit the tree at this distance."

"Good point." Kirsty shoved her gun in her waistband and Montrose did the same, then followed her out onto the gravel path. She brought out her phone and held it up towards the ruins. "Only tourists taking a shot," she said. "Don't stare at them, Connor. We'll just walk around the grass until we're close enough."

"Yeah. Pilgrim, can you hear me?"

The earphone crackled. "One moment," said Pilgrim.

"Shit, they're looking over." Kirsty pulled Montrose's arm and turned him away then held up her phone and reversed the camera. "Keep moving closer."

In the distance, he heard sirens. "I don't think we're going to have much time left. Pilgrim, we're going to do it."

"Do they have backup?" said Pilgrim.

"No idea. I've seen nothing."

"Then it's not safe. You could be surrounded."

"Shit," said Kirsty, looking around the ruins.

"He's right," said Montrose. "You could hide a company of men up here. We would have no idea."

"Abort the operation," said Pilgrim. "I have a feeling you've walked into a trap. Be very careful. I will inform the authorities about the two men. They have no targets in the sky, so the authorities can take care of them."

Montrose saw the fury on Kirsty's face. "He's right."

"No, it doesn't make sense," she said. "They don't drag

two suitcases to the top of the hill just to trap us. If they did, we'd be dead already. They must know the flights will be cancelled. So why are they here?"

The voice of Priti came over the line. "I'm at the bottom of the hill. Ready when you are."

"Priti, can you see a guy dressed as a Roman soldier looking like a total dick?"

"Yeah."

"We'll meet you there."

"Priti," said Pilgrim, "do you see any more fighter jets in the sky?"

"No, military flights don't give out a radar beacon and identifiers like commercial flights. But you can find them, if you know where to look."

"I'll check all military flights," said Pilgrim.

"Some internet trackers only monitor one type of beacon," said Priti said. "Not everyone uses the same frequency. USA flights are different from the EU. I'll try a different tracker."

"I have access to the NATO military tracker," said Pilgrim. "There is nothing over Rome. The fighter jets are out of range."

Montrose glanced over his shoulder. The two men were staring into the eastern sky. Then he saw it. At first just a speck of white amongst the blue, then a glint from the sun on a fuselage. "Then what the hell is that?"

Kirsty scanned the sky. "Where?"

"Oh, my days," said Priti. "I've found it. I can see the beacon on my screen."

"Connor," said Kirsty, "Stop looking at the bloody…"

"North east of Rome," said Priti. "It's not NATO or a civilian. The beacon code says YK40. What does that mean?"

"It's a ICAO code for the type of aircraft," said Pilgrim. "Hold on."

Montrose could hear him hitting the keyboard.

"It's a Yakovlev Yak-40. A Russian Air Force private jet. Used for state officials and military top brass."

"Hold on," said Montrose, "they're not going to shoot down…" He turned and saw the two men drop their binoculars and push the suitcase flat on the ground. "Oh, fuck."

Kirsty dropped to one knee and brought up her pistol.

One of the men looped a machine pistol around his neck.

"No, we need cover, we're out-gunned!" Montrose ran to the crumbling arches with Kirsty close behind. They dropped behind the shattered remains of a column and brought up their weapons.

The first man hosted the launcher onto his shoulder and the second man lifted the warhead from the suitcase, slotted in the second propellant section and carried them both towards the launcher.

"We're going to have to get closer," said Kirsty, and edged out on to the gravel.

"No, last time they…"

She skirted the column and sprinted across the gravel, then dropped prone on the ground and fired two rounds.

The second man spun around as the bullet caught him in the arm and dropped the warhead to the grass. He rolled flat and pulled a machine pistol from his jacket.

"Cover!" shouted Montrose, and fired six rounds at the man.

Kirsty rolled to the side then sprinted for the column. Gravel sprayed around her and she dived behind the stone.

"You okay?"

She grinned. "Yeah. I got the bastard."

The ancient red brick above them exploded into powder as a burst of automatic fire ripped over their heads.

Montrose kept low and ran to another arch then looked out.

The first man was kneeling down as the second stood behind him, lifted the missile with his good arm and hoisted it on to the launcher. It dropped into the mechanism and slotted home. The second man dropped to the side and lifted the machine pistol.

Kirsty steadied her weapon against the column and began firing, but several rounds slammed into the stone and she ducked back.

"Keep him busy!" shouted Montrose, and held his gunsight as still as he could and squeezed the trigger.

Another burst of fire scattered gravel at her feet. Kirsty leaned out and fired two rounds. "You're high and right!"

"I know. I'm not trying to shoot him." He leaned out again and fired. They heard the whine of a ricochet when the round hit the back of the missile and a thin white stream of propellant gas burst into the air, knocking both men to the grass. "Hit the suitcase!" They both stood and emptied their magazines towards to the metal suitcase, until a blue spark jumped into the air towards the gas. A fireball blew out from the bottom of the tree and they both threw themselves behind the stone.

Heat scoured Montrose's legs and flame burst over his head. Then the roaring in his ears stopped and he rolled onto his back.

Kirsty dropped onto his legs, smothering the flames, then pulled off her jacket, straddled his chest and threw it over his head. She held it tight then pulled it free.

He looked up.

She sat on his chest and wriggled her thighs. "You're still alive. How many fingers am I holding up?"

Blood ran down his face. "Now, that's just rude. How do I look?"

She rolled off and stood, holding her gun in front of her. "Like a shit Guy Fawkes on a bad day. A few cuts. You'll be fine."

He got to his knees and peered out. Above the burning tree, a huge mushroom cloud of black smoke drifted south through the blue sky over Rome. On the smoldering grass he could make out the two blackened remains of the men. Police sirens sounded from all directions. "Priti?" said Montrose. "Are you there?"

"I'm here," she replied. "And I'm very glad to hear your voice. Are you both okay?"

Kirsty pulled Montrose behind the red brick wall, and wiped away the blood from his head wound. "Slightly toasted and a bit bloody, but fine."

The voice of Pilgrim came over the line. "I take it that the smoke means the missile has been destroyed?"

"Oh, yeah," said Kirsty.

Montrose looked out. "Maybe it's still…"

"For fuck's sake, Connor." She made to pull him back and saw two Italian cops staring at them. One of them pointed to Montrose. "Oh, well done. No point hiding now. Why don't you walk over and say hello?"

"What is it?" asked Priti.

"Cops." said Kirsty.

"Then get out," replied Priti. "I'm heading for the road on the west side, I'm parked outside a big villa at the bottom of the hill. I'll be directly south-west from you."

"Look, I'm sure…" began Montrose. His throat dried when he saw the cop checking his phone and showing it to the other cop.

"Get ready," said Kirsty.

The cops brought up their guns and began running towards them. One of them levelled his pistol and took aim.

"Run!" She pulled Montrose back to the red arches and fired two rounds over the heads of the police then sprinted past him, through the rear of the arches, vaulted a set of low railings, ran across an ancient courtyard, and ducked behind a line of broken columns.

Montrose caught up with her and squatted down behind a column. "You okay?"

"Yeah, I'm fine, I just want to know exactly where we're going. This place is a bloody warren." She checked the map. "I got it. I know where Priti is going to be. Follow me." She ran around the crumbling remains of a villa, then slid down a grassy slope.

Montrose followed her, crabbing sideways as the slope became steeper. He could hear traffic behind a line of trees and saw a tiled roof at the bottom of the hill. He followed her through the trees, the ground becoming steeper, until they reached the wall of the villa. He followed her around into a courtyard and saw gates to the street where Priti was waiting.

Kirsty ran over to the SUV and pulled up the tailgate. "Connor, get in. And wrap my coat around your head, you're bleeding everywhere."

"Look, I don't…"

"They're looking for a man and a woman. And they recognized you. Don't be an arse."

He clambered in and lay down flat.

Kirsty pulled the retractable cover from behind the rear seat. "And frankly, you're still a fucking jinx." She slammed the tailgate shut.

All eyes were fixed on the TV screen mounted on the boardroom wall. The Director stood motionless as the fireball blew up into the air. The picture shuddered when the blast wave hit the drone and spun wildly until the operator regained control. The picture fixed upon the burning tree.

"Enough," said the Director. The picture froze. Behind him, he heard chairs being pushed back. He didn't turn around. "Sit down." He took a deep breath then spun around on his heel. "Tell me, gentlemen. What did you see?"

The old man leaned over the table. "An abject failure, Director. That is what I saw. How on earth could you describe it as anything else?"

The Director let out a low laugh. "And you all agree?" No one moved. He raised his eyes to the ceiling. "You look, but you do not see. Arthur Conan Doyle, gentlemen, creator of Sherlock Holmes." He gazed around the table at every man in turn. "Most disappointing. Or then again, absolutely perfect."

The old man sipped from his glass of water. "Please explain, Director. I personally can't wait to hear this. I've always been a big admirer of Sherlock Holmes, yet I always found his arrogance to be his weakness."

The Director closed his eyes and bowed his head towards the old man, in the knowledge that this irritation would soon cease. "I will tell you what you saw. A jet full of Russia's most respected statesmen, known as the moderates in the

143

Kremlin. The peacemakers, they are called, flying in to negotiate with the US Ambassador and the CIA to resolve this crisis and ensure the return of their property." He glanced back to the screen, showing the burning tree. "Blessed are the peacemakers, for they will be the first to die." He smiled. "And yet a jet full of Russians did not have to fall burning from the sky onto the innocents of Rome to achieve the objective. Focus on the objective, gentlemen. You are distracted by the vicissitudes of combat. Remember the British Army adage, no battle plan ever survives first contact with the enemy."

The old man choked on his water. He sat still for a moment, then looked up. "I think this plan may also be struggling with the second and third contact, Director."

"How amusing. Yet it does not alter my point. The Italians will find conclusive evidence that an attempt was made on the lives of Russian diplomats by a missile from the diplomats' own armories. A missile that is suspected to be in the hands of the CIA. Moscow has not yet seen the video of our friend, Connor Montrose, with two suitcases in his hand in the underground streets of Rome. But they will. They already know his name. They already have his details. And so does every policeman and agent in Rome. The trap, gentlemen, has been set." He turned to the technician. "Show them."

An image appeared on the screen, at first blurred, then resolved into the face of a man peering out from behind red brick columns.

"Voila! The elusive Mr. Montrose. You see, I now have an ex-CIA operative with the missile in every scene." He counted them on his finger. "One at the hilltop when a C-130 is blown from the sky, and out of all the attackers, he is the only man to survive. Two, we have him with the suitcases in hand, after they were bought by the CIA and collected by their operative in underground Rome. Three, at the scene of the crime on the Palatine Hill. And we will drip feed this to the Russians, then sit back and enjoy the games. It could not be more perfect."

The fat man shook his head. "It would be more perfect if Montrose was dead."

The Director laughed. "Every policeman and agent in Rome has his photo, and orders to shoot him on sight. Mr. Montrose has run out of lives."

"No, I think we will never see him again. They will not have the chance. He will know the odds against him. He will become a ghost."

"He may well try," said the Director, "but I have something that will bring Mr. Montrose out into the daylight. And then he will die."

CHAPTER 15

"**K**neel down and bend over," said Kirsty. "And drop the jacket in the bath. It's not as if I'm going to wear it again."

Montrose peeled it from his head and felt the blood soak through the fabric and stick to his fingers. The blast of freezing water made him jump.

"Got to be cold," said Kirsty, holding the shower head. "It'll help stop the bleeding." She drove the jet of water against the wound, and it flowed pink into the bath. "It's a clean cut. No big deal."

"Glad to hear it," he said.

"But you'll have a nice scar to show all the girls when you're pretending to be a super-spy."

"And a bald patch," said Priti, waving a razor in front of his face. "I'll stop the blood with some adrenaline gel then use butterfly stitches."

"You've done this before," said Montrose, blinking to keep the water out of his eyes.

"I come from a family of boxers," said Priti. "Part of growing up."

Kirsty stopped the shower and patted the wound down. "If we can't do a comb over, you're going to need a hat."

"Don't make me go there. I hate wearing a hat."

She tapped her fingers on the top of his head. "Well, don't let your irrational dislike for millinery stop you from getting shot on the street by some copper. You saw the cop's reaction, yeah?"

"Yeah."

"He clocked you. Big time."

In the corner of his eye, he saw Pilgrim maneuver his wheelchair through the bathroom door. "Clocked?" he said.

"Recognized him," said Kirsty. "And he checked something on his phone."

"Are you sure?" said Pilgrim.

Kirsty leaned down and spoke in Montrose's ear. "He's talking to you."

"Yeah," said Montrose. "I think he did."

Pilgrim tapped his fingers on the arm of his wheelchair. "Well, if a policeman has that information, this certainly gives us logistical issues. Priti? Any ideas?"

"I'm on it," she said, "Let me finish this first then I'll take care of it. Scalp wounds are always particularly bloody. Do you have any concussion, double vision?"

"No, I didn't even feel it hit me."

Priti patted down his head with a towel and cleaned the wound. "We can assume that if one cop has your photo then every cop does."

"Indeed," said Pilgrim. "But let us lift our heads from this particular concern for the moment. It was a risk, though given the potential outcome, one that was worth it, I'm sure you will agree. But from what Kirsty told me, the policemen were not there to arrest you. They were there because of the explosion."

"Yeah, they were wondering what had just gone bang, why a tree was on fire, and probably most of all, why there were two burning corpses below it. If Connor hadn't stuck his head out, we could have buggered off and no one would be any the wiser. Then cop number one sees him, checks his phone and shows it to cop number two. Then, would you believe it? The shooting starts. Again."

Pilgrim blinked. "No attempt at an arrest?"

"Nope," said Kirsty, "it went straight to the gunfight at the OK Corral."

"I understand. But if you had not been on that hill, we would have been dealing with a very different issue. It's clear the objective of the attack was to bring down a jet full of senior Russian intelligence personnel. And from what my contacts tell me, these are the moderates that are more sympathetic to western democracies. These are people who are often in conflict with the more hawkish and right-wing members of the Russian intelligence community and government."

"They may well be," said Montrose, "and that begs the question, if some element of the CIA is behind all this, like Linden keeps hinting at, then it makes no sense. I can't believe the CIA would want to take down a plane of Russian moderates."

"A valid point," said Pilgrim. "Then we have to consider who would benefit from the attack."

"Russian crazies," said Kirsty, "or whoever was paying for it."

Pilgrim nodded. "An astute observation."

She sat on the toilet and placed her feet on the edge of the bath. "If those guys were like the ones that Connor met up with, they're not fundamentalists. They are professionals. They're doing this for money. Someone is paying those two guys to fire a missile at that jet. Not just in Rome, but in the village, too."

"And it's like the village," said Montrose, "they expected to escape. I'm sure of it. So, they were working for someone. If this is an American or Russian operation, why do you need to hire someone? You have Special Forces. Guys you can trust."

"Deniability," said Kirsty. "And false flag. They can make it look like any country they want."

"Yeah," said Montrose, "but that only works if you can rely on the people pulling the trigger to keep their mouths shut. And the CIA or Russian FSB won't take that chance. The guy in the village, the one I spoke to, just before he was shot. He knew who he was working for. I'm sure of it."

"Maybe that's why he was shot," said Priti.

"Maybe, but he was pretty damn sure it wasn't him that was going to buy the farm. He thought it was me. He was part of a team. And they chose to shoot him. Why? I don't know. They had hidden transport waiting for them at the bottom of the hill. These guys weren't just hired hands, ready to pull a trigger. They were part of the team."

"Okay," said Kirsty, "what if it's not CIA or Russian FSB. Who the bloody hell could it be?"

Montrose winced as the adrenaline hydrochloride bit into the wound.

"I'll apply the butterfly stitches," said Priti, "and you can comb over your hair."

"You know," said Kirsty, as she stood up to check Montrose's stitches, "if you wanted it to be really deniable, you'd just pay someone else for the whole operation. And I mean, the whole thing. Steal the missiles, smuggle them out of Russia, set up the attacks, everything."

Montrose involuntarily shook his head.

"Don't move or I'll end up sticking this up your nose."

"Kirsty, what are you talking about?" he said.

She leaned over and spoke in a stage whisper into to his ear. "An agent provocateur. And not like the lingerie brand. Less deviant. But infinitely naughtier."

Pilgrim nodded. "An old-fashioned name for a very modern approach. Yet we are not talking about some anarchist faction. This is too direct, too focused. Too professional."

"It brings us back to the guys pulling the trigger," said Kirsty. "If Connor's right and they knew who they were working for, then the question is, who is the paymaster? And I mean the final paymaster. Not the guy handing out a wage packet for some asshole who shoots down planes. Who put up the money in the first place? The guys pulling the trigger could be a well-connected mercenary force, or criminal organization, but who is paying the piper? Is it the Russian FSB, the CIA, or someone else?"

"Cui bono?" said Pilgrim. "As the Romans would say. Who would benefit?"

Priti delicately placed stitches to seal the wound. "My first thought is an arms dealer. The price of those missiles must have quadrupled after the first attack. It is possible they have been stolen simply to be sold to the highest bidder. And if the Russians are behind it all, their profit would be worth the risk. After all, Russia needs the money."

"Could be," said Kirsty, "but would an arms dealer really bring down a whole US C-130 stuffed with combat troops? Because that was the more likely target. That's the plane that should have been in the sky."

"I would have been tempted by the arms dealer theory," said Pilgrim, "if it was clear that the transport plane that was shot down was the actual target. But the shooting down of a private jet full of Russian moderates does not sit well with that line of thinking."

"Agreed," said Priti, "but it had to be said. And I do not think it disproves the agent provocateur theory. If one of the members of the United Nations Security council is using a criminal or terrorist organization at arm's length for its own purposes and to commit atrocities. No, wait, that happens all the time. What I mean is using them to commit an act that could start World War III."

"I understand," said Pilgrim. "Therefore, the question remains. Cui bono. Who benefits?"

"The Iranians?" said Montrose. "The Saudis? They're up to all sorts of shit."

"No," said Pilgrim, "their ambitions are restricted to the Gulf. Though I am increasingly attracted to the agent provocateur theory. Which leaves us with several issues. Who are they, who is paying them, and what do they gain from these actions?"

"Money and power," said Kirsty. "It's always the same. Everybody wants to blame everyone else, and if you create a situation where all the weird and wacko conspiracy theories fit, you can sit back, collect the money, and watch everybody run around in circles. The US might lose a plane, but get what they want, or the Russians might lose a plane, but get what they want. And one thing is for sure. Whoever it is, they don't mind blowing planes out the sky."

Montrose stood up. "Maybe it's just me, but whoever is trying to hide in this mayhem is doing a really good job."

"Oh yeah," said Kirsty. "And I'd be very interested to see what the posh boy from MI6 has got to say."

"Good point," said Pilgrim. "I think we should set that up. Priti?"

"I'm on it." She handed Montrose a bath towel. "Leave your clothes here, I'll get you something else."

Kirsty jabbed Montrose in the ribs. "She means get your kit off. What is this outrageous attraction you have?" She followed Priti through the door before he could answer.

Montrose pulled off his bloodied and scorched clothes and pulled on a bathrobe. Priti was waiting with the phone when he entered the room.

"Remember, if I see a tracker getting too close, I'll just cut the call."

He took the phone. Priti held up a hand as she leaned over her laptop and gave him the thumbs up. He hit redial and speaker. The call was answered immediately.

"Hello?" the voice sounded surprised.

"It's Montrose."

"My God, you're alive?" said Linden.

"Still here."

"I saw the explosion on the news. It was caught on video by tourists. I did not think anyone would survive that."

Kirsty whispered in Montrose's ear. "How did he know we were there?"

"Yeah?" he replied. "Did they get me on video?"

There was a pause on the line. "No, your name came up

in a police report. They're still looking for you. And I mean every copper in town. You know, if you need some help to get out of Rome, I have some friends…"

Montrose glanced over at Pilgrim who raised an eyebrow, then shook his head. "Thanks, but I'm gonna lay low for a while. Wait until the cops have got something better to do."

"Understood. But be aware, the CIA and the Italians have got this place locked down tight. The CIA haven't yet found out who leaked the info on the second missile, but let's say they are looking at MI6 with renewed vigor. I have no doubt I'm being watched very closely. There's nothing I can do, but I have a lead that may be of interest."

"Go on," said Montrose.

"This is straight from a friend at GCHQ. It's RUMINT."

Pilgrim shrugged.

Priti looked over at Kirsty, who whispered in her ear. "Rumor Intelligence, or unconfirmed gossip."

"It's not gone through the usual channels," said Linden, "and the boys at Langley won't be told, or they'll know we're up to something. Poking our noses in when we were told to back off. I'll be frank, they are throwing a lot of shit around, and GCHQ is getting very pissed off. Right now, we don't know who we can trust."

"Understood. Go on."

"The two men you killed in the village, the ones that brought down the C-130, they both travelled from Monaco on the day of the attack."

"Monaco? The car they drove had an Italian plate."

"Maybe, but not when it crossed the border into Italy. We heard from a contact in Monaco that cameras picked it up then dismissed it as an anomaly. Then GCHQ trawled through the cameras and saw it crossing the border. We have access to the entire European ANPR camera network."

"ANPR?"

"Automatic Number Plate Recognition. Right across Europe. The car was rented from Nice in France and tracked back to the hotel in Monaco."

"You got the details?"

"Of course, I'll text them to you."

Montrose turned to Priti. She concentrated on the screen and gave a thumbs up. "Listen, Linden, when do you think the CIA will get this info? What's the process?"

"Look, we're not even supposed to know about the BMW, never mind that it came from bloody Monaco. But I do know this. They will find out eventually. There is a CIA mole in GCHQ. It's bad form, old boy. And we're going to use this to flush him out. This is the best chance we've had for years, given that the Cousins are running around with their arses on fire. When we find the little shit, I'm going to personally rip off his bollocks."

"How long?"

"No idea. There's been no reaction from Langley, so we're waiting for a shift change to try to nail it down to a group of people. We're scrabbling around in the dark. It could be ten minutes, could be ten hours. But we'll know, because Langley will go ballistic. When they do, I'll let you know. Until then it's all yours."

"Thanks. I mean that."

"No guarantees, though. It's the best I can..." The call ended.

"Tracked again," said Priti. "But I was a bit more prepared this time. Whoever it is, they know what they are doing."

Kirsty smacked Montrose on the butt. "Monaco, baby!

Let's go. I want a drop-top Jag, shades, and enough jewelry to make Liz Taylor turn in her grave."

Montrose looked over at Pilgrim. "Monaco?"

"It makes some sense. The Principality of Monaco has become a very appealing place for those who have amassed considerable wealth and prefer their networks to be less obtrusive. The secrecy and security around the whole principality is very attractive."

"And the whole country is smaller than Central Park," said Kirsty. "But it stinks of money."

"And it's four hundred miles away," said Priti, "so no drop-top Jag, I'm afraid."

"Spoilsport."

"Listen," said Montrose, "I step outside this room and I could get a bullet in my head. My face is on the phone of every cop in Rome. I'll never get through an airport, so four hundred miles is a long way to get lucky."

"Leave it to Priti," said Pilgrim, "I'm sure she'll think of something."

Napier watched the priest walk away, his footsteps muffled by the robes.

Faber stood to the side of the altar, a slab of stone covered with a thin white cloth. A threadbare tapestry bordered in gold thread hung on the wall above him. He looked down at his phone, but there was no signal. Two feet above his head, rough stones arched across the chapel.

The priest reached the open door and grabbed the handle, then leaned back to haul the thick wooden door closed.

"Why here?" said Faber.

155

"I wanted somewhere that can't be bugged. You checked?"

"Yeah. I ran a scan. And there's no signal."

"The walls are ten feet thick and held together without mortar."

Faber flicked his eyes from side to side.

"Relax. The priest tells me it's been here for over two thousand years. The stones fit so close together that you couldn't get a hair between them."

At the sides of the tapestry above the altar the stone was polished and smooth. Faber pushed the tapestry aside and saw the stone was covered in deep, ornate carvings, some with traces of paint. "Jeez, look at this."

Napier walked over. "No, not Jesus." He pointed to the symbol of a man plunging a spear into the neck of a bull. "Mithras. This place was built way before the Christians arrived."

"A Roman god?"

"It was a cult that spread through the whole Roman army. It wasn't for the faint-hearted. I wonder if the priest is sending a message."

"I thought this was a peaceful place. Now, I'm not so sure."

Napier stared at the door. "Yeah, peace. I don't think we're gonna see much of that for some time. But I'm going to let Dimitri know that his asshole country has gone too far. Shit is about to get real."

The door swung open and Saitsev marched in. "Napier. You stupid bastard."

"Hey, Dimitri, don't hold back, dude. You got something to say, just get it off your chest. Go on, tell me how you feel."

The Russian visibly shook with anger as he walked stiff-legged towards him. "You nearly started World War III."

Napier held out his arms. "What the hell are you talking about?"

Behind him, a bodyguard lowered his head to fit through the door and stood to the side, then unbuttoned his jacket.

Saitsev stood in front of Napier. "Whatever you are going to say, whatever argument, or explanation you have, you must explain why the FSB, or any of the Russian security services, would use one of their own missiles to shoot down a jet full of Russian intelligence personnel and military chiefs over Rome." He moved closer. "I am scared. I am scared that you will try to explain this action as some sort of rogue terrorist or anarchist faction, or some right-wing Russian plot, because then I will know that you are part of this malicious, murderous lie. Then there is no hope. You see, you and I are the last line of defense. The negotiators in that plane were coming here to work with you to bring this madness to an end." He rubbed his face and looked up to the ceiling. "But no more. They are returning home. We are all that is left. And my patience is at an end. Now, talk."

For a moment Napier stared at the red and broken veins on Saitsev's face. "If you think…"

Saitsev raised a finger and held it between their faces. "You bought that missile. You took it to the Palatine Hill. Your man was identified… Connor Montrose."

"He's not our…" He looked past Saitsev at the guard, who had moved his hand inside his jacket. "Hey, asshole. Don't get all Hollywood on me."

Faber opened his jacket to show a 9mm pistol in a holster. "Make your move or fuck the fuck off." The guard let his hand drop.

Saitsev edged closer until his spittle flecked Napier's face.

"Focus. You have to stop this. I want to believe that you have been duped. I want to believe that the CIA have all the missiles and are selling them on the Silk Road in some elaborate ruse, some crazy, idiot scheme and that they are keeping you in the dark. I do not know who stopped the attack. Maybe it is also part of your madness. But right now we are closer to war than we have ever been."

Napier looked down, shaking his head. "Dimitri, please, there is no way that we would attack your plane. Connor Montrose is..." He stopped and stood open-mouthed, then his voice came out in a whisper. "What... What do you mean, all the missiles?"

Saitsev's face tightened. "If I think for one moment that you are going to lie to me, I will beat seven different colors of shit out of you. Right here!"

"Dimitri, you said *all the missiles*." Napier could see his lips trembling. "How much is all?"

"We have Montrose identified by the police on the hill. And we are waiting for further information. Direct evidence of CIA involvement. Indisputable evidence. So, do not..."

"Please." Napier held up his hand. "*All*. How fucking much is *all*?"

Saitsev half-turned away. "This is pointless. I believe Washington have sent me an innocent."

Napier heard his voice becoming louder. "Dimitri. How many?"

The Russian laughed. Saliva flaked Napier's suit. He grinned and turned to the guard. "He doesn't know. Shall we tell him?" He faced Napier. "There are only two organizations on the face of this earth who could have stolen all those missiles. Yours and mine. And why would we break into our own secure underground missile storage, steal our own missiles, then irradiate the bunker to conceal your crime? Why? Why would we do that?"

"Dimitri, we…"

"It took us two weeks to clean that bunker and the rest of the armaments. We thought there was an accident. A radiation leak. But once we got inside, we found out what was missing."

"Just tell me, please. How many?"

Saitsev shook his head and stared at the floor. "Why don't you ask Washington? We tracked the truck to Ukraine. It would have been at a NATO base within hours." He looked up. "You know, I believe you. I can tell when you are lying. So, why don't you go back to your hawks in Washington and ask them, is there going to be another fifty attacks? Who will be first to die? Russians? Americans? Passenger jets? Which will be the attack that starts the war? Because they know. Ask them." His words came out in a whisper. "Only they know." He turned and walked towards the door, his shoulders slumped like an old man.

The clamor of the faithful around the Vatican became a hush as the armor-plated doors closed. Faber slid down in the rear seat.

Napier leaned forward to the driver. "Take a walk." He waited until the driver had closed the door then switched on the LCD screen embedded in the rear headrest.

"Do you think he knows?"

Napier said nothing and stared straight ahead. Campbell's face appeared on the screen. "Did you get all that?" said Napier.

"Yes," said Campbell. "A very interesting man, Mr. Saitsev. Very impassioned. Very imaginative."

"Cut to the chase, Director Campbell. Tell me this is a set up. Tell me we don't have fifty missiles hidden somewhere in Italy."

Campbell shook his head and looked down at his notes. "NATO defense chiefs have just concluded an emergency meeting. I'm sure you are aware that the original attacks were on a NATO plane, in a NATO country, and a direct violation of NATO Article 5. An attack on one member state is regarded as an attack on all member states. The Defense Secretary, the Secretary of State and the Vice President have been reminding the member states of their obligations. The point was firmly made that these were Russian missiles, being used against NATO. I'm afraid to say that there was not unanimous agreement on action, despite the overwhelming evidence that this is a Russian operation. They were, despite their own intelligence gathering, rather dubious about our conclusion." Campbell looked up. "I can assure you, the government in Washington made clear their grave disappointment at this weakness."

"Woah. Are they saying we set this up? We shot down our own plane?"

"They intimated that the evidence to prove or disprove this theory no longer exists, and if anything, it exists to the contrary."

"What evidence?"

"Tell me, Napier, in the first attack, who removed any opportunity to capture and question the perpetrators? And who stole the missile from under our nose, then appeared at the top of the Palatine Hill? Who is the man I stressed should be executed on the spot?"

"Yeah, Montrose."

"Exactly. The intelligence services of all NATO countries are talking to each other behind our backs. They know who he is. We have lost their trust, Napier."

"Yeah, I wonder how that happened? History, eh? Like the man said, it's just one goddam thing after another."

"Flippancy is…"

"Listen, Campbell, I'm at the end of my line with this shit. There are fifty…"

"No!" Campbell pushed his papers aside and jabbed his finger at the screen. "Montrose was with the two terrorists when they shot down the first plane, then he killed them. And when the attack on the Palatine Hill miraculously failed, he did so again. How many times does it have to happen before you understand? Montrose is working for the Russians, but they have given the game away. If they really wanted us to believe it was some mysterious terrorist organization that only exists in the minds of the madmen in Moscow, they would have shot down their own plane. But they didn't. This is Moscow's operation. One plane has been destroyed, yet the fabric of NATO has been irrevocably weakened. A classic Moscow operation."

"Yeah," Napier nodded slowly and fixed his eyes on the screen. "Trust in the US is at an all-time low. And Moscow has had some help from the succession of isolationist assholes in Washington."

"I think you've been in Europe for too long," said Campbell. "All that strong coffee is going to your head. You are thinking like many other NATO countries. It is a weakness. And the Russians are exploiting that weakness. Montrose is the key. Find him."

The screen went black.

Napier slid down in his seat and gazed out of the window. "Tell me, what do you think would happen if Russia aligned with Mexico, then parked a dozen fighter-bombers on the border with Texas?"

Faber switched off the screen. "We'd go ape shit. Like Cuba and Kennedy. What do you mean?"

"Look at the Baltic. Estonia and Latvia. Former Soviet states, now full members of NATO, and up to their ass in fighter-bombers with tactical nuclear missiles that can hit Moscow in fifteen minutes. We have tank regiments and artillery right on their border. And Germany, Poland, Turkey, they've all got tactical nuclear missiles pointed at cities across Russia. The next war isn't going to be a shooting match of ICBMs across the North Pacific and the Bering Strait. We know that. And so do the Europeans." He pointed out of the window. "That square with the fountain. A thousand people were killed there. Right here in the heart of Rome. The entire history of Europe is a litany of wars and conflict. Europe is currently going through the longest period without war since the Romans. These people aren't crazy. They've seen it all before. And when it comes down to it, they're not gonna be the battleground any more, especially not between Moscow and Washington. They're not gonna let it happen. And you know why? Because it all comes down to one thing. No one believes us anymore."

Faber felt sweat gather at the nape of his neck. "You mean the USA?"

"Vietnam, Afghanistan, South America. We've been fucking up Iraq since the 50s. Joe Public in Ohio thinks we are straddling the world like a colossus. But the Europeans have seen this all before. You know what they see?"

162

"No," said Faber.

"End of Empire. Everything we touch turns to shit. It started in Korea, then really came good in Vietnam. The black ops in South America, protecting democracy by propping up fascist juntas and murderous regimes. Then a whole line of clusterfucks in Iraq, Afghanistan, Syria. I tell you, the Europeans are not gonna be the next in line. We fill Europe full of American tanks, and make them pay for the privilege, that is what we do. And it is very good business. But they are sick of being the front line for American foreign policy. Russia and Europe were allies before the USA existed and way before the Soviets came to town. No one teaches that any more. And one day, they're gonna shake hands and that will be the end of the American dream."

The board members sat very still, stunned at what they had just witnessed.

"Death will claim us all, gentlemen," said the Director. The body of the old man was carried from the room like a rag doll. "I will have my staff ensure he is given all the respect he deserves."

Another man came into the room and picked up the shattered glass where it had slipped from the old man's fingers, before he had slumped in his chair and slid to the floor, his chin thudding off the edge of the table as he dropped from sight.

The Director had shouted for assistance and a guard had come into the room and applied CPR so violently that board members were sure if old age hadn't killed him then the attempted resuscitation most certainly had.

"I shall miss him," said the Director, "both his counsel, and his wisdom."

The other board members said nothing.

"Now, let us continue. We have one more death to consider today." The Director stifled a laugh at his own joke.

"Montrose," said the fat man.

"Indeed, our good friend and unwitting ally. I have carefully reassessed his potential, given his latest activities, and I am not prepared to release the video of him collecting the missiles until I see his body." He looked up at the table. "I do not underestimate his abilities."

"Then we are a hostage to fortune. Where is our plan, Director?"

"We are no hostage to fortune." He leaned over the table. "Do you think I have not planned for this? Do you think I would allow this operation to be jeopardized by just one man?"

The fat man said nothing.

"We will release the video at a time of our choosing."

"I understand, Director," said the fat man. "but I'm sure I speak for all of us when I say that Montrose is the wild card."

The Director turned away. "He dies today."

"You know where he is?"

"I am not concerned where he is." He looked back at the puzzled faces. "Because I know exactly where he's going."

CHAPTER 16

"I'm only doing this for you," said Kirsty, and rubbed sunscreen into her thighs. "I hope you're grateful." She arched her back and spread her arms over the stern of the boat.

Montrose poked his head out of the cabin, his eyes level with the deck, which thrummed with the two engines running at full speed.

She laughed when a spray of water burst over the deck and threatened to pitch her off the stern. "This is extreme sunbathing. How long do I have to keep this up for?"

"Kirsty, come inside," said Montrose.

"No way," she replied. "I've always wanted to do this, just not at this fucking speed." She wiped the seawater from her face. "Anyway, I'm not being hunted by every satellite above the Mediterranean. You hide down there and I'll distract the operators. With boobies."

"I can see the coast," shouted Priti. "I'll take her into port." She looked down. "Stay out of sight," she said, and leaned back on the throttle. "I don't want to come in too fast. We

165

are supposed to be rich layabouts cruising the Med, and I'm coming in like a commando at Juno Beach."

Kirsty stood and walked back to the wheelhouse. "Talking of commandos, unless you have some underwear on board, that's exactly what I'll be doing."

"All taken care of," said Priti. "There's a change of clothes in the cabin."

Kirsty waved at the sky. "Hello, I'm just a naked rich bimbo arriving in Monaco, and not in any way about to start shooting people. Maybe. Connor, throw me a towel. And some dry clothes."

Montrose grabbed a bag with jeans and deck shoes and pushed it out of the door towards her. The roar of the engines gradually subsided, and from the edge of the wheelhouse he glimpsed trees above a rocky beach and could hear traffic from the coastal motorway.

Kirsty shouted down into the cabin. "Hey, Mr. Pilgrim, you weren't winding us up, were you? There really is a spy satellite up there?"

"I can't be certain," he replied, "but when the CIA orders all available resources to search the area, that includes surveillance. My sources tell me that they have redirected the satellite missions since the first attack. They will be looking for Montrose in all modes of transport. But I'm sure you gave them the impression that this was purely a leisure craft."

"I hope so," she replied, "since I've just spent the last four hours going across the Med like a dolphin with its arse on fire while half-naked and clinging on for dear life. Mind you, I'm going to have a cracking tan." She squeezed past Montrose into the cabin. "Has this boat got a shower?"

"Over there," said Pilgrim, pointing to a narrow door set into the cabin furniture. His wheelchair was fixed to a chart table, surrounded on three sides by computer screens. "When we have docked, I will hand over to Priti." He pointed to one of the screens, showing a town square bordered by palm trees, with ornate white buildings on each side. "The principality of Monaco has more CCTV cameras per square foot than any other city in the world. We will require access to such cameras but that is not my specialty."

Montrose looked out a porthole near the roof of the cabin. "The whole place is covered in cameras?" He heard the note of the engine rise and fall as the boat edged onto the berth.

"I'm afraid so. The government of Monaco is obsessed with security. They have the highest density of millionaires and correspondingly, the largest ratio of police to population in the world."

"And we're going in? What if the police have got my details?"

Pilgrim looked up. "I'll be honest with you, Montrose, it would make for a very short visit. I will understand if you consider it too dangerous and I will leave it to Kirsty and Priti."

Kirsty stepped out of the shower and pulled her jeans on over her wet skin. "I can do it alone. You can stay here and make a nice pot of tea."

"Don't underestimate the risk, Montrose." said Pilgrim. "The Five Eyes are looking for you."

"The Five Eyes?" said Montrose. "The British and the US, yeah, but the Canadians, Aussies and Kiwis too?"

"Mate," said Kirsty, "You should do a World Tour."

"If I ever get out of this shit, I'm going to India."

"Namaste," said Kirsty. "So, you staying or what?"

"I'm going," replied Montrose. Through the porthole, he saw Priti step onto the pontoon with a rope in her hand to tie up the yacht.

"Just keep a baseball cap pulled down and keep your shades on. If the camera can't see your face you've got a chance." The boat slowed to a crawl and waves slapped against the hull. "We'll keep off the streets as much as we can. Priti has got us a room in a hotel, we can operate from there."

"I think," said Pilgrim, "from the information we have and the analysis, you won't have too much time to settle in."

"Okay," said Priti, climbing down into the cabin. "Check the map." She pointed to one of the screens. "I searched through the traffic camera records and found the original BMW as it left Monaco, heading for the Italian border. Then I checked the booking, but the names and credit cards led nowhere. But from the cameras, I found the BMW leaving an underground hotel car park. It was there for a day. I've booked you a room."

"Just one?" said Kirsty. "Oh, Connor, you romantic old fool."

Priti pulled open a drawer and handed them each an envelope. "Your new identities. Passports, Visa and Amex cards. Check your weapons."

Montrose instinctively reached for the pistol stuffed into his pocket.

"You need more magazines?" asked Priti.

"Sure, whatever I can get my pocket without looking like an 80s rock star in tight jeans. Is it too warm for a jacket?"

"I'll carry Connor's ammo," said Kirsty. "We need a change of clothes so you can fit right in and buy a man bag for your hardware. You can get away with it around here. Rich people have no style." She dropped the magazines into her bag.

"Transport?" asked Montrose.

"No," said Priti, "it will be quicker to walk to the hotel. Remember, Monaco is only three miles long and half a mile wide." She opened a sea chest at the side of the cabin and handed them each a new cell phone. "Dial in you when you leave the boat and I'll forward any messages from our man in MI6."

Kirsty leaned over the sea chest. "What else have you got? Do you have any exploding pens, or a wristwatch that makes a girl's knickers fall off? Connor's always wanted one."

"You know," said Priti, "I'm right out of those. But you'll need this." She handed Kirsty a canvas bag. "This is your comms equipment. Connect it up outside the boat or the feedback will deafen us all."

"You got my penknife?" said Kirsty.

"In the bag."

"Then I'm good to go."

"Not quite," said Pilgrim, and pointed to a screen. "I think you will find this very interesting. You see, when you start tracking, one thing leads to another. Priti?" He maneuvered his wheelchair out of the way, and she sat down at the chart table.

"Those cameras might keep all the rich folks safe," she said, "but you cannot move without being monitored and recorded." She brought up a video on each screen. "Monaco has over one thousand CCTV cameras in an area no bigger than Staten Island. Look here." She pointed to the first screen. "This is the day before the attack in the village. Here are the two men walking into the car hire office to pick up the BMW to drive to Italy the next day. You see, they do not have suitcases. Then they drive to a hotel and park in an underground car park."

"Maybe the suitcases are in the hotel?" said Montrose.

"No, the men arrived at the train station that morning. They had no luggage. They picked up the car and drove to the underground car park."

"There's a lot of miles between here and Italy. They could have picked up the suitcases on the way."

"I don't think so," said Priti. "They were here for a reason. The European train network is pretty good. They could have taken a fast train to Italy in comfort. But they went to Monaco and hired a car. Then they go to a car park under the hotel where the cameras aren't working. Tell me, Connor, you picked up the suitcases. Were they heavy?"

"Yeah. At least thirty pounds each."

She pointed to another screen. "Now, look at the BMW when it leaves the car park the next day. According to my calculations the rear wheel arch is three centimeters lower than when it entered. I believe the suitcases with the missiles are in the trunk."

"Okay," said Kirsty, "let's run with that. So, who delivered the suitcases to the hotel?"

"I can't check the cars," she said, "but I can check their license plates, and they were all valid. And I have checked every person that walked into that hotel for the two days before and none of them had that type of metal suitcase. It did not come through the front door."

"What about hotel delivery?" said Montrose.

"Nothing out of the ordinary," she replied. "It would not be impossible to smuggle two suitcases into the hotel then into the car park, but I can find no evidence of it. So, I followed the men and noticed this." She pointed to the screen and played a video. "You will see the two men leave the hotel after they have parked the car. They turn right, but do not go far. Look at the building next door."

"Looks pretty fancy. Is it a hotel?"

"No, it is a private club. The two men enter via the front door and that is where I lose them. Then they return to their hotel ten minutes later. But with no suitcases."

"What is that place?" asked Kirsty. "Like a posh club?"

"Yes, like a British gentlemen's club. Though it has no website. No email address. Just a phone number and I had to dig deep to find that."

"What about a network?" said Kirsty. "Servers? Wifi?"

"It has wifi, but with a very high level of security. Which makes me think, why? It's only a gentlemen's club."

"Well," said Montrose, "if the front door is anything like the network we're never gonna get in there."

"You read my mind," said Priti. "But I did get in. And it wasn't a pleasant experience."

"What do you mean?" said Kirsty.

"The wifi is being used almost exclusively to access particularly unpleasant internet pornography."

Kirsty leaned in. "How unpleasant are we talking about?"

"I shall brief you later. You may find a target for a different day."

"You better believe it."

"But there was an admin server and I found a membership list. Basic details, but names, nevertheless. I gave it to Mr. Pilgrim."

"I recognized several names," said Pilgrim, "mostly

Russian oligarchs and various international money men, but one name stood out above them all."

Priti pressed a key and a man's face appeared on the screen. "Sergei Blokhin."

"He's an ugly bastard," said Kirsty.

"In many ways," said Pilgrim. "He's also a wanted man in Russia. He fell foul of the politics of Putin and the rest of the Russian cabinet, and was discovered to be backing right-wing extremists in Hungary and selling weapons to Nazi organizations in eastern Germany. His specialty was funding murderous hate groups right across Europe."

"The Russians have been doing that for years," said Kirsty, "what makes him so special?"

"He was right on the edge. Even for the Russians, he was extreme. Though that wasn't his crime. Mr. Blokhin was a big name in Russian oil and banks. He was very well connected, especially to the old KGB, whom he used to make millions of dollars. And they were well rewarded. But if you want to play in Russia, you have to pay the piper. Vladimir Putin. And when Sergei was found to be selling Vlad short, he was sent a bill. He couldn't or wouldn't pay. So, he moved his billions to Switzerland and ran for Monaco."

"Tough life," said Montrose. "You sure about this guy?"

Pilgrim nodded. "I've been through all the names. Of course, Monaco is full of dubious characters, and this 'Gentlemen's Club' especially, but Sergei stands out like Charles Manson in a church choir. He's in another league. Now, let me show you…"

"Wait," said Kirsty. "Does he have a Twitter account?"

"How did you know?" said Priti.

"Because I've seen him before. I picked up the name in

London. He was involved in finding Syrian refugees and getting them to safety."

"Doesn't sounds like a crazy fascist to me," said Montrose. "You sure?"

Kirsty gave him a look. "Connor, you can't be that gullible. He set up a charity for orphans. Even brought in some Russians celebrities to front it. He got children out of Syria to turn over to UNICEF. Not all of them reached safety. Some went missing. Then the UN sent in observers. And they were killed in an artillery strike. Fog of war, they called it. But he wasn't rescuing orphans. He was trafficking children. And the only people who could prove it died that day. With the children."

Priti brought up a Twitter profile on the screen. "Is this him?"

"That's the piece of shit."

Pilgrim leaned forward and took Kirsty's hand. "We need to find where the missiles came from. You know what's at stake. Let him live for another day."

Kirsty nodded then stretched her neck and held her chin in the air for a moment. She breathed out slowly and lowered her head. "I'm cool."

"Thank you," said Pilgrim. He pointed to the Twitter account on the screen. "Sergei Blokhin is by far our most likely candidate as the middleman for handing over the missiles. The question is, where did the handover take place?"

"Where the cameras don't work," said Kirsty. "The underground car park."

"Exactly," said Priti. "You know how the French are obsessed with bureaucracy and paperwork? It turns out the Monaco civil service are the same. I hacked into City Hall and got the plans for both buildings."

"They share a car park?"

"No, not quite." She brought up an architect's drawing on the screen. "The two buildings are connected. The hotel was originally the residence of some Italian duke, two hundred years ago. And next door he built a home for his mistress."

"Jeez," said Kirsty, "he must have really liked her. Or didn't trust her."

"Maybe both," said Priti, "but there is still a connecting corridor between both buildings."

"The dirty old bugger," said Kirsty.

Priti pointed to the screen. "Here is the car park of the hotel, and here is the tunnel leading into the basement of the club."

Pilgrim edged his wheelchair forward. "Then I think we have our target. Sergei Blokhin."

"Yeah," said Kirsty. "I'd like to have a word with him."

Pilgrim lifted a hand. "We need to know where the missiles came from. That comes first."

Kirsty grinned. "Understood, Mr. P. Don't worry, I'll be all sweetness and light." She turned to Montrose. "Let's go clubbing."

"You can't just walk in," said Priti. "Remember, this is a private club." She pressed the keyboard and a Twitter account with Montrose's face appeared on the screen.

"What the hell is that?" he said.

"Your cover," replied Priti.

"What about mine?" asked Kirsty.

"You will be his secretary."

"Fuck that bollocks," said Kirsty. "Why isn't he my secretary?"

"Next time, sister. This is the Twitter account of Robert

Nohmark. He's a shadowy right-wing billionaire from Long Island, and he has links to every shady deal in New York and Washington. He likes to think he's a player, but he's just another fly on the dung heap of American politics."

"What's the connection?" asked Montrose.

"He's American and the right height," said Priti, "but then all you white guys look the same, so who knows?"

Kirsty laughed out loud. "That's you, paleface!"

"But the point is," said Priti, "this guy is seriously rich and is connected to all the right-wing crazies in the USA. The ones who wear camouflage to the grocery store and stock up on enough peanuts and toilet roll to see them through the zombie apocalypse. The Russians have been trying to pull in Robert Nohmark for years, but he's too smart. This time, I've planted rumors on the internet to make it look like he's working for a special group of patriots in America."

"Special?" said Montrose.

"Fantasists and fascists," said Priti. "I've hacked into Nohmark's Twitter account and he won't get it back for a few hours, until he goes through the recovery process. And you've just sent Sergei Blokhin a direct message on Twitter."

"Twitter?"

"Yes," said Priti. "Sergei is a big Twitter fan. Remember, he likes to tell everyone about his humanitarian work."

"I'll bet he does," said Kirsty.

"And Sergei knows that if he brings Robert Nohmark in for Moscow, he will earn big brownie points. I've set up a meeting. In the club. Because that's where Sergei is right now."

"Are you sure I look like him? What if they've met?"

"Nohmark stays in the shadows. He's very reclusive. Likes

to think of himself as the spider at the center of the alt-right web. But he's almost exclusively despised in Washington, which is no mean feat, and any serious politician won't meet him."

"And this Russian guy is going to believe me?"

"Your references will be the best. Tell him you are a friend of Jonny Grieg."

"The guy that got put away for sex offenses with underage girls?"

"Yes, the billionaire pedophile and former defense contractor. He's just out from two years in a rather comfortable federal prison. The FBI turned him and he's been fully cooperative, informing on all his rich and powerful friends. It's the only thing keeping him out of a high security jail. Rich, white pedophiles don't last long in that environment and he knows it."

"Okay, who else?"

"Let me work on that. I have an idea, but I have to do some research into Blokhin. If asked, talk about Grieg. I'll send his private number to your phone. If Blokhin tries it, it will be engaged."

Kirsty brought up a picture on her cell phone. "Robert Nohmark. I've got him here. Not too bad a resemblance. Apart from one thing."

"Yeah?"

"He's got a really dark monobrow."

"A mono what?"

"His eyebrows nearly meet in the middle." She pulled a tube of black mascara from her bag. "Come here, I'll make you look lovely."

Montrose leaned forward. "This better be worth it."

"Okay," said Kirsty, and carefully penciled his eyebrows. "We walk into the place and meet Blokhin. What then?"

"My concern," said Pilgrim, "is not getting in, but getting out. Monaco is very secure and easily sealed off."

"Do we make a run for the boat?" said Montrose.

"Only as a last resort. We will keep that in reserve." He tapped his wheelchair. "From a purely selfish point of view, I am unable to make any other form of escape. If you are discovered, then running down to the harbor will only mean police speedboats and helicopters. The Mediterranean is too small to hide. I very much doubt if we could make it to the north coast of Africa in time, or whether we would want to. No, you need a less dramatic exit."

Priti tapped on the keyboard. "Once you have gone, I will follow you and leave a hire car in the underground car park. I will place the key behind the driver's side front wheel."

"Good," said Pilgrim. "Your documentation and passports are for Irish citizens, so you may move freely across Europe."

"And this guy is going to meet us?"

Priti checked the screen. "He says he will find time today."

"We need to force the issue," said Pilgrim. "Make a booking at the heliport for Robert Nohmark and his secretary for a helicopter flight in the next thirty minutes, then send another message to Sergei Blokhin. Say there is a very small window of opportunity and a very large budget."

"I'm on it," replied Priti.

Montrose nudged Kirsty, who was staring out the porthole towards the city. "You good to go?"

She turned and fixed her gaze on Montrose. "Oh, yeah. I'm good to go."

"I've seen that look before."

"If I'm on your side, you got nothing to worry about."

Pilgrim backed his wheelchair against the bulkhead. "Keep the meeting as short as possible. You have three routes of escape. Use the car or the helicopter. Let me be clear. I want to know if Sergei Blokhin supplied the missiles. If he is the middleman then I want to know if there are more. I personally doubt that is the case, but I have to be sure. If he is, I can direct the CIA or the French DGSE to pick him up and extract the information. But primarily, find out if he is the source or middleman for the missiles. That is a tall order, yet it is our objective. Do you understand?"

Kirsty smiled at Montrose, then faced Pilgrim. "I hear you, boss, loud and clear."

"I take it I'm posing as a buyer or a broker," said Montrose. "So what if he wants to sell?"

"I can offer things that the CIA cannot," said Pilgrim. "If he is willing to deal, then move your flight and we will continue to talk a little longer. If necessary, call me and pretend I'm the client. If Blokhin is proving reticent and we think he is the middleman, or an agent provocateur, then I will direct the CIA to pick him up. There is too much to lose. I will alert them to make sure they are in the south of France, but omit to say that the target is Monaco. Let's be clear. We have a great opportunity. I will give you a chance to escape before the CIA arrive. We'll see if that is necessary."

"If you do, put in a good word for me," said Montrose.

"Of course."

"You never give up," said Kirsty. "I like that."

"It's my country," mumbled Montrose. "Maybe one day they'll know the truth."

A screen beeped. "He's responded," said Priti. "He says *'Meet in his club, twenty minutes.'*"

Montrose patted the gun in his jeans. "Let's go." He followed Kirsty up onto the deck, then stepped onto the dock.

She rummaged inside the canvas bag and handed him a baseball cap and sunglasses. "Put these on." She pulled out a smaller canvas bag. "Comms equipment."

"Maybe not," said Montrose, walking towards the line of palm trees along the road and the white ornate buildings behind them. "We can't walk into a meeting wearing earpieces and looking like Secret Service goons."

"Oh, you Luddite. There are ways and means." She held him by the elbow. "Stand still." She took out a small pill box. It opened to reveal what looked like two tiny watch batteries. She lifted one up on the end of her finger. "Friends, Romans and Connors, lend me your ear." She gently pulled down on his ear lobe with one hand, then dropped the metal cell into his ear with the other.

He felt the metal fall into his ear canal. "What the hell is that?"

"An earpiece. The smallest that money can buy."

"Is this some weird spy shit? That's never going to work."

"I wouldn't say that around Priti. She gets very touchy."

He pressed his palm against his ear and felt the metal cell as it dropped further into his ear. "How am I going to get it out?

"KY Jelly and a crowbar. How the hell should I know? Stop being a wimp."

"Did Priti make them?"

"Don't be daft. Why would she make them when you can buy them on Amazon?" She reached into the bag and pulled out a thick silver cross on a chain. "Put this around your neck. It's the microphone and transceiver. It connects to the earpiece and the Bluetooth on your phone."

He held it in his hand then lifted it over the cap and onto his neck. "It's a bit gangster."

"Chinese technology has yet to catch up on your fashion requirements, Connor, but they're doing their best. It's either that or a big disco medallion and a hairy chest wig. Your choice."

She handed him a phone. "Priti has set it up. It runs in the background even when the phone is switched off."

He stopped under the palm trees beside the road and looked down at the map on her phone. "How far to the club?"

"About a thousand yards," said Kirsty. She took the other cell from the pill box and dropped it in her ear, then fixed on heavy earrings. "Now turn up the volume on your phone, but slowly. Or you'll blow you ear drum right across the harbor. Ready?"

He pressed the volume control to one bar.

"Priti, this is Kirsty. Test please."

The voice of Priti grew and seemed to echo around his head. "Mary had a little lamb…"

Kirsty grinned. "She kept it in a bucket."

"I don't think we need to know how that version ends," replied Priti. "Montrose, can you hear me?"

"Loud and clear."

"Mr. Pilgrim will monitor comms," said Priti. "I will arrange your hire car. Good luck."

"Thanks, sister," said Kirsty and she nudged Montrose. "We need to get you some proper clothes. If they check any of his photos, you've got to look the same. Like a rich idiot."

"There are shops on the way?" He ran after her as she weaved between the traffic and down a side street.

"This is Monaco, baby! Everything is for sale. You need

180

pastel shirts, cashmere and over-priced chinos. No Ralph Lauren or Lacoste polo shirts. There must be no branding on your clothes. That's how the super-rich roll."

"You know these things?"

"I do."

"I hate shopping."

The assistant held open the door and Montrose hurried into the street.

"Dump your clothes in the next bin," said Kirsty, "Priti will leave new gear in the car."

He caught his reflection in a shop window. "Jesus."

"Stylish," said Kirsty, "in a friendly, fascist kind of way."

Montrose looked down at the sky-blue cashmere pullover, the white chinos and tan Gucci loafers. "I don't want to die today." He held up the polished leather man bag. "Not like this."

Faber threw the door closed behind him so hard it rattled in its frame. "We got a tip-off."

"You found him?" said Napier.

"No, but the missiles could be in France."

"France?" Napier got up from his desk and stared at the map on the wall. "That's crazy. But crazy is the new reality." He walked over and traced his finger north from Rome, along the Mediterranean coast of Italy. He tapped his finger on the red line separating the Principality of Monaco from France. "You know, I wouldn't be surprised if Montrose was on his way right there. Maybe he made it out of Rome. And there's only one route by road. Right along the coast. Otherwise he'd have to take a detour through the Alps. And he isn't Hannibal. What did this tip-off say?"

"That the location of the missile source may be in southeast France, and we should be prepared to move."

"Prepared to move? Who gives a tip-off like that? Is this kosher?"

"The source is unknown, but has a very high hit rate. And it's well informed."

"Yeah, like an intelligence service. Like some tea-drinking Herbert in GCHQ."

"Or maybe our guy in GCHQ?"

"Yeah," said Napier. "Maybe." He stood before the map. "Southeast France. We're talking Marseille at a push, Toulon is a big naval base, then it's all sun cream and film stars. Cannes, Nice and St. Tropez."

"And Monaco."

"That's not France, but it might as well be." He closed his eyes and placed his palms flat on his face. "This is a Russian missile. Where are the Russians in the region?"

"They've got spies at the naval base, the rest are fat gangsters with plastic wives spending their money in the sun. All along the coast."

"Where's the money?"

"Nice, Cannes and Monaco."

"Yeah, but where's the real money? The private banks, the yachts registered in a hundred different shell companies, the place where you can do a deal to sell a fucking missile?"

"Monaco."

Napier stabbed a finger onto the map. "Forget the rest. We won't get a better chance, but if we're wrong…"

"We have time," said Faber. "Montrose can't have made it to Monaco already. Maybe we can set up a border post between France and Italy."

"Yeah, that'll please everyone. They haven't had a border post there for thirty years. The whole freeway will grind to a halt."

"Maybe not a bad idea. Flush him out. Maybe he's going to lead us right to the missiles."

Napier shook his head. "He's too smart for that. There's a whole network of back roads and mountain passes between Italy and France. None of them are manned. What about the sea? A boat could make it in four hours."

"We checked. Only a pleasure boat and a few guys ripping up the water to impress the chicks."

"Forget it. Let's hit Monaco. Then if we hit the jackpot, Montrose walks right in. Who have we got?"

"We have eight teams around Europe." He pointed to the map. "But that exposes us elsewhere. We have a tactical Learjet in Barcelona with ten men. They've been on alert since the first attack. We can have them on the streets in Monaco in thirty minutes. We'll get airport priority. Then transfer to a police helicopter, because they'll be dressed to kill."

"They can't fly to Monaco?"

"Too small for an airport. Everyone uses choppers down there."

Napier edged closer to the map. "Do it. And warn the Monaco police. We want the whole damn force looking for him."

"Yes, sir. One last thing. Do we try to take him alive?"

"I no longer care."

*

183

The fat man glanced at the empty place at the table where the old man had sat. He paused, then began. "He told me just before the meeting. He thought the exposure was too great. Montrose could bring all this to an end in seconds." He turned to the Director. "I do not think I speak for everyone at the table, but you said you knew where he was going, Director."

"I am beginning to lose patience with this obsession."

"Entertain me for a moment more," said the fat man. "So, Montrose made it out of Rome. That was unexpected, no? Your ruse was to tempt him out into the open and into the waiting arms of the police and security services. Not to actually make it all the way to the Principality," said the fat man.

The Director pursed his lips, then let out a slow breath. "Unexpected, yes. Unplanned, no. Worrying, gentlemen, is a misuse of the imagination. Yet I see you still don't understand that. Very well, let me update you on the fate of Montrose then we can move on." He nodded to a technician.

A picture appeared on the screen, showing two people standing at the corner of a street.

"Monaco, gentlemen."

"Is that…?"

"Yes," said the Director, "that is Connor Montrose. And it seems he has a charming assistant. No matter."

"How did he…?"

"His method of arrival is irrelevant. Though he did get there very quickly. However, we were prepared."

The fat man leaned into the screen. "I know that street."

"I'm sure you do," said the Director. "It leads to your private club. Mr. Montrose is about to have his final meal.

The fly is walking straight into the web. And we will hear no more from him. Now if we can move on…"

"Director, if we can see that image then so can the police. You know Monaco, there will be someone watching him right now."

The Director slammed his hand on the table. "Do you think I am an idiot! Of course they can fucking see him!"

No one moved.

The Director stepped back from the table. "Gentlemen. One last time. Let me explain. Then we *will* move on." He walked over to the window and looked out over the fields. "Montrose is wanted by every force in Europe. You want him dead before he can talk, even though he has nothing to say. And this, gentlemen, is exactly what I am going to do. This is what I had planned. This is what is going to happen." He turned to face the table. "Montrose will enter the club. It will be seen on the cameras. After a short period, he will leave the club via the hotel car park next door, as a passenger in a taxi. It will be seen by cameras. Then he will be driven away from prying eyes and his body will never be found. That will not be seen by cameras. The police will come calling and the club will tell them he visited, asked for accommodation, but had no business there and was asked to leave. He was given the courtesy of a taxi. And that is the last they heard of him. The club has a relationship with the police. Everything will be above board. The circus will move on and the club will be forgotten."

"A taxi?"

"Yes, with a man beside him pointing a gun at his stomach. And as soon as the taxi has crossed into France, he will pull the trigger."

CHAPTER 17

"I look like an asshole."

"I'm afraid that you look very much like an asshole, but that's important." Kirsty stuffed their jeans and shirts into a polished metal garbage can attached to a streetlamp, then faced the entrance to the club on the other side of the street.

He felt the weight of the Glock in his polished leather man bag. "What if they search me?"

"What if they do? Remember, you're a right-wing Christian and the only thing you believe in more than Jesus and money is guns. Just hand it over and tell them to take good care of it."

He looked down as she opened her bag and unwrapped a cloth. "What've you got there?"

She smiled. "Just a little letter-opener." In her hand was a long, thin dagger. The wooden handle was stained with age. The blade was dull but the edges gleamed silver and blue.

"What the hell is that?" said Montrose.

"It's a Sykes-Fairbairn. A British commando dagger. Standard wartime issue for the Royal Marines. They still use them. A very nice Welsh Guardsmen taught me how to use it."

He shook his head. "What if they find it?"

"It will be at the bottom of my bag, covered in sanitary towels and panty liners, and if anyone gets near it I'll say I need my bag back and the nearest ladies toilet immediately." She placed the knife deep in the bag. "Men are such wimps."

He heard Priti laughing in his ear. "Your car is ready. There will be radio silence from both Mr. Pilgrim and I unless it is an absolute necessity."

"Let's do it." Kirsty strode out from the curb.

"Wait," said Montrose. "I'm supposed to be the big shot. I walk in front."

Kirsty growled.

"You're the secretary, remember?" He stepped one pace ahead of her.

"Yeah, I'm the secretary. But I've got a knife, so remember to be a considerate employer, or I'll cut your goolies off."

"Jeez, it's tough being a boss." He looked up at the club. "I can't see the cameras."

"Correct, and I'll bet that they are watching us all the way, so walk like the God-fearing gun-toting right wing racist Nazi bastard that you are. This shit is about to get real."

They both stepped up the curb to stand in front of a high wooden door. "How long do you think we're going to last?" said Montrose.

"Oh, ye of little faith. Let's concentrate on what that piece of shit knows, then get the hell out. If he is the middleman then he knows where the missiles came from. Or where the next attack will be."

"Oh, right. Nothing too tricky, then? He's not going to just spit it out."

She patted her bag. "He might need some persuasion."

"Kirsty, he's not going to be on his own."

"I didn't think he would be. So, we might have to get him on his own. If we do, leave that to me."

"Look…"

"You do what you have to do, and if it all goes to shit, I'll do what I have to do."

There was no nameplate or doorbell. "We do it my way first, yeah?"

She didn't look at him. "Oh, yeah. Absolutely."

Montrose knocked on the door. He felt the mascara sticky where Kirsty had darkened his eyebrows. "Okay. We're about to walk into a club run by terrorists, arms dealers and pedophiles. I've got a gun, a handbag and I'm wearing make-up."

"Welcome to my world," said Kirsty. "Fuck the patriarchy."

"Oui?"

Montrose looked down at a small metal grille.

"I have an appointment with Monsieur Blokhin."

"Entrez."

The door clicked open. Montrose felt a jolt of adrenalin as he stepped through the entrance. In front of him was an old-fashioned revolving door of etched glass and dark wood, lined with polished brass handles. Through the glass he could see a figure sitting behind a desk about twenty feet away. Kirsty stood beside him. "Ladies first," he said.

"Gee, thanks, I'll be the first to get shot. No, you're the right-wing alpha male, and I'm just eye candy, so you go first. That's how it works in the great white America."

"Yeah." He shoved the brass handle and stepped in. The door revolved smoothly then slammed to a halt. Montrose almost smacked his face off the glass. He felt a puff of air and the door started again, and he emerged into a wide hall lined with ivory marble. The sweat chilled on his skin, and he heard the hum of aircon above and from brass vents set into the floor.

He felt a shove in his back as Kirsty came behind him. "Sorry."

She smiled sweetly and spoke softly, her voice masked by the aircon. "Stop acting like a nice guy, you fascist prick."

He stuck out his chin and marched towards the long desk at the back of the hall. In the corner he could see a high wooden door, flanked by two guards. Behind the desk, a man with close-cropped hair watched him approach. Montrose placed a hand on the marble top counter. "Mister Robert Nohmark. I'm here to see Mister Blokhin."

"He is *expected*," added Kirsty, in a low, southern drawl.

Montrose stopped himself giving her a sideways look for channeling Scarlett O'Hara.

The man nodded. "For security reasons, I must ask you if you are carrying a weapon. I hope you understand. We have many important club members who insist on discreet but very strict security."

Montrose caught the Russian accent. They had this place sewn up. "Of course, my club is exactly the same. It is not an issue." He took the Glock from his bag and placed it on the marble counter.

Kirsty stepped forward and placed her Glock beside it. "I just feel so naked without my piece." She lifted her arms dramatically in the air. "Do you want to search me? You never know what you might find." She pinned back her shoulders and her breasts jutted out through the thin cloth.

"Enough," said Montrose.

She let her arms drop.

A man approached from one of the doors. "Your bag."

Montrose opened his bag and the man felt around inside.

Kirsty held her bag open and he glanced in, rummaged around then pulled his hand out and turned away.

"Follow me."

From behind the high wooden door, Montrose heard a lock snap back, like a bolt action rifle. The door opened and another guard in an identical suit and haircut stood to the side.

He stepped through the door. The frescoed roof was thirty feet high, hung with sparkling chandeliers. The long, high windows each side of the salon were covered in thin, translucent curtains, diffusing the light. It occurred to him he'd seen photographs of similar rooms. They were usually fin-de-siècle Parisian brothels. The room was full of silver gilt furniture, lined with red velvet. It was a monument to bad taste. It would suit the Russians perfectly.

The door closed behind them. The guard positioned himself with his back to the door, facing the room. Two more men stood at a marble-topped bar at the side of the room, sipping water. The white-coated barman looked straight ahead.

The room was several degrees warmer than the hall. At the far end, below a fading medieval tapestry, a short, fat man sat perched on a chaise longue, wearing an expensive crumpled suit. His left arm was draped over the back of the couch and he held a fat cigar in his right hand, trying to give an air of louche sophistication, while his stubby legs barely reached the carpet. He regarded Montrose through half-shut eyes. In each corner of the back wall there was a low archway, leading to identical dimly-lit corridors.

Montrose lifted his chin into the air as he walked.

"Jeez," whispered Kirsty, just behind him, "we've walked into Madonna's knicker drawer."

Blokhin got to his feet, splaying his legs wide and thrusting out a hand.

"Oohh," murmured Kirsty, "it's handshake power play time. You men are so impressive."

Montrose ignored her and stepped over, taking Blokhin's hand in a tight grip. "Robert Nohmark. A pleasure to meet you, Mr. Blokhin. I appreciate your time." Blokhin began to pump his hand up and down and Montrose freed his little finger to tap twice on Blokhin's wrist.

Blokhin let go of Montrose's hand.

Work that out, thought Montrose. You'll be thinking P2 Masonic Lodge of Rome, and I'm thinking Long Island Cub Scouts. "If I may introduce my secretary, er, Scarlett."

Kirsty began to move forward, but Blokhin spoke without looking at her. "She can wait at the bar. I'll not discuss business with pretty little things."

Montrose nodded towards Kirsty, and she smiled and turned away. He watched her step gracefully between the furniture and heard her voice whisper through his earpiece as she walked.

"I'm going to rip his fucking lungs out and make him eat them."

She sat on a bar stool next to the two men, and faced Montrose, smiling sweetly.

"Can I offer you a drink?" said Blokhin.

"Perhaps later. I have a very tight schedule and I'd like to get straight to business."

Blokhin gestured towards a chair.

"Let me come straight to the point." Montrose sat down. "I understand that certain hardware has come on the market. Both I, and the people I represent, would like very much to have access to this hardware. I also understand that the first time it came up for sale only two buyers were permitted."

Blokhin said nothing and tapped the end of his cigar on his chin.

"On our side of the Atlantic, the opportunity to access similar hardware is considerable, but we are not convinced, shall we say, that the normal market is sufficiently secure. Too many people would be involved. Too many tongues wagging. Now, some of my friends have access to the heart of US government agencies, and have recommended that I take a more direct approach."

"The hardware?" said Blokhin. "Normal market?"

"The Silk Road."

Blokhin didn't react. "And you think I can help?"

"Yes, I think you can. So, let's not flirt like a couple of teenagers at their first dance. Because I don't have time for that shit."

Blokhin grinned. "And where did you get my name?"

"From two of my friends. Each separately confirmed your, shall we say, *abilities*."

"And they are?"

"Jonny Grieg in Washington. He sends his regards."

"Ah, you know Jonny?"

"We share some interests. He's just got out of prison and I'm flying back to the US today to arrange a little private party. I always make sure he has a good time when he's in New York. You know what he likes." Montrose flicked his eyes behind him towards the bar. "Pretty young secretaries are fun, but there's nothing like a younger vintage."

Blokhin laughed. "Fruit is always freshest when it has just fallen from the tree."

"Call him, if you need to be reassured."

"No," Blokhin shrugged, "that won't be necessary." He lowered his chin, which disappeared into the folds of fat around his neck, and regarded Montrose closely. "You know, you should join our club. I'm sure you could find something to keep you entertained."

"That would be very interesting, Mr. Blokhin. Very interesting indeed. Perhaps when we have concluded business." His phone buzzed in his pocket. He brought it out and read the message. "Ruslan Shevchenko also sends his regards."

Blokhin sat very still.

Montrose held out the phone, showing the Crimean phone number.

"Turn it off," said Blokhin.

"Of course, I understand." He held the phone out so that Blokhin could watch and thumbed the power button.

Blokhin sat back. "Now, let us talk freely, Mr. Nohmark. Let us pretend your assumption is correct. And let's also assume that I, a simple businessman, am someone who can help you. But I will not assume that you know of the exclusivity and value of this market. Or perhaps you do know the current price of this hardware?"

Montrose closed his eyes and nodded. "I know that the last successful bid was two billion US dollars, so let me assure you, I know the market and I have access to the funds required, not only from my own resources. We have sympathetic members of our organization within the security services of the United States, and they keep us informed. So, let me be clear. Thanks to the seniority of people in my organization, I have gained security clearance to fly through US and NATO military airspace all the way to my private airfield in upstate New York, and if we can seal the deal today, I can make a very generous offer."

Blokhin held up a hand. "Let us step back for a moment."

Montrose shifted in his chair.

"Humor me, Mr. Nohmark. This is a seller's market. You and I are businessmen."

"I am under no illusion that this is a buyer's market. We want to get in before the rush. And there will be a rush. But do you really want that hardware to end up in the hands of Russia's enemies?"

"Our enemies?" Blokhin grinned. "And you are a friend?" His eyes closed to slits and his whole body jiggled as he began to laugh.

Montrose smiled and sat back in the chair. "More than you know, *tovarishch*."

Blokhin took out a handkerchief and wiped his eyes. "What do you want to do? Start another war on terror?" His chest began to heave and he leaned forward. "The last time you did that, you set fire to the entire fucking Middle East." The tears were streaming from his eyes. "You know, my friends in the Kremlin, they couldn't believe it. They have spent so many years dedicated to undermining your democracy, your foreign relations, your military alliances, and government structures, but then you go and bomb every fucking village with an idiot and you do all the work for us!" He wiped his face and took a deep breath, then stuffed the handkerchief in his pocket. "I mean, what was the one in Mosul? You dropped a bomb from a jet to kill a sniper. One man. You used a million dollar smart bomb and you collapsed an entire building and killed hundreds of people. You feed the war. Your country feeds the war on terror. You are a martyr machine."

"Not me, my friend. Not me."

Blokhin leaned back on the couch and stared up at the roof. "Your country is being more productive in its own destruction than all the spies in Moscow could ever hope to be. Every time you kill someone, or create more orphans and widows, or kill another sniper, you create another hundred enemies and terrorists longing for the destruction of the USA. We are more than happy to leave your country to eat itself alive and suffocate in its own shit. All Moscow needs to do now is sit back with their arms folded, order some vodka and tune into CNN and Fox to see you winning hearts and minds across the globe. Your love of democracy in Libya and Iraq created the charnel house that bred ISIS. They are the bastard child of your foreign policy." He pushed himself forward. "You have lit fires across the world that will not be extinguished for generations."

Montrose shrugged. "When did Russia start handing out lessons in politics? You barrel-bombed half of Syria and destroyed Chechnya."

"Yes, but we control Syria and Chechnya. We have an endgame. A purpose. Syria gives us the Mediterranean port we have always desired. So, tell me, what are you planning to create with your world tour of democracy?"

Montrose shook his head. "What can I say?" He looked up. "You're right. There has been no gain. We should have stripped Iraq and Afghanistan of their resources. Not to do so would be a waste of all those American lives. What we need is our own East India Company. Then both Russia and

America can work together. But, that is for another day. My people, my organization, are not immediately concerned with war in Kabul or the mountains of Pakistan. No, as far as myself and my friends are concerned the whole Middle East can burn itself to the ground."

"Really? Then tell me, this hardware you speak of, what new war is coming to our screens next? Who is about to get a dose of democracy?"

Montrose looked him directly in the eye. "War is coming, and sooner than you or Moscow think. But not on foreign shores. This time it is an American war."

Blokhin said nothing.

"War on America, Mr. Blokhin. And my organization wants to know whose side Moscow will be on. My blessed land is being strangled by its own constitution. America has never been more divided. It has never been more on the point of civil war. The left wing, the secularists, the socialists, the godless sinners that weaken our country and our resolve and make us targets across the globe. Well, no more. War is coming to America. And at a time of our own choosing. Our civilian army is already armed, many with assault rifles. Then we will cleanse America of the degenerates, the weak, vile scum, sucking at the teat of welfare handouts, thanks to the deluded electorate voting for compassionate government. Well, they'll find out about compassion when we have them in camps." He closed his eyes and pushed his chin into the air. Kirsty's voice whispered in his earpiece.

"For fuck's sake get to the point before you go the full Adolf. You should never go the full Adolf."

Montrose relaxed his shoulders and smiled at Blokhin. "It's time to throw the crates of tea into the water and set fire to the ships." He saw the quizzical look on Blokhin's face. "My friends need that hardware to bring down the most important airplane in America. If that hardware can go through the defenses of a combat plane, then we can blow any moronic President and his plane out of the sky. There will always be a useful idiot to take his place. And when the troops are on the street we will make sure that the Democrat and Antifa scum are blamed. Then the armed revolution will begin. They'll be begging our troops to protect them. And once they are under our control, emergency powers will ensure that's where they stay." He leaned forward. "That is why my friends need this hardware. And we will not forget the help that Russia gives us."

Blokhin paused, looking up to the thin sunlight diffused through the windows. He shook his head. "Russia cannot help you with this." For a few moments he covered his face with his hand, rubbing his eyes with his thumb and forefinger. "But perhaps I can." He let out a deep breath and leaned forward, elbows on knees. "Do you realize how popular and how expensive this hardware is about to become?"

"Yes, I do. I don't doubt it for a moment. I have immediate access to a military budget. We have friends in very high places. I can outbid any country on the planet. But I have no intention of doing so. Getting into a bidding war will generate an intelligence SIGNINT feeding frenzy. We don't need the CIA or NATO and the Five Eyes interfering."

"I'm sure you don't. The intelligence service of the British Empire is still a force to be reckoned with. But I hear you, my friend. Let me be clear too, the Russian government has no say in this matter. Business is business." He took a cell phone from his pocket and typed in a message.

"As to your current activities," said Montrose. "I wish you well in your operation against the fabric of NATO. I assume that is your goal?"

Blokhin waved a hand, concentrating on his phone. "That is none of my concern. That is for Moscow to deal with. These attacks mean a war on Russia or the destruction of NATO. And Russia cannot afford a war. For all their bluster and firepower, they could not win a war in Europe and they know it. They would be wiped off the face of the earth." He faced Montrose. "The government in Moscow is a cabal of ex-spies longing for the Cold War, when their sad little lives had some meaning. Now they are just administrators. They fill their lives with gold and compensate for their impotency by undermining the governments of their ex-vassals and taking some of the Ukraine that was already full of Russians. It's like watching children fighting in a playground."

"I was always surprised they stopped at the Crimea. It showed a weakness in their resolve. You could have taken Ukraine in a week and NATO would have done nothing about it."

Blokhin shrugged. "The reaction of Moscow is a disgrace. They chase around playing their spy games in Washington and the Balkans, but they keep an eye on their Swiss bank accounts. What we have seen in the past four years is the death rattle of democratic Russia." He looked Montrose in the eye. "You are not alone in your ambition and vision for the USA. We will also bring Russia back to its former glory. And when it is done, NATO and the Moscow government cabal will be history. Some of them are here now, in Monaco. They fill the restaurants, barely able to use a knife and fork." He smiled and sat back. "But I talk too much. You have touched a raw

198

nerve. You are a clever man. Perhaps our countries will work together in the future before the Chinese ruin everything. Our hands will stretch in friendship across the Bering Strait."

"I hope so. We have strong men who are prepared to do what is right to make our country great again. The new America will not forget this. You will always be welcome on our shores."

The phone buzzed in Blokhin's hand. He looked down and smiled.

"Good news, I hope?" said Montrose.

"We will know very soon. In the meantime, let's have a drink." He nodded towards the bar.

Montrose sat back in his chair and glanced up at the ancient tapestry on the wall. The sound of Pilgrim's voice in his ear made his eye twitch. He rubbed his face to cover his reaction.

"Listen to me. Your cover may be blown. Robert Nohmark has been arrested in New York. Source says a tip-off came from Europe. It may have been Blokhin. Get out of there. Now."

Kirsty stared at the back of Montrose's head as Pilgrim's words echoed through her brain. She got up from her bar stool.

The barman came out from behind the bar, unwrapping a bottle of champagne.

She walked casually to the center of the room then lifted a compact from her bag and pretended to check her lips as she spoke. "That's not going to be easy. There are four armed guys in here. We're in the big salon, ground floor. Priti, do you have a map of this place? A route to the car park next door?"

"Yes," said Priti, "I'll send it to your phone. There is a

corridor at the end of the room, same side as the bar. Go to the end, there are stairs down to the kitchens. At the southeast corner of the kitchens is a door to a corridor that leads to the car park."

"I have more news," said Pilgrim. "It's not good."

"We have to lose the goons," said Kirsty. "We are outnumbered and unarmed." She thought of the knife in her bag and wished it was a Glock. She kept her gaze glued to the back of Montrose's head. His neck was tight. She knew he could hear every word.

"Message from my source in Langley," said Pilgrim. "There are an estimated fifty missiles for sale. We are monitoring Monaco police channels, and the CIA are on their way to your location. I don't care how you do it, but get out. The operation is aborted."

Kirsty glanced around at the bar and saw the barman pop the champagne and began to wipe the froth from the neck, ready to place it on a silver tray. She whispered into her hands. "Connor, listen to me. Tell him you'd like to celebrate. Invite me over. Offer me as a gift. Tell him you'd like to watch." She wiped her lips and covered her mouth again. "I know what this place is. Just go with me. Do it. Right now. Tell him I'm the best fuck you've ever had."

She dropped the compact in her bag, strode over to the bar, then lifted the tray with the champagne and glasses. "I'll take that. They're expecting me."

The Director read the text one more time to be certain. "Good news, gentlemen." He looked up and saw the empty chair at the end of the table, then nodded to a technician who pushed it from the room. They didn't need an empty chair to be reminded how transient life could be. The space at the table would serve that purpose. He gazed around the table at all the eager faces and smiled. "Some of you were concerned about the whereabouts of Mr. Connor Montrose. I have decided that he will not be leaving at the point of a gun after all. Instead, his corpse will be leaving the club in the trunk of a taxi. We will deal with that issue later. The Monaco police will do as they are told. His secretary can share his fate. They are being entertained while our disposal team arrive. They were delayed by a security alert. Probably some leather-skinned American émigré has lost her purse. In the meantime, Montrose has four armed men guarding him. So, you may no longer concern yourself on his account. I'm told he is something of a confidence trickster and that his impersonation of an American businessman was quite convincing. It is a shame. We may have had use for a man of such talent, but he has, to a very great degree, outlived his usefulness." The phone buzzed on the table. "Ah, it is our friend in the Monaco police." He picked up the phone and read the message. His hand trembled and he dropped the phone onto the table.

One of the men leaned forward and peered at the screen. Three letters stood out. "The CIA? In Monaco?"

The Director lunged forward and grabbed the phone. "Yes, that is an unusual development. I assume Mr. Montrose may have inadvertently led them there. No matter." He glanced at the screen. "According to the police, they are landing in Monaco and will be at the club in ten minutes. They have asked the police to secure the area." He began to type into the phone.

201

The fat man stood up. "Director, we must…"

"Shut up!" He resumed typing. "There is time. The taxi with Montrose will leave as planned. Our police contact will be waiting to ensure that it leaves the area. Montrose's corpse will be in the trunk." He pressed send, then placed the phone in the table. "You know, when I am on my deathbed, I will regret only one thing. That I was not the man who put the gun against Montrose's head and pulled the trigger."

CHAPTER 18

"**C**hampagne, gentlemen?"

Montrose twisted his head and saw Kirsty approach with a bottle in an ice bucket and two glasses wobbling around on a silver tray.

The barman hurried behind her, but Blokhin waved him away.

She stood beside Montrose. "I just popped over to remind you, sir, that your helicopter is waiting. Now, I'll leave you alone."

"Kir…. Scarlett," said Montrose, "why don't you join us? The helicopter can wait."

"And your jet, sir?"

"They can find another slot. I have more important business to attend to." He turned to Blokhin. "As I said, certain friends in the Defense Department have given me a NATO access and clearance with French air traffic control. It's very useful." He placed a hand on Kirsty's waist. "While we're waiting, my dear, why don't you be nice to Mr. Blokhin? You know, very nice."

She gasped and placed the champagne on the table. "Wow, do we have time? Oh, yes please!" She held out a hand to Blokhin.

He stood and kissed her hand, then smiled at Montrose. "She has many talents then, as a secretary?"

"Oh yes, she certainly does. She's a good girl. My secret weapon."

Blokhin stepped forward and placed a fat hand on the side of her head, then let it slip down, and gently wrapped his fingers around her neck.

Kirsty gasped.

"Are you a good girl?" he said, his teeth clenched.

"I'm a very good girl," said Kirsty, then gently bit her lip. "But sometimes, I'm bad."

He took a step back. "Just how bad?"

She held out a hand and ran her finger up the front of his pants.

Blokhin grinned and summoned a bodyguard.

"Is he coming to play too?" said Kirsty. She turned to Montrose. "Please tell me he is."

"That's up to Mr. Blokhin. But I'll let you play on one condition. I like to watch." He grinned at Blokhin. "I'm sure she will be very accommodating. The more the merrier."

"He never lets me play alone," said Kirsty. "But I like him seeing me punished." She licked her lips. "Will you tie me up?"

Blokhin's right eye twitched and bubbles of saliva appeared at the edge of his mouth. He grabbed her breast and Kirsty squealed. "Come with me," he said, "I have something to show you."

Montrose stood and elbowed Kirsty out of the way. "Bring the drinks."

"And the ice," said Blokhin. "You'll need it."

"Yes, sir." She lifted the tray and followed them to the corner of the room.

Leading the way, Blokhin led them into a narrow doorway and down a dark corridor, lined with doors.

Montrose glanced towards Kirsty, and saw her flick her chin to the end of the corridor. He saw the double doors leading to the kitchen. Now? he mouthed.

Blokhin stopped at one of the doors in the middle of the corridor and unlocked it with a brass key. He pushed it open and moved to the side. "After you, my dear."

Kirsty stepped inside and squealed.

Montrose followed her. A wide bed covered in plastic dominated the room. The curtains were closed and the only other object visible in the room was a six-foot high wooden cross fixed to the wall, made of solid dark wood, with manacles and restraints attached to it. Fixed to the wall was a rack of wooden canes, of varying thickness and lengths.

"Oh my God," she said. "This is perfect."

Blokhin stood proudly in the middle of the room and took off his jacket. The bodyguard closed the door and turned the key in the lock.

Montrose tried not to pace around, but slapped his hands off the thick wood of the cross. "Very nice. It might give me some ideas for New York."

The bodyguard backed against the door and folded his arms across his chest.

Kirsty pointed to the canes. "Which one are you going to use?"

Removing his cufflinks, Blokhin rolled up his sleeves. "All of them. Until they break." He grinned at Montrose. "As

I said, the hardware you seek is very expensive." He pointed to the bodyguard. "Then we will give you everything you desire, you little slut."

Kirsty gasped. "I'm going to need my lube." She rummaged in her bag and at the same time backed towards the bodyguard, wiggling her bottom. "Please, undo me." She pushed her backside against him.

The bodyguard looked down, searching for a zip or tie, and placed a massive hand on Kirsty's shoulder. She gave a sigh of pleasure, then dropped her bag and spun around, blocking the guard's arm with her forearm and burying the seven-inch blade deep into his eye socket. The bodyguard jerked upwards then slumped to the floor, his mouth wide open. Kirsty ripped the dagger out as he fell, turned and hurled it at Blokhin. He threw up a hand in front of his face and the blade sliced across his knuckles and flew past his head.

Blokhin roared, crouching down to charge as Montrose slammed into him, knocking him to the side of the bed. They both bounced off the edge of the mattress and lay at Kirsty's feet. She brought her heel down hard onto Blokhin's neck. He gasped for breath, but shot out a fat hand and grabbed her leg, pulling her to the ground then rolling on top of her.

Montrose reached up and grabbed Blokhin's chin, hauled back with all his might and pulled him off Kirsty.

She scrambled to her feet, seized the champagne bottle and swung it high above her head, then smashed it down onto Blokhin's face. He slumped to the floor and the champagne turned pink as it spewed around his head.

Montrose stood up, his hands shaking. He shoved Blokhin's head with his foot. There was no reaction.

"Shit," said Kirsty. "I wanted him to talk."

A voice rang in their ear. "It's Priti. The CIA are close. Police are blocking the roads. You need to get out right now."

Kirsty hauled Blokhin onto his back and stamped on his groin. "Wake up, you bastard."

Blokhin's eyes rolled back in his head. He began to cough as Kirsty repeatedly stamped down on his groin. He gasped in agony and rolled to the side.

"Get his phone," said Priti.

Montrose shoved a hand inside Blokhin's jacket and pulled out the phone.

"Give it to me," said Kirsty.

"It's locked. Do we cut his finger off?"

"Urban myth. Doesn't work with a dead finger." She pressed the phone against Blokhin's index finger and the screen burst into life. "Priti, give me a number. I'll text you and then you reply with a worm. Then you can clean this bastard out."

"I'm on it."

"You tell us where the missiles are," said Montrose, "and you get to live."

"Live?" said Kirsty. She stood over Blokhin as he spluttered blood onto the carpet. "Connor, you know what this place is, right?"

"I don't care. We just have to…"

She jerked a thumb back at the heavy wooden cross. "You don't care, yeah? Look at those restraints on the spars of the cross. Look at the distance between them."

He glanced over.

"They're for kids. This is a place for torturing and abusing kids. And you think he's going to get out of this place alive?" She heard Pilgrim's voice in her head and stopped in her tracks.

"Kirsty. Focus."

Priti spelled out a number and Kirsty typed in a blank message. Almost immediately the reply came back. She opened the attachment in the message then threw the phone under the bed and leaned over Blokhin. "He's right," said Kirsty. "You tell us where the missiles are and you get to live. You better listen to him." She walked over to the bodyguard, lying slumped against the door, and hauled him to the side.

"Where are the missiles?" Montrose leaned in so close he could smell the blood streaming from Blokhin's nose and lips.

"No," said Blokhin, "I don't think you understand. If I die, then you die. You are a dead man walking."

"You know," said Montrose, "I've been told that by bigger, badder bastards than you, but here I am, still standing."

"Get out now. They are closing the roads."

"Last chance," said Montrose. "Let's see if you can redeem yourself. Where are the missiles?"

Blokhin began to laugh, blood and spittle spraying from his mouth. "I'm just a delivery service. You're asking the wrong man."

"Then you're fuck all use to me." Kirsty held the bodyguard's gun against Blokhin's head. "Unless you tell me where I can find the kids."

Blokhin looked up at her. "What?"

"The ones who died in here. The ones you took from Syria and Iraq."

"The police are at the front door. Go now!"

"You'll never know if you kill me," he said. "Then you will die too."

Kirsty stepped back and pulled a pillow from the bed. She placed it over Blokhin's head. He began to shake and she straightened her arm and forced the muzzle of the gun into the soft, white cloth. "I don't fucking think so." She pulled the trigger.

Blokhin's corpse twitched, then lay still.

Montrose stood up. "Okay. So. Got any plans?"

"Yeah. Run like fuck." She unlocked the door and stuck her head into the corridor. Voices came from the salon. "Go."

He ran after her to the end of the corridor and through the double doors, into a dimly-lit stairwell and down several flights of stairs, emerging into a long, wide kitchen.

Two men were busy washing plates, moving to the sound of the North African music that thudded off the tiled walls.

"Southeast corner," said Kirsty, and she ran for a swing door. It opened into another long corridor and they both sprinted towards the end. "This is where they brought the kids," said Kirsty. "I know it."

"Check it's clear," said Montrose.

She stopped and glanced through a porthole window set into the door. "Seen."

"Who?"

"Some dick standing beside a Mercedes taxi with the doors and the trunk open. That will be our ride. And I bet we weren't getting to ride in the back seat holding hands." She brought up the bodyguard's gun. "Ready?"

"You want me to distract him?"

"Don't be daft, just stay behind me. Let's hope he's on his own. I'm not tooled up for a movie shootout." She kicked open the door.

The taxi driver twisted his head towards her then dropped to one knee and raised a gun.

Kirsty put two rounds in his chest and he slumped to the

ground. She ran over and put another round in his head and crouched below the hood, sweeping the sights of her gun across the garage. "Clear."

"I'll take his weapon."

"No, leave it," said Kirsty. "Priti will make sure we are well equipped. Priti? Can you hear me?" There was no reply. "No signal." She kicked the taxi driver's gun across the garage floor and under a car. "There's a lot of cops out there, Connor. Carrying a gun is not going to help." She reached under the wheel of a Porsche and pulled out a key. "They're looking for two people, so I'm going to take this Porsche and play the rich chick, and you can be a taxi driver. Follow me. Once we're clear we can dump the taxi." She got into the Porsche, fired up the engine and hit the roof release. The roof folded backwards and the exhaust note rolled off the walls. She adjusted the rear-view mirror and pulled out towards the exit ramp.

Montrose stepped over the taxi driver and got into the Mercedes. He drove forwards, following Kirsty up the ramp and into the sunshine. From the ramp he could see the tops of several police vehicles across the street.

A policeman stood at the top of the ramp where it crossed the sidewalk and joined the street. He glanced at Kirsty and held up a hand.

Montrose saw her flex her shoulders and reach down into the door pocket. "Jesus, don't do it." He pressed the horn, and the policeman turned around. He nodded to Montrose and stepped aside, waving Kirsty into the traffic then heading towards the club.

Priti's voice came over the line. "Can you hear me? Come in, come in, can you hear me?"

"Loud and clear," said Montrose. "We're out, heading to the harbor."

"No," said Priti, "head for France or Italy. There are police boats patrolling the harbor. We can't put Mr. Pilgrim at risk."

"Understood," said Kirsty.

"I need to ditch this taxi before the border," said Montrose.

"There is no border post," said Kirsty, "but there may be some nosey cops. I'll pull in ahead. You park up and meet me. Nice and calm."

"Understood," Montrose slowed and stopped at the curb. He stepped out and walked forward to where Kirsty was waiting. She pushed open the door for him and he dropped into the seat. "Let's go."

Kirsty grinned. "You got it." She pulled out and accelerated down the street. "Priti, we're heading east and north. I'm just going to take the fastest road out of town. If I see anything, I'll try to find a quieter route."

"Okay, but if you do get stopped, you do not want to be searched. Is that clear?"

"Understood."

"I have left you weapons and equipment in the trunk."

"Thanks, quartermaster."

"We are leaving the harbor," said Priti. "Maintain radio silence until you are clear of France."

"Roger that."

Montrose shielded his eyes from the sun. "Which way to Italy?"

"That way," Kirsty said, and pointed down the road. "Eight miles east."

He saw a line of police cars pulled into the side. "Maybe we better find another way."

"No, that's good news. Those are French cops, not Monegasque. That's the border with France. Blink and you miss it. And French cops don't give a shit."

As they got closer, he saw the cops standing by their cars, watching the traffic.

"We're cool, Connor. We're just another couple of rich, parasitical, good for nothing bald monkeys who shouldn't be allowed to breed or vote."

Montrose turned towards her.

"Sorry, all my friends at school were Marxists. Or Trotskyists. Something like that. I could never tell the difference. Welsh valleys, you see?" She dropped a gear and pulled into the fast lane. "But I could tell you one thing about them. They never got laid."

CHAPTER 19

Priti's voice came over the line. "Head north. Now!"

A police car sped past, heading for the center of town. Montrose resisted the temptation to turn and look. "What's going on?"

"I've noticed activity on the road cameras at the Italian border, and more police cars are heading for the motorway. They're going to block the roads."

"Where are you?" said Kirsty.

"Heading for Corsica," said Priti. "We just made it out before the police closed the harbor."

"So where are we going?" said Montrose.

"Germany," said Priti.

Kirsty and Montrose stared at each other. "Germany?" said Kirsty. "How long is it going to take us to get there?"

"Too long," said Priti, "they'll have swamped the roads. Listen to me, head north on the D2566."

Montrose switched on the satnav. "Got it. Shit, next exit!"

The car swung hard right, narrowly missing a concrete lane divider, and down a steep slip road. Kirsty gripped the wheel hard and the tires bit into the tarmac as the road swept 180° and under the road above.

Holding on to the door and the top edge of the windscreen, Montrose checked the map. "Okay, we're on it. Just."

"Keep heading north and take the D93," said Priti. "Look for a place called Roccaverde, it's right on the Italian border."

"I'll find it on the satnav."

"Why there?" said Kirsty. "Are we crossing on foot?"

"No, it's a mountain rescue heliport. I've chartered a helicopter from Monaco to pick you up there. It's too dangerous for you to come back into town."

"Love it," said Kirsty. "I'm going to miss this Monaco life." She kept her foot hard down as the roads became tighter, climbing up the foothills of the Alps.

"We'll be there in fifteen minutes," said Montrose. "Why Germany?"

"Blokhin's phone," replied Priti. "When Kirsty opened it in the hotel room, I sent a worm message. Once she opened it, we sucked the phone dry. We have Blokhin's movements, contacts and call records. Amongst other things."

"Like Germany?"

"Yes," replied Priti. "I tracked his number through the cell phone masts around Monaco. He arrived at the hotel two days prior to the attack on the C-130 in the Italian village. And we know that the two men who brought down the plane left the hotel one day after Blokhin arrived."

Montrose held on tight as Kirsty swung the Porsche into another tight curve. "You think he delivered the missiles to the terrorists?"

"It seems likely. Then I checked back through the locations. He came from Germany the day before."

"How did Blokhin get here with four suitcases?" said Montrose. "There were two used for the village attack and two for Rome. He must have found a way through airport security with…"

"He didn't fly. He drove to Monaco."

"All the way from Germany? This guy is a billionaire. Why would he drive twelve hours across Europe when he could have taken a private jet, or helicopter?"

"Makes sense," said Kirsty. "Even though it was an internal EU flight, and he could skip Customs, there are too many prying eyes at airports, and too many cameras. It only takes one cop or nosey customs dude to ask what's in the suitcase and then the gig's up. And this is one thing that you'd want to take care of yourself. Whoever he was dealing with, they won't be Boy Scouts. This wouldn't be something you could trust to some flunky."

"And I can track him," said Priti. "Every cell phone mast his phone connected with on the way. I've got a lot of information to get through, but the headline is that he stopped in Germany for about five minutes and then drove to Monaco. I checked the date and time when he arrived at the cell phone mast next to the club. Then I checked the cars at that time and I found his Mercedes Maybach. That kind of limo stands out. And it's registered to one of his companies."

"And those things are big enough to carry four heavy suitcases in the trunk."

"Exactly. But I need time to process the information from all of the cell phone masts and the distances between them. Once I have his cellphone connections compared against them, I can triangulate his speed and location to the nearest yard. I'm going to make sure he didn't stop on the way from Germany. Then I can focus on what could be the pick-up point. And that is where the rest of missiles could be."

"Okay," said Kirsty. "Looks like we're going to Germany."

"When I've worked out the exact location, I'll send a message to the helicopter company and they can redirect the pilot. They think you are rich business people going hunting."

"They've got it half right," said Kirsty.

Pilgrim's voice came over the line. "Priti has been concentrating on the location records on Blokhin's phone and I have passed on the remainder of the information to friends who can compare it with existing intelligence. We know Blokhin was well-connected to Moscow. But the wealth of contacts was wider than we expected, and include some very unsavory characters."

"I want to meet them all," said Kirsty. "Just once."

"Perhaps one day," said Pilgrim. "Mr. Blokhin has been very busy, especially with extreme right-wing groups all over Europe and Russia. The people he was working with are not the usual suspects. I will pass the information to the CIA when I am more certain."

"Maybe the CIA know already," said Montrose. "Just maybe not the guys you're talking to, the whistleblowers, or whoever they are."

"White Hats," said Priti. "Just call them White Hats."

Kirsty grinned at Montrose and held a finger to her lips.

"There are two bags in the trunk," said Priti. "I had planned to give you more, but the harbor wasn't safe to hang around."

"Guns and ammo?" said Kirsty.

"Yes. And new phones. Ditch the phones you have. If we can track them, they can track us."

"That's all I need. Thanks, quartermaster."

The sound of rotor blades made Montrose look up. A helicopter flew low overhead, heading north. "That's our ride."

"I hear it," said Priti. "I have told the pilot to take you to Berlin. But it could be anywhere in southern Germany. I'll give you as much notice as I can. Be ready."

Faber pushed open the door.

Napier looked up from the desk, his mouth slightly open.

"Two dead Russians," said Faber.

"And?"

"No Montrose. He's gone. The cops are looking everywhere."

Napier leaned forward and held his head in his hands. He opened his eyes and his head jerked up. "Fuck Montrose. Two dead Russians? Who?"

"I just got the report." Faber checked his phone. "Fully classified. The French DGSE have told the Monaco government to say nothing."

"Whatever. Who were the Russians?"

Faber flicked the screen. "Some ex-military goon, low level, and Sergei Blokhin."

"Blokhin?" Napier stood up and pushed back his chair. "That piece of shit?"

"Yeah. Who is this guy? I'm just pulling his files now. I've got a request in."

"Sergei Blokhin is one evil motherfucker. Well, he was. If it was Montrose that killed him, he did us a big favor. He used to be one of Putin's billionaire oligarchs. Made a fortune in money-laundering through British banks in Hong Kong and real estate in New York. If you had dirty money, Blokhin could clean it. For a price. When he wasn't doing that, he was into people trafficking and arms deals. The list is very long and very dirty."

"So, we can connect him right back to Moscow?"

"It's possible, but not that easy." Napier slammed the table. "Dammit! If we had caught Blokhin and Montrose together we could have nailed this shit."

Faber checked his phone. "The cameras caught him going into the club where we found Blokhin. They didn't see him come out, but there are other exits."

"Yeah, I'm sure. Montrose is way ahead of us."

"There was a girl with him."

"Yeah? Have we ID'd her?"

"Not yet. We don't have her face on record. She was wearing shades."

"Let the geeks work their magic. We'll find her." Napier turned and looked out the window, down to the busy street. "The tip-off was right, whoever it was. Maybe they didn't want us getting too close. All they said was South of France. We guessed Monaco. And we guessed right. And then we find Blokhin."

"Maybe he was the middleman. Selling the missiles to Montrose?"

"No, we have a video of Montrose picking up the missiles in underground Rome. If he had them, why would he have gone to the club? Something about Montrose isn't making sense, no matter what that asshole Campbell says. Whatever. Just shoot the bastard."

"Yeah, but was Blokhin still the middleman for Moscow?"

Napier rubbed his face. "I don't know. See, the reason Blokhin was in Monaco, was because he would be a dead man if he ever went back to Russia. He got caught selling arms to ISIS in Syria. And they were Russian weapons that were used against their own army. Worse than that, he didn't give a kickback on the deal to Putin. Probably only a very large payment to Putin's cronies kept him alive. You know, this guy was a real piece of work. I can't say I'm sorry he bought the farm."

"Maybe he was working for Moscow whether he liked it or not. You know, part of the bargain to save his life."

"It's possible, but if there's one thing you could trust about this guy, it's that he would sell his mother's bones to the highest bidder. I can't believe Moscow would be trusting him on any operation."

Faber looked down at his phone. "Even as an expendable delivery boy?"

"You know, that's a tempting thought, but if Sergei Blokhin had all those missiles, then there would be planes dropping out of the sky all over the Middle East, and he would be chilling on a yacht in Monaco. Delivery boy maybe, but that's as far as it goes. I just don't get Moscow ever trusting him again. It doesn't smell right. How did he die?"

"On his ass. Shot in the head at close range. They used a pillow to mask the sound. I don't think he was killed for what he knew. He was just rubbed out. Maybe someone was cleaning up."

"You mean Montrose? Could be." He sat at the desk. "I don't think Montrose is working for Moscow. He's a loose cannon. A crazy guy. It's not Moscow's style."

"So, if it's not Moscow calling the shots, who the hell is?"

Napier pressed the tips of his fingers against his mouth for a moment, then looked up. "That's the million-dollar question. I know that fucking weasel Campbell is going to point the finger at Moscow, but my gut tells me some weird shit is going on and Moscow might not be in the loop." He stood up. "I need to speak to Dimitri Saitsev."

"Sir, Director Campbell is following our every move. If he finds out…"

"Yeah, if he finds out that I've got an unofficial back channel straight to the FSB while some asshole flying a desk in Langley is trying to pin this on Moscow, it won't look good on my end of year appraisal and I might not get my performance bonus. Yeah, got that. Fuck it."

"Sir, are you sure about Saitsev? He…"

"I'm sure about nothing. Except that this stinks. Campbell stinks. The whole of Washington stinks. They're playing politics when we should be stopping innocent people being killed." He looked over at Faber. "Listen, I appreciate your support. Things are about to get… If you want to walk away, I totally understand."

Faber shook his head. "Tell me what you need me to do."

"Thanks. I need you to contact Saitsev. Campbell's watching me more than you. Just tell him *Tin Can*."

"*Tin Can*? That's it?"

"Yeah. Then I want you to go across the street and buy two pay-per-use cell phones. Program each with the other's number. Bring one to me, and take the other and hide it behind the cistern in the men's restroom in the Ristorante Cornelia in Via Grossi. It's not far."

"*Tin Can*? Saitsev will know what that means?"

"Oh yeah. Years ago, we were both working in Syria. It wasn't exactly a fun time, trying to defeat and undermine ISIS despite the shitstorm of misinformation from both our countries. We were being bugged at every move. By ourselves, the Russians, the Syrians, the Turks. The Iranians had a whole network running on the ground, and the British were listening to every word from RAF Akrotiri in Cyprus. Even the backchannels had backchannels. Saitsev and I said the only way we could talk in private was if we had to two tin cans and a piece of string. And we made a deal that if I ever needed to talk to him, I would leave a phone taped behind the cistern in a restaurant. Just like in *The Godfather*, except that was a gun. You know the scene?"

"Yeah, I know the one."

"Okay, do that, then send him the message." The phone rang on Napier's desk. Faber went to pick it up, but Napier placed a hand on top of the receiver. "Just go. I know who this is."

"I'm on it."

He watched Faber close the door behind him then picked up the phone. "Yeah?"

There was a slight pause on the other end then he heard a familiar voice. "This is Director Campbell. I'd appreciate it if you would identify yourself correctly, Director Napier."

"Depends if I want the caller to know. I get a lot of weirdos calling me. So, Director Campbell, what can I do for you?"

"Where is Montrose?"

Napier rolled his eyes and looked up to the ceiling. His grip tightened on the handset. "We missed him by about five minutes. Right now, we are searching every…"

"Director Napier, I'm finding it increasingly difficult to believe that you do not understand the importance of finding

221

Montrose, but let me spell it out. He is central to finding these missiles. He is a terrorist, and a clear and present danger to this country. If you cannot find him then…"

"Goddammit! Don't lecture me, you fucking desk jockey. You can sack me any time, but you won't get anyone better on this operation. You know that, I know that, and any post-op enquiry will know that. This is my turf."

"Napier, do not dare to make ultimatums or threats to me. I can guarantee you that…"

"Yeah, whatever. I'm not on your Christmas card list. If you even celebrate Christmas. You're probably down with the fucking Grinch. Let's stick to business, yeah? Montrose has gone. We are turning over every stone to find him. And if you want, I will personally drop his fucking corpse on your desk. But before I shoot him, I might just shake his hand."

"What?"

"He killed Sergei Blokhin. In a private club in Monaco."

"Sergei Blokhin? The arms dealer?"

"Yeah, exactly. And Blokhin is just the kind of low-life snakeshit dealer that would sell missiles to terrorists. Montrose did us a favor. We've found Blokhin's phone, but it's been wiped. From checking his number, we know he only arrived in Monaco a few days ago, so while we're looking for Montrose, we have to track Blokhin's movement. It could lead us right to the missiles. Montrose killed him for a reason. I want to know why, because this is looking increasingly unlike an FSB Moscow operation, and more like right-wing lunatics causing mayhem for the highest bidder."

"Napier, you are making assumptions way above your pay grade, you must…"

"Don't shit me, this operation is exactly what I'm paid

for. You know it, so let's not shuffle around like a couple of kids squaring up in the playground. I don't give a shit how you paint this to the Chiefs of Staff or the President in the Situation Room, but I'm betting that if Sergei Blokhin was involved, then this shit just went right off the weird scale. So back off and let me do my job." He listened to silence on the line, imagining Campbell gritting his teeth, wondering how he was going to explain to the President how a Russian billionaire mobster, pedophile and arms dealer, hated by Moscow and on the run in Monaco, fitted into this shitstorm.

"Napier, whatever I tell the President is none of your business. Do you know where the missiles are?"

"Not yet."

"You failed to pick up the missiles in Rome. Do you know where Montrose is?"

"You know that…"

"Then you have singularly failed in every task I have given you. You have also failed to make any tangible progress. I will instruct the section head of France and Germany to take over this operation, and I expect you to give them any assistance and full cooperation. They will be in your office within the next thirty minutes. You will hand over all information and give a full briefing. Don't do anything stupid in the meantime."

Napier stood open-mouthed.

"You see, Director Napier, you may be an expert at running around Rome in blacked-out SUVs, talking to Russians, swapping information, and generally looking busy for the cameras, but post operation enquiries are my specialty, and so are the politics of the CIA. I guarantee you, I will squash you like a bug." The call ended.

Napier stared at the phone.

The door opened and Faber walked in, holding out a phone in his hand. "It's done."

The Director stood quite still, staring out of the window across the forest canopy to the spires of Dresden, his hands clasped tightly behind his back.

The other board members said nothing. Some picked up their glasses of water, before changing their minds, and some checked their phones, even though they knew that the raid on the club would be unlikely to be on the news.

At the end of the room, below a wide TV screen, a technician worked at a laptop. He sat back and the Director turned around.

"I've managed to access the cameras outside the club. We had to break through some security and the camera was locked. We may be detected, but they won't be able to trace it back here."

The Director nodded. "Let us see."

The screen flickered into life. Several board members leaned forward. The picture showed several police vans and unmarked SUVs at the door of the club. Policemen stood at the doorway, semi-automatic rifles lowered.

"Director?" said one of the members.

The Director smiled, but his eye twitched.

"Can we be sure of Montrose?"

The Director tried to laugh but it caught in his throat. "Gentlemen, the brave Montrose walked into the lion's den. The last report said he was disarmed by security at the front desk. Then he met with Blokhin in a room full of

224

heavily-armed men. Montrose was surrounded, unarmed and helpless."

"But can we be…?"

"Be quiet!" The Director fixed his gaze on the screen. "Show me the hotel camera. The exit to the car park. Then roll it back."

The technician brought up the requisite camera, then rolled back the frames, showing a policeman and two cars on the ramp.

"Stop." The Director walked slowly to the screen. "The taxi, gentlemen. As planned, it left the hotel with Montrose's corpse and was waved through by a policeman. There!" He jabbed the screen with his finger. "There, gentlemen, is the stuff of your nightmares, his corpse thrown into the trunk." He faced the table. "It seems the CIA got there a little too late to rescue their friend." He squared his shoulders and raised himself up on the balls of this feet for a moment, then faced the table once more. "Now, with the demise of Mr. Montrose, we will release the video showing him sneaking through a Tuscan village, collecting the stolen Russian missile from the streets of underground Rome, and his visit to the Palatine Hill." He nodded to the technician. "I'm sure conspiracy theorists around the world will have the time of their lives. I estimate that it will take intelligence communities around the world ten minutes to identify him and leak his name to the media. This will be, I have no doubt, the worst day in the history of the CIA. But who knows, perhaps in the next few days we can improve on that." He allowed himself a wry smile and looked around at the board members. "Any questions?"

"Sir?" The technician spoke, still hunched over his laptop.

His tone sent a chill down the Director's spine. "You… may speak."

"I have a report from our Monaco contacts. Sergei Blokhin is dead. Gunshot wound to the head. Suspected assassination."

There was complete silence in the room before all the board members began to talk at once.

"Silence!" The Director leaned forward, placing his hands on the table to steady himself. "Anything else?"

"One other casualty."

The board members sat completely still.

"I see." The Director turned slowly. "Montrose?"

"No. Not Montrose." The technician reread the message. "Montrose has gone."

The Director looked open-mouthed at the screen, his voice reduced to a whisper. "The taxi. Focus on the taxi."

The technician leaned over the keyboard and the picture zoomed in, blurred at first and then sharpened. A face appeared behind the wheel of the taxi.

The Director edged forward until he was only inches from the screen. *"Montrose."* He could hear his own teeth grinding. Any sign of weakness now and he would not see the end of the day. A shock of adrenalin burst through him. He spun around and faced the table. "What a talented man." He thrust out an arm towards the technician. "Do not send the video. We have a little housework to do before we can progress. And tell every resource in Europe I want Montrose's head on my desk. Literally. One million dollars."

A cell phone rang. The board members stared at the Director's phone on the table. It vibrated and moved across the polished wood. One of the board members leaned over and held it still.

The technician looked up. "It's St. Petersburg. They have hidden their number."

"I'll take it in the …" The Director walked over, but the board member pressed the answer key.

"I think we should all hear this." He pressed the loudspeaker button and placed it in the middle of the table.

"I want to talk to the Director."

The Director cleared his throat. "Speaking. Go ahead."

"We have had news of the death of our colleague in Monaco. Therefore, we require immediate confirmation that all hardware is secure and ready for distribution. We are sending a man to assist you, and to protect our investment."

The Director nodded. He breathed out slowly through his nose. "I understand. I can confirm that all hardware is secure and ready for distribution. Funds will be transferred as soon as they arrive from the customers. And I look forward to meeting your new representative. They can witness the next stage of the operation."

"We also require assurance that Connor Montrose, who has come to our attention, is not a threat."

His hands were clasped behind his back so tightly they began to shake. "Montrose is over one thousand kilometers away with the police forces and security services of three countries in pursuit."

"Are your certain that he does not know the location of the hardware?"

"Yes. My planning ensured that Sergei Blokhin did not know, therefore there is no way that Montrose would have found out."

There was a pause on the line.

"And what if you are wrong?"

The Director stared at the phone. "You are sending a new representative. He can witness operations for himself. The next few hours will see the hardware disposed of across the continents and through a network of transport and exit points to the Middle East. Then this site will no longer exist."

"We look forward to his report." The call ended.

"Gentlemen," said the Director. "Time is short and so is my patience. We are at the end of the game. Focus, gentlemen. Put aside anything that distracts you from the objective. Some of you may be aware that as an expert on military history and strategy, I have a wide collection of military uniforms and weapons. Amongst these is a pearl-handled revolver carried by General Patton during the Second World War. If I find anyone leaving this site before the operation is complete, then I will go down to the cellars, find Patton's gun, bring it up here and shoot them between the eyes."

The phone rang. Napier stared at it for a moment, then lifted it to his ear.

Saitsev's voice was low. "Since you are using this method of communication, I assume you are trusting me with information that, shall we say, you're not at liberty to share through normal channels."

"Yeah."

"Then I am listening."

"Did you hear about Sergei Blokhin?" said Napier.

"That piece of shit?"

"Yeah, that piece of shit."

"I know why you were in Monaco. It's not hard to work out. Did you kill him?"

"He was killed by an ex-CIA agent. Connor Montrose. We think Blokhin was involved in the distribution of the missiles. We don't know how he got them or where they came from, but he arrived in Monaco the day before the attack in the Tuscan village."

There was silence on the other end, then Saitsev spoke. "You know what this means?"

"That depends on who Blokhin was working for."

"*Tovarishch*, that would be a short list. I have a longer list, that of people who would like to see Blokhin cut open and thrown in a sewer. That's what happens when you try to fuck a cabinet minster's fifteen-year-old daughter, and sell Russian arms to ISIS in Syria. If Blokhin had those missiles, he could have personally handed them over to the Russian president, accompanied by the Red Army choir singing the national anthem, and he would still have been dead within the hour."

"You're saying there's no way they could kiss and make up?"

"Let's say they would extract a very high price for that reconciliation. And more money than Blokhin ever had. Then they would kill him anyway. And Blokhin would be under no illusions. He was a dead man walking."

"Well, when you put it like that…"

"If Sergei Blokhin was involved, then we are looking at a very different picture. Let me make some enquiries of my own. I need to see what kind of company he has been keeping. I'm sure it will prove very illuminating." Saitsev let out a low laugh. "Unless of course, that I find that he was working for the CIA. That would be very disappointing."

"Listen, Dimitri, that would be news to me. But I have

to tell you, there's gonna be a new CIA sheriff in town, and when that happens, and I find out that Blokhin was working for us, then I'm going to phone you on this number and tell you straight."

Saitsev said nothing.

"I'm not shitting you. If I find that there was someone in Langley or Washington involved in a false flag operation, using a piece of crap like Blokhin, that resulted in the murder of US service personnel, then I will regard these people as traitors to my country and I will do anything in my power to stop them. Including passing on information that results in their exposure. And if I have to go to the Russian FSB to do it, that's exactly what I'm going to do. Do you understand me?"

Saitsev paused before answering. "I understand. My objective is to find and destroy or recover the missiles. If we do not stop this, then there will be planes dropping out of the sky. Both Russian and American. *Tovarishch*, if they end up in the hands of the lunatics in the Middle East..."

"Let's concentrate on finding them. But you know what I think? The remaining missiles are not in Italy."

"How can you be sure?"

"Logistics, my friend. They were delivered to Rome from somewhere in Europe. And I'm thinking the same as you. Blokhin and Monaco. But that was the end point of Blokhin's most recent journey. I want to know where it started."

"I hope you understand, if we discover them before you, then we will take action."

Napier heard the steel in his voice. "What you mean?"

"I mean, if we discover them and we cannot recover them, then we will destroy them."

"In a NATO country? You know how that could look?"

"Yes. But we are staring down the barrel of a gun. If Moscow thinks it is going to be blamed for these atrocities in Europe, then military action will not be a deterrent to them. They will strike anywhere and hard. They are damned if they do and damned if they don't."

"You know it may be seen as an act of war?"

"If it stops a civilian airliner dropping out of the sky, then it will have been worthwhile. Then we will send in the diplomats."

"Yeah."

"Luckily, they survived the Rome attack. It is no coincidence that they were a target."

"I hear you. I hope to God it doesn't come to this."

"We have to be ready. Russia will not shrink from military action in Europe if it is the only option."

Napier squeezed the phone tight in his hand, "Dimitri, you have to talk to these people, if they think that NATO is going to…"

"*Tovarishch*! Let me explain the Russian mindset. We are pariahs. The US sanctions have crippled our economy. We have NATO armies camped on our border in our ex-Soviet states. The Ukraine will be next, it's only a matter of time. Then it's checkmate. Until then, Moscow will never stop doing what it can, anything it can, to undermine the west and NATO. It is the most important mission in the FSB. Nothing else comes close. Our enemies are armed, ready and on our border. Destroying NATO is our obsession."

"Well, given the assholes you put in the White House, you've had some success."

"We cannot always rely on the United States providing us with a succession of immoral, greedy imbeciles. Though sometimes, it is too tempting. No offense, *tovarishch*, but in your free democracy, we have freedom to create havoc."

"Yeah, we got that."

"So, we look out over the border and we see the future. There is absolutely no doubt that the US and their allies would use these missiles to blame Russia for military aggression and state terrorism. Then what would happen next? Would it be an excuse for NATO armies to cross our border? I do not think so. Even the hawks in Washington don't want to see their pension fund threatened. No, I think you would harness your outrage to drive us to starvation. All it would take would be for the missiles to end up in the arms of Russia's enemies, then our markets would crash and Washington could sit back and watch the Russian bear eat its own children. And when revolution has burned everything to the ground, then NATO can don their blue helmets and walk in with their food parcels to distribute democracy at gunpoint."

"Dimitri, sometimes I think…"

"I have to go. Listen to me. Someone is trying to set fire to Europe. And it's either your tribe, or mine."

The upper room was thick with cigarette smoke as Saitsev reached the top of the worn wooden stairs. "Open the window. Sit down."

One man opened a window onto the noisy street, and the restaurant tables below, then took his seat with the others in front of their laptops.

Saitsev stared out of the window for a moment, then looked at each man in turn. "I am convinced that the missiles are in northern Europe. I want a company of Special Forces in the sky, ready for immediate deployment. If we can recapture them we will do so, if not, we will destroy them."

One of the men stood up. "Sir, do you mean deploy a Special Forces team in Europe?"

"Yes, I do. In a NATO country."

"What will…? Do you want me to call Moscow? Tell them?"

"No, I'll call the President myself. He's going to ask a few questions. And I want a cargo plane in the air and minutes from the European border."

"Will the cargo plane pick up the missiles?"

Saitsev gave him a thin smile. "No. The Special Forces team will collect the missiles, if it is possible, though I think it unlikely. The cargo plane will be delivering a cargo, not collecting it. I'll come to that later." He stared down at the floor for a moment. In the silence, the noise from the restaurant drifted up the narrow staircase, and he turned and closed the door. At the end of the table, plates of pastries and cold meats lay untouched. Beer fizzed in open bottles. He pointed to the food. "You eat, I'll talk."

The men got up from their seats, filled their plates, then sat and began to eat methodically.

The bare wooden floor creaked as Saitsev stepped slowly around the room, his hands behind his back. "The CIA have been on a day trip to Monaco."

The men didn't stop eating, but looked up expectantly.

"But they got there too late for Sergei Blokhin."

All the men started talking at once, spraying beer and food across the table with their mouths full. "That bastard! I'll…"

"Eat," said Saitsev. "As soldiers, you should know your next meal is never guaranteed."

"Blokhin," said one of the men, "Do they have him?"

"They have his corpse."

The men laughed and clinked beer bottles across the table. "God bless America!" said one. "Maybe the CIA can help us kill them all."

"No," said Saitsev, "it was not the CIA who killed him. It was a man called Connor Montrose. I want background on him. Eat first."

"His name has come up several times," said one. "Who is he working for?"

"That I don't know. My enemy's enemy is my friend. For now."

"Why did Montrose kill Blokhin?"

"I do not know. But Blokhin may have been involved in delivering the missiles to the terrorists."

"In the name of Christ! We should have shot that treasonous shit and fed his body to the dogs in Syria!"

"Well, let's just say karma caught up with him." Saitsev leaned over the table. "We are about to get very busy." He pointed to one man. "Brief our team in Moscow about Blokhin. Highest priority. We know who his friends are. I want them all tracked and monitored. I want men in their faces. House visits. Kick the toilet door down if they're having a crap. I want to see who starts to panic. I want to see who starts to run." He pointed to another man. "Blokhin was killed in his club in Monaco. I want to know where he has been for the past two weeks. Every step. Find his number, and break into any system to track his movements. Credit card, cell phone masts, border records, anything. Phone calls, texts and emails. The French DGSE have several harvesting cell phone masts in that area. The CIA probably don't know they are being monitored. Get onto our French contact. I want to know everything that the CIA do. Every map that they look at online, every website. They are desperate to find the missiles, not save the reputation of Mother Russia. Do whatever you have to do, but I want Monaco to be sucked dry. If Blokhin was involved in delivering those missiles, then they came from somewhere. We must find them before the CIA."

One of the men looked up.

"Talk."

"If we do find them, and the Special Forces are sent in to recover them, that might be…"

"It might be considered an act of war if people start shooting. Yes, I have no doubt. But if we don't find these missiles, then I have a feeling that it really won't matter any more." He pointed to another of the men. "Get me the cargo plane. When you have it, I want to speak to the pilots. Two at most. They must be Special Forces trained. Other air crew will not be required. There will not be a return journey."

CHAPTER 20

He tightened the headphones against his ears to suppress the roar of the engines. The helicopter swung north east and picked up speed, and Montrose could see the peaks of the snow-covered Alps in the distance. Opposite him, Kirsty wriggled her bottom deeper into the leather seat and grinned. He made to speak, but she pressed a finger to her lips.

The chopper climbed high and fast and he clamped the kit bag tighter between his legs to stop it sliding on the floor.

As they reached cruising altitude, Kirsty loosened her seatbelt then leaned forward and unzipped her bag. She pulled out a pair of jeans and Dr. Martens boots, then kicked off her heels. She undid the seat belt, pulled on the jeans and laced up her boots.

Montrose looked down at his bag. He unzipped it and his hand brushed against the cold metal of a 9mm pistol. Beside it lay a phone. He brought it out and held it up to Kirsty.

She took it and switched it on, then connected his Bluetooth earpiece. Once she had finished her own, she connected the call and handed it back. "Can you hear me?"

"Can we use these phones up here?"

"Yeah, they don't interfere with aviation systems, that's total shit."

Priti's voice came over the line. "Welcome back. I've fed Blokhin's phone history into a database and I ran a triangulation of his number to all the phone masts around the club and then found the nearest cameras."

"You saw him arrive?" said Kirsty.

"Not in person, but I didn't need to. I saw a black Mercedes Maybach arrive and drive into the underground hotel car park. Then the masts lost the signal, so it had to be him."

"That's a big limo, right?"

"Yeah, and it's easily big enough to get four large suitcases in the trunk. I think it's certain he delivered the missiles to Monaco himself. That way there would be no weak links in the chain. Then I scrolled back two days before the attack in the village. He left Monaco in the Mercedes and I tracked his phone and his car through all the phone masts and all the way through Italy, into Austria and then Germany. I could work out where he would be by his average speed then check it against the camera. He never broke the speed limit at any time. Now, in Italy, that's a crime in itself. And he avoided the most direct route through Switzerland."

"Why would he do that?" asked Montrose.

"Borders," said Kirsty. "Switzerland isn't part of the European Union. More chance of getting stopped by the border cops. Yeah, I think that nails it. He was the delivery man."

"Did he take the back roads?"

237

"No," said Priti. "You've less chance of being stopped on an autoroute. He entered Germany and headed straight for Munich, but he didn't stop, he kept going towards Nuremberg, then stopped fifty miles from the city."

"Where?"

"A service station and truck park. I am trying to access the cameras right now," replied Priti. "He stopped for five minutes and when the signal began moving again, it shows he returned to Monaco using exactly the same route. The bad news is that I can't get into the cameras at the service station. I can see them on the network, but they are either switched off or pointing at the sky."

"Yeah," said Kirsty. "That's what I'd do."

"Priti," said Montrose, "I have an idea. If Blokhin was there for five minutes to make the pickup, then whoever delivered the missiles to him had to either be waiting for him, or arrive at the same time, yeah?"

"Makes sense," said Kirsty. "Let's make an assumption that you wouldn't be hanging around in a service station with stolen missiles in your trunk, and let's make an assumption that the service station is a mid-point on the road. So, we're looking for someone who arrived from the opposite direction in a vehicle big enough to carry four suitcases, within twenty minutes of Blokhin's arrival."

"And then that vehicle would then return the way it came," said Montrose, "minus the missiles, yeah?"

Kirsty leaned forward. "How many vehicles would drive to a service station, then turn around and go back the same way? In the middle of no place?"

Pilgrim's voice came over the line. "I appreciate your reasoning, but if I may exercise a note of caution, a lot of traffic can travel down a motorway in twenty minutes, even if you have cameras."

"Not just cameras," said Priti. "Thanks to German efficiency, that road is lined with ANPR cameras. They can read license plates."

Kirsty clapped her hands. "The UK motorways are covered in them. Priti are you accessing the database?"

"I'm on it. I'll be back as soon as I can."

Montrose looked out of the window and the snow-covered valleys of the Alps. "If Priti finds this vehicle, and tracks it, that's where we're going, right?"

"Oh, yeah," replied Kirsty. "And if we can read its license plate, we can discover a whole lot more."

"What about false plates?"

Kirsty wagged a finger at him. "That's why there are ANPR cameras. If they can't read a plate, it alerts the cops. The computers read every plate that goes past and it's checked against a database. If it has no insurance against that number, it alerts the cops. If it has no vehicle tax, it alerts the cops. You see where I'm going with this?"

"Yeah. If you wanna hide, stay legit."

"You got it. Isn't technology wonderful?"

"I will let Priti deal with that conundrum," said Pilgrim. "In the meantime, I have researched the contacts on Blokhin's phone. It's a rogue's gallery of unsavory characters and gangsters in every country. Interestingly, the last call record activity was to a number of men who are fugitives of the government in Moscow."

"Politicians?" asked Montrose.

"This is Russia," said Pilgrim. "Oligarch, politician and corrupt gangster are much the same. I'm not giving you

239

any news when I say that Russian organized crime and the government in Moscow are closely linked, because they both need each other. The same names keep popping up in both camps. The government lets the Mafia thrive, because the Mafia's aims are aligned with the government. Control, enrichment and power."

"Just like America," said Kirsty. "Except you call it freedom."

Montrose ignored her. "So, who he's been talking to in Moscow? The CIA should know…"

"No," said Pilgrim. "If this is Moscow, they would be one step removed. The people Blokhin was talking to are black sheep. The ones who got too greedy and thought they could operate independently of Moscow. Nearly all of them are linked to a multibillion dollar raid of a US hedge fund operating in Russia. The Russian Mafia faked documents and stamps to gain complete control of hundreds of billions of dollars and then Moscow threw in some trumped-up charges against the company. The original directors fled back to the US and most of the Russian ones are in prison awaiting trial. So far, they've had a very short lifespan. The last lawyer who tried to investigate was beaten to death by burglars in his own home, despite million dollar security. In the meantime, the Russian judiciary keeps the entire investigation locked up in the courts and going around in circles while people drop dead and the money disappears. You can't do that without the government being absolutely complicit. But some of them got a little greedy."

"Blokhin's friends?"

"Yes. They stole billions, then forgot to give Moscow their cut. But Moscow didn't forget. Moscow never forgets.

Then Blokhin's friends start dying all over the world. And Blokhin knew he was top of the hit list. I suspect Blokhin and his remaining friends are trying to appease the beast and commute their death sentences."

"Yeah," said Kirsty, "but what if Blokhin wasn't working for Moscow? What if he was working for Washington?"

Pilgrim paused before answering. "Let's stick with what we..."

"Dresden!" shouted Priti down the line.

"Where the hell is that?" said Montrose.

"North of Nuremberg, on the road to Berlin. I found a truck. There were only three trucks that turned around in a twenty-minute slot and went back the same way. One was a panel van from a sandwich company. The other was a delivery truck that stopped at another station, delivering ice cream. And only one other truck. I'm still tracking it down, but I know it took a turn off towards Dresden."

"Priti," said Kirsty, "how long until we get there?"

"About an hour. You can go straight to the airport. I'll tell the helicopter pilot. I'm out."

Kirsty reached into her bag and pulled out a 9mm pistol and stuck it into the waistband of her jeans. "In the meantime, I'm going to get some shut-eye." She took off her seatbelt, stretched out over the seats and looked over at Montrose. "Tip from an old sergeant major. If you're a soldier, eat when you can and sleep when you can. You never know what's around the corner."

Montrose gazed out of the window. The snow-covered peaks were gone, and green fields had opened up below. He reached into the bag and pulled out the pistol, glancing over at Kirsty as he sat back. Her eyes were closed, and her lips set slightly apart. Then he saw the specks of blood on her neck. Tiny, deep red dots. Blokhin's blood.

The helicopter swung to the north, and a ray of sunshine flooded the cabin. Her eyelids flickered, but she didn't move. Her skin turned golden in the light and the red spots became darker.

In his heart he knew it would not be the last blood spilled before the sun set.

Faber closed the door behind him. "We have another message. Same source."

"You sure?"

"Reckon so. Someone is being very helpful." He placed a sheaf of papers on Napier's desk. "We are keeping this off the system."

"Good. Campbell is going to be all over us. You trust the source?"

"It has a high hit rate. And they were right about Monaco."

"They were right about the South of France," said Napier with a wry smile. "We were right about Monaco. I get the feeling that this source knows more than they are telling us." He looked down at a list of names and numbers. "What is this?"

"Blokhin's contact list from his phone."

"That phone was wiped when we found it," said Napier.

"Maybe, but someone got there before us."

"Montrose? He kills Blokhin then sends us the contacts from his phone?"

"I'm not going to even try to work that one out. But we're cross-checking the numbers and it's bringing up a whole list of Russian Mafia figures. All of them on the wrong side of the government in Moscow."

Napier slammed a hand on the desk. "This is driving me crazy! If someone is trying to help us, I could do without cryptic clues. They must know what will happen if the missiles get into the wrong hands. The Middle East and the Balkans will go up like a tinderbox, and Moscow will sit back and point the finger." He scanned the list of names. "Some of these might be customers. Can we bring down the Silk Road? Stop the sale of any more missiles?"

"Maybe. But not for long. It would just pop up elsewhere. And if they can keep us out of the loop, we will have no idea if there are any more for sale or where they are going. The normal shit we can track – arms sales, drugs, but this little dark hole we have never been able to crack. The NSA has been searching for ten years. They have teams of people dedicated to it. It disappears overnight then comes up somewhere else. The IP address is changed by the minute and there are layers upon layers of security. Everything they work out in twenty-four hours becomes useless. One of the guys likened it to a shape shifter. You think you see it in the corner of your eye and when you look, it's gone."

Napier read down the names on the list. "You said these guys are not in Moscow's favor, right?"

"Yeah, as far as we can see."

"What if this is a Moscow hit list? What if Moscow is using these guys to do the dirty work?"

"Or Washington is using them to get back at Moscow?"

"Shit, yeah, like that has never happened before." He pushed the paper across the desk. "This tells me nothing. We are no nearer to finding to the missiles."

"But we should track them, right?"

"Oh yeah, I want to know where they are. Someone sent us this list for a reason. Maybe it was Montrose. Maybe he wants us to do his dirty work for him, but whatever the reason, I want to know where each one of these assholes is, and what they had for breakfast."

"Campbell's going to see that activity."

Napier sat back in his chair. "I don't care. I'll send the order. You stay in the background. Because if I see Campbell trying to suppress the monitoring, then I'll know whose side he is on. And I will go back to Washington and shoot him myself. And I will enjoy it."

Dimitri Saitsev watched each man in turn, hunched over their laptops. He stepped over to one and placed a hand on his shoulder. "Where are they?"

"We are close, but the wifi is too slow."

"I understand." Restaurant noise drifted up the staircase and through the closed door. "And these are all Blokhin's contacts?"

"Yes. We are tracking their movements. And we tracked Blokhin's phone along the autoroute to Germany. Then it stopped and returned."

"A pick-up point?"

"I think so."

"Where does that road lead? The cities closest to the eastern border?"

"Leipzig, Berlin and Dresden. We cross-referenced Blokhin's phone history with the current location of all the contacts he called in the past two weeks. But it is strange. At first I thought that the tracking was not working."

"Why?"

"Because in the past week, hardly any of them moved." His screen beeped. "It is done." He pointed at the screen. "Look, this is what I mean. We tracked the location of everyone he spoke to, and there's a tight grouping somewhere near a *dacha* outside St Petersburg."

"Who owns the *dacha*?"

"General Timoshenko. It is his second home. I have a picture of it here. It's pretty big for a *dacha*."

"Timoshenko? The head of the Southern Tank Brigade? A man who has access to missile storage sites?"

"Yes. They are all there, that's why I thought the tracking wasn't working. But there is one anomaly."

"Show me."

"Grigor Mikhailov. He left for Berlin airport in a private plane."

"Berlin?"

"Yes, but the plane made an unscheduled detour to Dresden and then continued to Berlin."

"And Mikhailov?"

The man leaned in closer to the screen. "He's somewhere outside Dresden."

Saitsev stepped back. "Dresden. Blokhin is dead, so someone had to go to Dresden. Again." He turned to one of the men. "Are the Special Forces in the air?"

"Yes, they are circling near the border."

"Sir?" Another man pointed to his screen. "Moscow is panicking. If they get the blame for the attacks they will retaliate. I'm getting the news now."

Saitek squeezed his eyes shut. "We cannot fool ourselves. If we have worked out the significance of Dresden then the CIA may already have done so. And they will be there, on their own territory, much quicker than us, and in numbers. We will need more than a planeload of Special Forces. By the time we made it halfway across Poland, there would be an army waiting for them." He looked at each of the men in turn. "I want the Special Forces directed to St. Petersburg."

"Yes, sir. I'll call them right now."

"And the cargo, plane, sir?"

"I want that headed for Dresden. After all, accidents happen."

"Sir, it is done."

The Director clapped his hands and stood in front of the board table. "Gentlemen. All missiles have been sold and the money is being transferred at this moment. You see, as I predicted, we had no need to advertise. We will begin loading immediately. Once collection points have been agreed, then the birds will fly the nest. We have already determined where these collection points are and our customers will have to work out how they are going to get there. It will not be difficult, but I'm not having our transport hang around while some idiot works out how to use a satnav. Understood?"

"And the video, Director. When are you going to...?"

"That part of the plan is postponed. For the moment it is no longer relevant or necessary. I will save that for the *coup de grace*. I have evidence from several sources, with independent witnesses, that Mr. Montrose's fingerprints can be found in the village in Tuscany, on a scooter found near the explosion on the Palatine Hill, at the scene of a brutal murder in Rome and in Monaco. He can say what he likes to anyone, he is a dead man, and everything points to the CIA."

"When will this information be released?"

"I will present it to our new man from St. Petersburg who will be here shortly. He has excellent connections to the Russian intelligence community, as you would expect, and he knows where to leave the information so it can be easily found. Let the journalists do their job."

"What about Montrose?"

"Dead man walking. He can live for today. He is no longer relevant."

The fat man leaned over the desk. "He has a habit of turning up in the wrong place."

"I don't care if he walks through the front door." The Director's phone buzzed. "Ah, our new man from St Petersburg is here."

The fat man looked around at the others at the table. "Director? How can it be safe for one of the St. Petersburg men to know our location? Who knows who he could lead here? It is madness!"

"It is also irrelevant. How can you be so naive, my friend? Of course this location will be discovered. The combined intelligence services of NATO won't take long to work it out. But by the time they do, then you, I and the missiles will be long gone. I suggest we adjourn this meeting while you pack your bags and find the transport I have arranged for each one of you. Because I have laid enough explosives under your feet to wipe Rhiandorf from the map. And when the last missile leaves through the gates, that's exactly what I'm going to do.

CHAPTER 21

Low clouds obscured the view as the helicopter descended. Montrose looked down at his bag then rummaged through the array of items and pulled out a tightly-wrapped waxed cotton jacket and shook it out.

Across from him, Kirsty sat up just as the airport appeared in the distance. She pulled out an identical dark green jacket and began to fill its pockets with items from her bag.

Montrose did the same, picking out a multi-tool and spare magazines for his pistol.

"You okay?" said Kirsty.

"Yeah." He gazed out the window at the broad, green plains to the west of Dresden.

Kirsty pulled on her jacket. "Priti's normally a bit more generous. She must have been in a rush, or low on supplies." She examined a plain cardboard box, then stuffed it in the bag. "Running about in a boat probably doesn't help."

"Plastic explosive?"

"In your dreams."

Montrose looked down. "Well, I'm grateful for anything."

He pulled a prismatic compass and a pair of sunglasses from the bag.

"Do you know how to use that?" said Kirsty, grinning.

"No." He pushed the sunglasses on his head and dropped the compass back in the bag. "And I don't want to be in a situation where I need a damn compass."

"Stick with me," she said, "I know where I'm going. Even when I don't."

Priti's voice came down the line. "Kirsty? Connor?"

"Loud and clear."

"I think I've found the delivery truck."

"Where?"

"A big truck depot," replied Priti. "A few miles from the site of an old town called Rhiandorf."

"Priti," said Montrose, "you sure? The truck's at a depot?"

"I can't be absolutely certain, but there's nothing else for miles around. When the truck left the autoroute I worked out where it could be by average speed on a radius, matched that to road locations and then checked every camera. I found the truck on a back road, then it disappeared into a forest and never came out. But I could see the truck's license plate and checked where it was registered. That's where I found the truck depot in the forest. It's registered to that address."

"Rhiandorf," said Kirsty, "I swear I've heard that name before."

"And it's just a truck depot?"

"I checked it out on satellite images and on the internet," said Priti. "Big warehouses. Trucks come and go, distributing all sorts of cargo. That's all that happens. It could be that the missiles were transferred to the delivery truck and that they came from somewhere else. This could be a dead end."

"How far?" asked Montrose.

"It's about five miles from your location. But this is where it gets weird. It depends which map you look at. On some maps, the old town of Rhiandorf is right on top of the truck depot. But on modern maps, Rhiandorf seems to be in the middle of a forest, though there's nothing there except trees."

"Maybe just a map error," said Montrose.

"No," said Priti, "Rhiandorf exists. Or existed. I trawled the web and found some old photos. It shows wide streets and gothic buildings, a school, several churches and a big town square. If you use Google maps and zoom in on the forest, all you see is a small pile of stones. But it doesn't make sense. Rhiandorf would have been a prosperous market town. All the roads would have led there. But all the roads lead to the transport depot. Then I found an old map from the 1930s. I had to hack into academic websites to do it, but I found them. Rhiandorf is exactly where the transport depot now sits. No question. Not two miles away in the middle of a forest. So why have so many modern maps got it wrong?"

"And where did a whole town go?"

The helicopter touched down, yet Kirsty didn't seem to notice. "I think I know."

"Kirsty. Let's go." He grabbed his bag.

A white Porsche pulled up alongside and a young man stepped out holding a clipboard.

Kirsty jumped from the helicopter and hurried towards the driver's door. "I like your style, Priti." She stood beside the young man and held out her hand. "Keys."

He stared at her for a moment, then placed the keys in her hand. He held out the clipboard and pen and began to speak as Kirsty took the pen and scrawled a signature at the bottom.

"Sweetheart," she said, "I'd love to stay and listen to your sexy German accent, but we really have to go." Ignoring his protestations, she dumped her bag behind the driver's seat and jumped in.

Montrose got in beside her, threw his kit and shades in the back, then saw a zip code come up on his phone. He programmed it into the satnav.

Kirsty took the sunglasses from her head and tossed them onto the rear parcel shelf. "Summer's over." She fired up the engine, pointed the car at the gates and hit the accelerator.

Mr. Pilgrim's voice came down the line. "I have some disturbing news. This comes straight from a MI6 monitoring station on RAF Akrotiri in Cyprus, and has just been distributed to the Five Eyes. There is evidence of Middle Eastern operatives moving towards Germany. The intel is heavily encoded and details are sparse, but persons of interest are heading your way in an array of transportation. I feel the distribution of the missiles is about to take place. This may now be out of our hands."

"Jeez, give me a bloody chance," said Kirsty. She turned through the exit in the airport fence and a straight road opened up in front of them.

"These persons of interest," said Montrose, "are they coming here? Because I think we're headed for a link in a delivery chain, not the location of the missiles. It's a truck depot. Stuff comes and goes all the time."

"No, there is no information detailing exactly where they are going, but they seem to be a heading to a number of different locations in Germany."

Kirsty turned off the main road and headed west. The road in front was straight, bordered by a high, thick pine forest on either side, blocking the sun. She opened up the throttle and they drove into the semi-darkness.

"Why don't the German police just stop them?"

"It'll be like looking for a needle in a haystack. The sheer volume of transport is what alerted the Brits in Cyprus. And we would have to mobilize an entire army to intercept them all."

"You mean like NATO?"

"Good point, and you can be assured that it is underway with some considerable urgency, but they are not going to catch them all. One missile is enough to cause havoc."

The trees flashed past, and Kirsty stared straight ahead. "I've got a bad feeling about this."

He turned his head. "Hell, yeah…"

"No, I mean this place. I think I know what happened here." She flicked down through the gears and drove along the edge of the road until she saw a gap in the trees. "The depot is through those trees." She hit the brakes and swung the nose of the Porsche into the middle of the road, then reversed back into the gap between the trees. She got out and dumped her bag on the hood then held up the car key to Montrose. "Just in case one of us has to make a quick exit." She placed the key in the grass beside the front wheel.

"One of us?"

"You're right. I mean me. I want the car to be pointing in the general direction of 'get the hell out of here'."

"Kirsty," said Pilgrim, "report back what you see. If Montrose is right and this is a red herring, just a truck depot, then the operation will be cancelled. Do you understand?"

"Loud and clear, Mr. P."

"I'm going to contact the CIA to ensure they have the capability to deal with this quickly. If I give the order, then you must withdraw immediately. We will let the CIA and the Germans take care of this."

"Understood," said Montrose. He checked his gun.

"Mr. P., we're going to dial out. If there is anybody monitoring for phone activity, they'll spot us a mile away. We'll dial back in when we have anything to report."

"Agreed. Good luck." The call ended.

"We need some camouflage," Kirsty said. "If there are cameras, they would give you points for fashion." She reached into her pocket and took out a make-up compact. "Eyeshadow. Chanel has a color for every occasion." She spat into the compact and rubbed her fingers hard into the dark powders, merging them together, then smeared it across her face then checked the mirror. *"Gorgeous."* She closed the compact and tossed it to Montrose. "Get your war paint on."

"This is the second time I'm gonna be wearing make-up today. Frankly, I'm getting worried about myself."

"Channel your inner bitch, big boy, and follow me." She slung the bag over her shoulder and headed into the forest.

He pulled on his jacket as he walked, ducking under branches. The mossy ground became soft and spongy under his boots. "What did you mean back there? About this place?"

Kirsty looked down at the map on her phone. "Years ago, when I was in London, I was big into urbex. Urban exploring, yeah?"

A picture flashed into his mind of him hanging on

desperately to the frame of a tiny, ancient train engine, hurtling through a dark tunnel, its sides inches from his face, and Kirsty laughing and winding up the power. "Yeah, I remember. That's not an easy thing to forget."

"There was a guy I heard of. Total urbex legend. He told a story about a town in Germany that he'd discovered. It was online for a while, if you knew where to look. This was like the Holy Grail of urbex. He said his grandfather was a bomber pilot who was shot down in the war. Not the big, heavy Lancaster bombers, but the fast, fighter-bomber Mosquitos. They did the tree-top raids in France, taking out Nazi command posts and busting open prisons." She pointed east. "Dresden isn't far. He talked about that raid in 1944, when they fire-bombed Dresden. The problem with the big bombers was that they were flying too high to be able to identify their target in the dark. If they flew lower or in the daytime, the Germans shot the shit out of them. This guy's grandfather was in a Mosquito, flying ahead of the bombers. His job was to mark the target. He would fly in fast and low, identify the target and then drop barrels full of flammable chemicals that would burn a bright color. Red or green, usually. The barrels of liquid ensured the fire spread over a large area which made it very difficult for local firefighters to extinguish the flames. Then the heavy bombers higher up would see the burning target at night and unload their bombs."

"But you said he was shot down?"

"Yeah, his Mosquito never made it to Dresden, the target. The night fighters got him. This guy tracked the war records that night, and the Luftwaffe records in Germany. That's how he found out how his grandfather died." She looked around between the trees. "He came down somewhere in this forest.

The records said he avoided Rhiandorf but crashed just outside. His plane exploded when it hit the ground."

"But he missed the town?"

"Yeah, but the whole forest was burning with the colored chemicals he was carrying, and behind him were four hundred bombers looking for their target. And they found it."

The Director waited until all the board members had left the room, then opened a small cabinet and took out a bottle of whisky and two glasses. He poured two shots, and held a glass in the air as Grigor Mikhailov walked into the room. "Welcome to Rhiandorf."

Mikhailov walked around the table and took the glass. *"Na Zdorovie."* He sipped on the whisky. "Your taste in whisky has improved."

The Director smiled. "One of the benefits of being at the heart of a transport hub. It's amazing what comes in and out on those trucks."

"I'm sure," said Mikhailov. "How are the sheep?"

"Panicking over Connor Montrose. What an admirable pain in the ass that man has been. If I wasn't going to kill him, I'd offer him a job."

"Any concerns? Blokhin was quite a shock."

"No, not really. I think Montrose got lucky. As for the sheep, if we didn't need their funding and their capacity to tell tales, I would have killed them already. One of them got a little too clever. He was old enough to know better."

"Is he still here?"

"Technically, yes. He's in a freezer truck full of frozen fish. I'll have his body dumped as part of the delivery."

Mikhailov downed his whisky. "When do we start?"

"Very soon. We need all the money safely in our account before the trucks begin to leave."

"And then?"

"Then, a helicopter will be arriving from Dresden airport. It will land in the truck park to pick us up. The sheep will be ready to leave in their cars. I have them all in a warehouse, luggage loaded and ready to go. Then they'll find out why I've been storing so much nitrate fertilizer."

Mikhailov stared at the drops of whisky in his glass. "Do you think that some of the missiles will actually make it to the Middle East? Iran or Egypt?"

The Director shrugged. "I don't care. Some will probably get lucky. It's irrelevant to achieving the objective."

"As long as the customer is happy."

The Director finished his whisky. "Well, the customer who's paying the most money. The other customers will not be alive to complain."

CHAPTER 22

He watched her move quickly between the trees, noticing how she avoided the branches and twigs beneath her feet. "Who taught you fieldcraft?"

She looked back for a moment and grinned. "The same sergeant-major who taught me to use a knife." After a few hundred yards, she came to a halt beside the trunk of an ancient pine tree.

Through the trees, Montrose could see a chain-link fence and hear truck engines.

"This is near enough. Get down behind me." She took out her phone and steadied it against the trunk of the tree and expanded the picture until they could see the ground at the bottom of the fence. She moved her head to the side so Montrose could see the picture. "Look," she said, "that's not just one fence."

He leaned in towards the phone and saw steel mesh in front of the chain link.

She lifted her phone and showed the top edge of the fence. "No razor wire," she said. "But they don't need it. No one is getting over that fence." She lowered the phone. "Look at the ground."

Montrose could see a strip of grass closely cropped either side of the fence.

"You only do that if you need the grass to be short for detectors."

"Motion sensors?"

"Yeah, probably, and pressure pads. The place is as big as six football pitches. If they have that all the way around, that's going to take a lot of wiring and security to monitor. It might look like just a fence, but this is a very professional set up."

"Then the only way in is the front door."

"Maybe," said Kirsty, "let's find out."

"We don't have time to recon the entire…"

"Technology, Connor. Get with the times." She reached into her bag and pulled out the plain cardboard box.

"What is that?"

"It's a drone for cell phones." She ditched the packaging and pulled out a plastic phone harness with fold-out rotor blades at each corner. She handed him a piece of paper. "That's the address for the app, download it to your phone."

He typed in the address and started the download, then watched her clip the phone into the drone. A text popped up on his screen and he opened it to see the image of an old map, roads clearly visible on it and Rhiandorf in the center. "Kirsty, it's from Priti. Check this out." He brought up Google Maps and tapped the screen to zoom in on his position, then held it out to her and swapped the screen to show her the text message. "Look at the shape of the roads. They're the same." He looked around the trees. "This is Rhiandorf." He flicked back the map and saw the roads and the warehouses amongst the trees but no reference to the former town.

"I see it."

The app completed loading and he brought it up on screen. "This could all be a wild goose chase. There could be no missiles here. They could be anywhere in a hundred mile radius."

Kirsty flipped a switch and the rotor blades at each corner of the drone spun into life. "That's not security for a truck depot in the middle of nowhere." She held it in her hand and stared through the trees towards the fence. "Look, Connor. The office building."

He saw a brightly-lit building between two warehouses. "Yeah? Doesn't look too secure to me."

"Hiding in plain sight." said Kirsty. "Check out the top of the building."

He looked up at the roof of the office block. "So?"

"The air-conditioning units. How many are there?"

He scanned along the edge of the roof. "I don't know, fifteen, twenty?"

"If those things are switched on, and those are just the ones we can see, then that place will be ten below zero inside. Why on earth would they need so many air-conditioning units for an office?" She reached into the bag and took out another small box. "I'm going to find out." She pulled a small clip-on camera from the box and fixed it to the cell phone.

"What's that?"

"Infra-red camera. I'm going to see why they need all that aircon."

"Refrigerated warehouses?"

She handed him the drone. "And the aircon is installed on

a different building? Makes no sense. Go over there." She pointed to a gap between the trees. "Hold it above your head. Give me your phone."

He took the drone and keeping low, shuffled over to the gap then lifted the drone.

Kirsty fired up the app and the drone lifted into the air. It climbed straight up above the tree canopy and disappeared from sight.

Montrose scurried back towards Kirsty who was staring intently at the screen. "What can you see?"

She edged in closer to him. On screen the tree canopy retreated as the drone climbed higher and the buildings came into view. "I doubt if they're using radar, but I don't want to signal that we're here." The drone climbed higher and they could see a wide expanse of concrete office buildings, and groups of warehouses with lines of trucks outside. "Check the border," she said.

"Yeah, professional job. No overhanging branches. Someone takes good care of security."

"And look at the trucks," said Kirsty. "I don't see many refrigeration units. I don't see any aircon vents on the warehouses." She thumbed the controls. "Okay, let's have a different view. She tapped the cell phone screen and it switched to a black and white picture. The warm hoods on some of the trucks glowed white on the screen. "Holy shit," said Kirsty, "look at the office block."

Montrose could see row upon row of glowing white squares where the air-conditioning vents stood. "There's no way an office block needs that amount of air. This makes no sense."

"Unless," said Kirsty, "there's something underneath that office block generating a massive amount of heat."

"Like what?"

The drone moved back over the trees then began to descend. "I doubt if it's going to be a cannabis farm. That size, you'd be able to smell it from Monaco." She looked up between the branches and watch the drone return to the clearing. "Get your urbex head on, Connor." She turned to face him. "I think we just found the Silk Road."

He stared through the trees. "Kirsty. C'mon, that can't be..." He watched the drone settle onto a cushion of dry pine needles. "You think all that heat is generated by servers?"

"Connor, the Silk Road has got to be somewhere. And you know how much heat they generate. There could be acres of computer equipment under the office block and anyone with enough knowledge could make them appear to be anywhere in the world."

Montrose sat back against the tree and gazed up at the branches. "If that's true, if it is the Silk Road, we could just bomb the place. If the missiles are there, then..."

"I like the way you're thinking," said Kirsty. "But let's make sure we are not in the vicinity when it happens. Look." She held out the cell phone, showing Google Maps. "There," she said, pointing to the phone, "on the map that Priti sent you. That's where Rhiandorf is supposed to be, at the road junction. Right here. But on the modern map it's two miles away, in the middle of no place. That's crazy. Rhiandorf was a market town. All roads led there. The roads are still on the map. And they all go to one place." She pointed through the trees. "Those warehouses."

"So why would someone go to all the trouble of making sure Google Maps pointed in the wrong direction?"

"The Silk Road. That's why they never found Rhiandorf."

"Who?"

"That urbex guy I told you about, remember? He disappeared off the face of the earth, plus his blog, and any reference to what he'd found. But the guy was a legend. I read the story."

"You remember it?"

"It's still famous around urbex dudes." She looked at the screen and laughed. "He said he had found the cellars of Rhiandorf by going through a German bunker. It was four-foot-thick reinforced concrete, and about the only thing to have survived. You can still see them today, scattered across France and Germany. They're just too strong to destroy."

"The Russians didn't blow it up?"

"Waste of explosives. There are still Nazi submarine pens in France. Huge, concrete structures the size of a football pitch. The concrete is twenty feet thick in places and reinforced with steel rods. The Allies bombed the shit out of them, but it was a waste of time. It would take years to destroy them, so they left them there. Now, look at this." She showed him a web page, and a picture of a bunker.

"That's it?"

"No, that's in the forest where Google Maps and," she jerked her finger over her shoulder, "whoever runs that place, wants you to think is the location for Rhiandorf. This is the weblog of another urbex guy who went searching for it to try to prove the story. He found what he thought was the bunker, but the floor was too thick to get through. He searched the forest for signs of destroyed buildings but there's nothing there. So, he called the story a hoax."

"I get it. He was looking in the wrong place. He was two miles away."

"Yeah, now check out the bunker in the forest."

"It's just a bunker."

She grinned. "If it was a German bunker, why are the gun slits facing west?"

Montrose looked closely at the screen. "Maybe the Russians…"

"This guy has done some research. When the Russians got here they covered the place in concrete to have somewhere to put their trucks and tanks in winter. They were advancing fifty miles a day. They didn't need to set up bunker defenses. Any place around here covered in concrete? Like a truck park?" She pointed through the trees, then down to the screen. "But this guy thinks that because the bunker is facing the wrong way and there's no trace of the buildings, or the concrete, then the original story was a hoax. I mean the guy who originally wrote it was never seen again." She stood up.

"But you mean that the bunker in the forest is a hoax? Not the original story?"

"Yeah, someone read the blog, built a bunker two miles away to throw people off the scent, then built it facing the wrong way."

"So, if there was a real bunker…"

"Some of it will still be here. Because those things are an absolute bastard to destroy." She thumbed the app and the drone lifted into the air again.

Montrose stood beside her. "My bet is that they broke it up. These don't look like people to go to all the trouble of building a decoy bunker and not get rid of the original."

"Maybe," said Kirsty, "but if they did, I'll bet they didn't get rid of the foundations. Because that's where the urbex

263

guy said he entered the cellars. And if it's still there, it'll be four feet thick, so no trees are going to grow through it."

The drone lifted higher into the air.

"Kirsty…"

"Sshh, I'm trying to …"

"Kirsty." He pointed through the trees to the clearing where the drone had been. "The clearing. There are no trees there."

Kirsty looked up, locked the controls so the drone would hover, then moved through the trees. The clearing was an uneven carpet of moss and pine needles. She kicked up soft earth with her boot, and hit stone.

Montrose knelt down and pulled away at the earth. He grabbed a rock and rolled it over. On the underside were pebbles protruding from a lump of concrete. In the center was a scar where a pneumatic drill had punched through. "This is it."

She kicked away at the earth, shoving moss to the side. "And this isn't the original bunker floor." She pointed down at a grey surface. "That's modern concrete." She held a misshapen fragment in her hands. "That's World War Two shit. I know, I've seen enough of it in the UK." She stepped back. "They sealed this up tight. There's no way we'll get through there."

He dropped the concrete. "Maybe he found a way in, maybe there's another..."

"Where?" She threw her arms around, pointing to the thick green forest floor and the dense branches. "It's like looking for a needle…" She stopped, open-mouthed, staring at the trees. "Oh, you beauty."

"What?"

"The aircon units!"

"What?"

"Heat flows like water. If they need all those aircon units, then I'll bet my sweet Welsh arse…" She tapped the screen and lifted the drone into the air. "We're going to need a better map. Hold this. Give me your phone."

"What are you going to…?"

"I'm going to take screen shots of the two maps, then superimpose the old 1930s map of Rhiandorf that Priti gave us onto this position. Then we'll know where we are. Keep an eye on that screen."

She took his phone and brought up an image editor, then merged the two pictures. "What do you see?"

The infra-red camera showed three white shapes. "That's you, me, and…"

"And a heat leak sticking out like a priest in a playground. Either that or someone is having an invisible barbecue, ten feet from here."

"According to the map, we're in a schoolyard off the market square." Montrose had a mental glimpse of children sleeping as incendiary bombs and burning phosphorus fell from the night sky.

Kirsty watched the drone moving over the trees.

"You said this guy found the cellars. You think they survived?"

She pointed to the screen. "I think we're looking at them. That's not as crazy as it sounds. Even new London buildings are built on old pre-war cellars. Looking at Priti's info, rich mediaeval market towns like Rhiandorf had loads of substantial buildings centered around the main square. The cellars could go down three levels, for storage. Everything came through a market town like Rhiandorf. This was like the Amazon of the region."

"You reckon they go that deep?"

"Yeah, Germans buildings went deeper than those in London. In cities like Berlin and Hamburg, they didn't have an underground to hide in and nothing like the network of shelters built in the UK during the Blitz. They all went down to the cellars and they'd knock through from one cellar to another, covering the holes with paper, so that if one cellar was breached then they could escape to another."

"But this was no ordinary bombing."

"No. They could not have prepared themselves for what happened that night." She pointed through the forest. "North of the airport where we landed. I read about what happened to Dresden. They were supposed to be targeting a major railway junction, but they were loaded with more incendiaries than explosives. It was a firestorm that lasted for days, and even if people survived the bombing, they suffocated in the heat. The inferno sucked in winds from around the countryside to feed the flames. It was so strong it pulled people off their feet and into the fires."

Montrose could hear branches creaking in the slight breeze.

"And that night, in this forest, the bombers found what they what they were looking for. The target marker. They had the same mixture of high explosive and incendiaries. Enough to burn the entire city of Dresden to the ground. And they dropped it on the market town of Rhiandorf."

He stared through the trees, standing where the people had once stood.

"When the Russians advanced they found nothing. Just blackened lumps of stone. Everything for miles had been incinerated."

Montrose stepped into the clearing. The ground was uneven

and at one side, near to where the heat signal showed, he saw an upended tree, its roots spread into the air. He looked down at the hole the trunk had left and saw the jumble of stones where the tree had once stood. "This isn't the bunker. These stones have been shaped. Building stones."

"This is it," she said. "They may have closed the bunker, but the weight of the tree has pushed through the rubble from the collapsed buildings."

He checked the map. "The schoolhouse?"

"Maybe."

He stepped into the depression, trying to keep his balance on the loose rubble. "I know why the tree fell." He raised himself up on his toes and dropped down. The ground was rock hard. He jumped into the air and slammed his boots onto the earth. "The roots couldn't penetrate. They couldn't go deep enough. Because of the stone."

Kirsty knelt and started to scoop away moss and earth with her hand, then pulled jagged fragments of stone from the ground. Around her knees the earth began to subside and she scrambled backwards.

"Let's go carefully," said Montrose.

"Get behind me," said Kirsty. "Hold me tight. I don't want to become Alice in Wonderland." She scooped up more earth and threw it to the side, exposing a flat rock. "That's too big to lift." She got to her feet and stepped back. "Ready?" She stabbed the rock with her boot.

It dropped an inch and Kirsty shoved a boot forward and gave it another kick. With a raw scraping sound, it dropped out of sight, exposing a black hole. They both stumbled backwards, watching loose earth disappearing into the darkness.

"You first," said Kirsty. "Age before beauty."

Montrose looked into the black hole. "Yeah, I think we should…"

"Never mind," said Kirsty. "I'll go. Just keep a good tight hold of my boots." She knelt down then lay onto her chest, edging closer towards the edge of the hole, then pulled out her cell phone and shone the torch into the blackness. "Wow!" She pushed forward and let her head drop forward.

"What can you see?"

"Absolutely bugger all, except what might be a floor. But I'm not going head first." She pushed herself out then spun around and held out a hand to Montrose. "Let me down slowly," she said, "you know, like one of your many girlfriends."

"Kirsty…"

She lay down and let her feet drop into the hole, then wriggled forward on her backside. "Okay, let go."

Montrose slowly released his grip and she slid out of sight.

"Kirsty?"

She did not reply.

"Kirsty!"

A voice came from below. "Yeah, I'm here. Throw my bag down."

Holding her bag, Montrose slid towards the hole and sat at the edge. He felt Kirsty's hands on his calves.

"It's a six-foot drop," she said. "Go for it."

He let go and dropped into the darkness. A shaft of light lay at his feet and Montrose looked back up at the sky. He played his phone torch around the room. A solid brick wall stood on three sides and the torchlight disappeared into darkness on the other. "Looks like dead ahead is the only way." Damp earth lay at his feet, but the walls looked dry.

Kirsty brushed off her jeans and slung her bag over her shoulder. "Let's go."

Montrose shone his torch past her and followed close behind. To one side he saw a stack of crates. The markings had faded, but he could make out a Wehrmacht eagle. "Kirsty." He played the torchlight across the wooden slats. "This is it. This is wartime Rhiandorf." He heard her blow out a breath. "I thought this was just a market town," he said.

"The whole of Europe was at war, Connor, army kit was all over the place." She lifted her torch to the roof. "The fire didn't come down here. At least, not this far."

"Is this where they hid? All the people?" he said.

"I guess those that could. I don't suppose they had much warning."

"Do you think they made it...?"

"Connor, if Rhiandorf was anything like Dresden, it burned for fucking days."

He said nothing and kept close behind her. The torch shone through a dark doorway and onto a brick wall.

"Dead end?"

"No," said Kirsty as she stood in the doorway and shone the torch at her feet. "We go down."

The steps were smooth with age. In front, Kirsty's torch showed a short corridor, where the remnants of a door lay scattered across the ground. She shone the torch into the doorway, but the room was filled with rubble. Ten feet away another door hung from its hinges, forced open by a jumble of stones tumbling through the doorway. She shone the torch past the door to another wall, and the black void on the floor. "Down again."

"This might be a dead end, Kirsty."

She shook her head. "The heat was coming from somewhere. Can't you feel it?"

The air was warm and dry. "Yeah. They built these places real solid."

"Doesn't matter how solid, a bomb from thirty thousand feet will go down twenty feet. They are still digging them out all over Germany." She stood at the top of the stairs. "The people would have known that. They would go as deep as they could. Even though they knew they might be buried alive."

Montrose followed her down the steep steps. At the bottom the air was warmer and a faint noise came from the darkness.

"I know that sound," said Kirsty.

"Me too," said Montrose. "Server cabinets. Each blade server with a fan. I worked next door to a computer room. It was deafening."

"Yeah," she said, and held up the torch. "I think we just wandered into the Death Star." They both pulled out their pistols. She looked down at her weapon. "You know, if this is the Silk Road, the biggest illegal arms market on the planet, I think we just brought a rubber chicken to a gunfight."

Montrose felt the metal warm on his hand and tightened his hand around the pistol grip. "Yeah. Let's see what we see. If we find the missiles then we'll report back to Pilgrim. Then it's his problem."

"Oh, yeah. His problem."

He could tell she was smiling. "Kirsty…"

Her torch shone on a doorway to the side. In front, a mound of earth and rubble filled the corridor to the roof.

"Looks like…"

"Connor, turn your torch off."

He shoved the pistol into his waistband and killed the torch. "What…?"

"Wait. Let your eyes adjust."

The white noise was louder and just below the roof a faint glow appeared over the rubble. He heard Kirsty edge forward, feeling her way, then climbing to the top. Rocks and earth rolled down behind her. The silhouette of her head cut through the faint glow. "What do you see?"

"Lights in the distance. Too far." Her torch beam shone at her feet as she slid to the floor. "It goes on for about twenty feet, I think. There's no way past it. We'd never be able to crawl through. But that's the heat source." She shone the torch at the edge of the rubble, then across their feet to a door set into the wall. "Last chance. Everything else is a dead end."

The door was unpainted with an iron handle. Montrose took hold. It didn't move, then with a grinding sound, it slid slowly down. He pushed, but the door remained shut. "It might be bolted from inside."

"Give it a kick."

He put his shoulder to the door and shoved hard, and it scraped open an inch. "There's something blocking it." He took a step back and booted the wood.

They heard metal hitting the floor. Kirsty shone her torch into the gap. A steel German helmet lay on the ground.

"Shit," said Kirsty.

They both stared down at the helmet, then Kirsty lifted her foot over it and squeezed through the gap.

He saw her shine her torch to the floor.

"Oh, man."

Montrose shoved his way into the gap. He stood behind Kirsty and looked down at the bottom of the door. The mummified body of a German soldier lay with his back to the wood. The skin on his face resembled parchment, tightly

271

drawn over his skull. Across his chest lay his Mauser rifle. The eyes had dried and sunk into their sockets.

"He didn't leave his post," she said.

"I think there was nowhere to go."

Kirsty shifted the torch beam to the side. "He didn't burn."

"But his skin…"

"He suffocated," said Kirsty. "The firestorm above would have sucked the oxygen from miles around. Then he was sealed in. The heat must have dried him." She looked away. "We have to move."

Montrose shone his torch to each side and saw old furniture and boxes stacked against the wall. "If we can find another door…"

"Oh, sweet Jesus." Kirsty shone her torch onto the floor where a child's doll lay broken.

Montrose glanced down. At first, he thought they were bundles of rags. Then he saw the shoes, and lifting the light, the mummified faces sunk into the clothes, and the smaller clothes, still held close in withered arms.

The bodies stretched back as far as his torch beam and disappeared into the darkness.

"I can't look," said Kirsty.

Montrose shone the beam along the wall. He came to the top of a door and let the beam drop. He saw the body of a boy lying on his side, clutching a rifle that was longer than his own body. "Follow me, I see a door." He reached back and led her past the outstretched feet and hands, then stood before the door and looked at the boy. "Give me a moment." He bent and placed his phone on the ground, then took the rifle from the boy, leaned it against the wall, then gently lifted the boy to the side. The skin and bones felt weightless in his hands. He picked up his torch and pulled open the door. It swung slowly on its hinges and they stepped through into darkness.

Kirsty pushed past him, blowing out a breath. "I could see their faces."

Montrose closed the door.

"The heat," she said. "They would have been sealed in by the collapsing buildings. It must have been like an oven." She switched on the torch. "When this is over…"

"Yeah, I know."

Kirsty lifted the torch beam. "What the fuck?"

In front of them was a tall glass cabinet, its door open and a naked mannequin on the floor. Montrose lifted the torch. Two rows of cabinets stretched into the distance, with doors open and mannequins lying on the ground.

Kirsty walked between the glass cabinets. "Say something, Connor. Say something reassuring, because I'm all weirded out for one day."

He pointed to the bottom of the glass case and lifted a thin piece of metal and read out the inscription. "Field Marshal Montgomery. Sicily, 1944."

"Eh? What the hell is a nameplate with Monty's name on it doing three floors below a bombed German town?"

He tapped the glass. "This isn't a wartime cabinet. This is modern plate glass."

Kirsty walked over and checked the next cabinet. "Gaius Julius Caesar." She moved forward and slowly read another. "An-Nasir Salah ad-Din Yusuf ibn Ayyub." She looked up. "Who?"

"Saladin." He picked up another. "George S. Patton. *Generalfeldmarschall* Erwin Rommel."

"Bloody hell, this is the weirdest Facebook group I've ever seen."

"Generals," said Montrose. "They're all famous generals." He walked between the rows of cabinets.

"I know the smell in here."

"Yeah."

"Gun oil and army clothing. I used to work in an army surplus shop in the East End of London. Good kit for homeless people. It smelled the same."

He shone his torch up on to the wall and saw metal racks stretching down behind the cabinets. They were empty, apart from name tags. He leaned over and began to read. "Brown Bess."

"I know what that is."

He looked along. "Martini-Henry. Sten. Garland. Lee Enfield SMLE. World War Two weapons?"

"Oh, yeah, baby. I've landed in Day of Honor."

"What?"

"It's a computer shooter game. Like *Call of Duty* for World War Two. That's how I know about these guns. But that begs the question. What the hell is this place?" She walked forward and saw stacks of plastic crates against the far wall beside a door. "Okay, I've found the way out."

He tightened his grip on the pistol. "Right, we have to make sure… Kirsty?"

"Not yet." She stood in front of the crates. "I've got a funny feeling…" She pulled open a lid and saw a black beret on top of a khaki jersey. "Bloody hell. That's Monty's hat. Or a copy of it."

"You sure?"

She lifted it up. "He was the only man allowed to wear two

badges on his hat. His general's rank on a Tankie's beret."
She replaced it back on the jersey. "It's amazing the things
you learn when you play computer games." Opening the next
case, she found a steel helmet with two white handled pistols
in leather holsters, and a belt studded with ammunition.

"Patton," said Montrose.

"Cowboy guns," said Kirsty. "No good to me." She
dropped the lid.

"Wait, was that ammunition real?"

She opened the next lid. "Oh, come to Mama."

"What is it?"

She lifted out some khaki webbing, holding long magazines
on a strap. She swung them over her shoulder. "This is the
motherlode." In her hand she held a short rifle.

Montrose recognized the dark wooden stock and the
stubby barrel. "A Thompson submachine gun?"

"Christ, this is heavy." She pulled back the cocking handle
and checked the breech, then slotted in a magazine.

"Listen, Kirsty… a tommy gun?"

"Connor, if some loony wants to keep mannequins dressed
up as famous generals in glass cases and collect military
weapons, I have no issue with that." She reached into the
crate and pulled out a parcel wrapped in oil cloth. It fell
away and showed the barrel of a semi-automatic. "Colt 1911.
WWII issue. Big ass 45."

"You don't need that."

"You're right, I've got a Glock, but this is a very cool
dinosaur." She dropped it in the crate, then pulled out a
wooden box, stained with age and gun oil. The letters BSA
were stamped into the top. "Made in Birmingham?" She
opened the lid. "Oh, heaven."

"What the hell is that? A pistol?"

She pulled it out, and looked down the long, fat barrel. There was no trigger guard, just a flattened piece of metal and a short pistol grip.

"That looks like it was made for a school project," said Montrose. "It'll blow up in your face."

"I think not. This is a Welrod. Possibly the quietest pistol ever made. The British developed it for the SOE, for assassinations in WWII. But they were still using it in the Falklands and even in the last Gulf War. I am so having this." She popped out the magazine, and pushed down on the rounds. She turned to him, clasping it to her chest and striking a pose. "This is the best present a girl could wish for."

"Now you're scaring me."

She shoved the Welrod into the waistband of her jeans and then hefted the Thompson in her hands and sniffed. "This has been cleaned recently. It's reeking of gun oil. And there's another smell I recognize."

"Yeah. Burnt propellant."

"Somebody's been firing weapons around here." She shone her torch into the corner of the room and saw an open door. She stepped over and flicked a light switch on the wall. As she stepped through, a bulb lit above the door, just over her head, and another on the far wall flickered into life. A knee-high line of sandbags lay halfway across the floor. The bulb illuminated as far as a 50 meter sign, then faded into darkness. "I've found the firing range."

Montrose ducked his head through. "Dead end."

"Yeah." She flicked off the light switch and turned back to the crates.

He looked down at the Thompson. "You know how to use that?"

"Mate, I'm expert level on *Day of Honor*. This is my personal weapon." She checked the safety catch and tried to make the magazine holders more comfortable around her neck. "But they don't tell you how heavy these things are in real life. Jesus..."

"Maybe you could..."

"What, find a more girly gun?"

"Kirsty..."

"If we go through that door and things get a bit fruity, I want to be holding a tommy gun, not a Glock 9mm pea shooter."

"I hear ya."

"So, you better get tooled up. Check the boxes."

"I... I've never fired any weapons other than a 9mm. Not all Yanks are gun nuts."

"Really? Have you ever played shoot-em-up computer games?"

"Not much, I..."

"Look, Connor, there's more to the internet than pornography. You got to live a little, you..."

They heard a noise behind the door.

Kirsty dropped the lid on the crate and ducked into the darkened doorway of the firing range. They looked out as strip lights buzzed into life over the crates, illuminating the cellar. She brought up the short barrel of the Thompson. They looked out from the darkness and saw two men enter the cellar.

The first man pulled the trolley towards the door. "Leave it open," he said. "The sooner we get this shit moved, the better. It's making me nervous." Both men pushed the trolley out the door.

The room returned to silence. Kirsty edged out and stood in front of the crates.

Montrose held the Glock in front of him. "We better be fast."

"You think they're here?" she said.

"The missiles?" He shrugged. "If they are, we just need to eyeball them then get the hell out. Pilgrim can take care of the rest."

Kirsty jammed the butt of the Thompson into her shoulder and stuck her head around the door. "Clear."

Montrose followed her into the low, stone corridor, and heard the familiar hum of computer equipment and the whirring of hundreds of small fans in server cabinets. "Machine room." At the end of the corridor they saw a long, dark room adjacent to the firing range, lined with server cabinets, glowing with thousands of pinprick lights.

"The Silk Road," said Kirsty.

"Wait." He pointed to the ground and a thick green cord running near the wall. "I've seen that before." He walked forward, following the cord until it came to the foot of a server cabinet.

Kirsty shook her head. "Are they running network cables along the floor? Very naughty."

"It's not a network cable," said Montrose. "It's det cord."

"What?"

"Detonation cord. It's filled with plastic explosive." He shone his torch down between the server cabinets, where the green cord looped in and out. "This place is wired to blow."

"Oh, shit."

He turned towards her, her face lit up by the thousands of tiny colored lights. "And I think we've got as long as it takes for those goons to load those boxes. After that I've got no idea."

"Then let's move. Missiles, yeah?"

"Yeah. But they're not gonna blow the place with missiles here."

"They're here or they're not. Let's just check this shit and go."

"I'm with ya." He backed out and down the corridor. "The trolley they used. We'll hear them coming."

"Wait." She held a finger to her mouth. "That's an elevator."

He heard the whine of the motors. "Yeah. Service elevator for the computers."

"And maybe missiles."

"Maybe."

She pointed to the end of the corridor then jerked a thumb right.

He nodded and crept towards the corner, then flattened his face against the wall and moved his head to the edge. He saw another corridor stretching around thirty feet. At the end a guard sat behind a small desk covered in security monitors, next to an elevator's wide steel doors. He heard the rumble of wheels and two men emerged to the left of the guard, each hauling two metal suitcases.

Faber walked into the room and shook his head.

"Nothing? Nothing at all?" Napier closed his eyes and looked up at the roof.

"Every one of those names has restrictions put on it. Files

locked, traces jammed. And as soon as we tried, we could see alerts going off all over the place."

Napier stood, forcing back the chair across the floor. "You know, if I was a cynic, and I am, then I'd say that it's as if someone knew we were going to look for those names. Someone called Campbell."

"A little bird told me he's on the warpath."

"I don't give a shit. He wants my job? If I don't stop those missiles, then I don't have a job." He pointed at Faber. "Remember, everything goes in my name."

"Understood. And appreciated, sir."

"You can come and visit me in prison. Bring beer."

Faber sat down. "What if Montrose, or whoever it is, sent them the same information? The same names?"

"And they set all those blocks up in time? I doubt it. And why would they do that? No, someone knew and blocked the search." He pulled the chair back and sat facing Faber over the table. "We're being taken for a ride. Washington is letting this happen. And I think Campbell is behind it. All of it."

"Sir, that can't be..." Faber looked down at the table. "They're going to let this happen, aren't they?"

Napier said nothing.

CHAPTER 23

Montrose pulled his head back from the edge of the wall. "Kirsty, I've found them."

"What?"

"Two men. Each hauling a suitcase. Just like Rome. They got in the elevator. I saw where they came from."

She lifted the Thompson.

"No, let them go. We only need to know for sure that the rest of the missiles are here. Taking out a few suitcases won't help."

"Okay." She lowered the barrel and they heard the elevator doors close. "We can use the explosives and det cord. Blow the place sky high."

"Det cord is not a like a fuse. That's not gonna work."

"What about the guard at the elevator?"

"We take him out. We need to see where those suitcases came from."

Kirsty moved forward and looked quickly around the corner. "Sorted." She swept the Thompson to the side and pulled the Welrod pistol from the waistband of her jeans, then tugged back the breech and loaded a round.

"Kirsty…"

She stepped out into the corridor and held the pistol in front of her, keeping it steady and walking quickly towards the man. She was halfway down the corridor before he looked up. The pistol coughed, and a red dot appeared on his forehead. He slumped beneath the desk.

"That went well." She nodded to the elevator. "They'll be back. We need to hide him."

"Kirsty." Montrose pointed through an open door, where they saw broken wooden crates stacked haphazardly against the wall, some stamped with Cyrillic script.

"There are no suitcases," said Kirsty.

"What?" He gazed around at the broken crates. All empty.

"No suitcases," she said. "They've used them all. Because there are no more missiles." She shook her head. "We're too late, Connor. We have to go." She ran back towards the elevator. "Bring him. The other goons will be back for the... Oh, Jesus. Look." She pointed to a TV screen by the desk. It showed a line of panel vans and trucks being loaded with suitcases.

"They're still here," said Montrose.

"We need Pilgrim. He can arrange an airstrike."

"You sure?"

"Connor, once those wagons start rolling, they'll be all over Germany in twenty minutes. We'll never get a better chance."

He pulled out his phone. "No signal."

Kirsty grabbed a phone on the desk and listened to the tone. "I've got an outside line. Give me Pilgrim's number."

He held up his phone. "Tell him it's compromised."

She dialed the digits. "He'll know."

"Let me talk…"

"Mr. Pilgrim? Listen to me carefully. We have no time. The missiles are here. They are being loaded onto trucks right now. They are ready to go. Your number is now compromised. We are leaving. Bomb my position. I repeat, bomb my position. Please confirm."

Montrose felt his mouth drop open.

"Understood," said Kirsty, and dropped the phone. "Connor, time to bugger off."

The elevator whined and they heard the car stop. Montrose looked down the corridor. He realized they'd never make it to the end without being spotted. "Missile room. Now!" He grabbed the guard by the coat and dragged him from behind the desk.

Kirsty ran in front and waited inside the door, then dragged the guard's corpse through as Montrose made it inside. The elevator pinged.

Montrose pulled out his Glock and listened to the sound of wheels in the corridor. "Let them take another load of crates. Then we go. If we start a shooting match they'll think they're being attacked and send the trucks out ASAP."

"Yeah. Connor, how long before NATO bombers get here?"

"Airbase in Germany. Five minutes? Ten? Depends if they're in the sky."

Kirsty lifted the barrel of the Thompson. "They'll be in the sky."

The technician leaned over the laptop and silenced the alarm.

"What is it?" said the Director. He fought the urge to run and slowly got to his feet.

Grigor Mikhailov placed his whisky glass on the boardroom table and stood up.

"The system has detected that a call was made to an outside number. It took a few minutes for the system to track down exactly where the call was made, but it was from the security guard's phone, next to the elevator door in the cellars. I have tried to contact him. There is no answer. And we have also detected an unauthorized cell phone on the wifi."

The Director walked to the window. "Has it penetrated the wifi?"

"No, sir. I can block it if required. But we have it triangulated to near where the outside call was made. The guard's station, near the elevator."

"You have the number that was called?"

"Yes, sir, it is recorded on the telephone system. It was registered in Italy three days ago."

The Director laughed.

Mikhailov walked around the table towards the technician. "Director, do you have a spy?"

"If we do, then they're too late. And rather reckless." He turned to the technician. "Block all outside calls."

"Yes, sir."

"And block all the cell phone masts within a mile of here. We can talk through wifi calling and the routers. I don't want this unknown cell phone finding a signal. Understood?"

"All outside calls are now disabled, sir. The phone masts will be cut in a few minutes, once their systems shut down."

"And what of the person who made the call?" asked Mikhailov.

"They are too late, whoever they are."

Mikhailov came closer. "And the missiles?"

The Director sat at the boardroom table, and waved an arm towards the window. "I've always enjoyed that view. Such a pity." He faced Mikhailov. "In ten minutes the trucks will disperse as planned to the agreed transfer points, and the drivers will destroy all evidence and disappear throughout Europe. They know the penalty for being caught."

"But what of the missiles? If the missiles don't reach…"

"It is of no consequence if most of the missiles are captured. It's not central to the objective. Ideally, we require just one to get through and take down a plane, but it's really not necessary. Cherry on the cake, you may say." He stood up and stared out of the window, towards the spires of Dresden. "Never under estimate the desire to return to the past. To rebuild. As we will rebuild."

"Where will you go?" asked Mikhailov.

"It matters not. We can bring up the Silk Road anywhere in the world. But next time, I am very much attracted to China. A truly great civilization. Endlessly fascinating. And always ready to do business." His phone rang and he held it to his ear.

A refined British voice spoke. "I've just had a message from MI6. An airstrike was ordered for this location. Rather unfortunate, really."

The calm demeanor of the British always infuriated the Director. He squeezed the phone tight in his hand. "It is indeed."

"However, I informed them that they were very much mistaken and were being fed false information."

"That is refreshing news."

"In fact, I told them that I was close to the location, having followed a tip-off from a Russian contact, and that they can tell the CIA that there is nothing here but warehouses full of nitrate fertilizer which would give the impression of being an arms dump if the CIA were idiot enough to bomb it. I made it clear that they were being duped by the Russians, and that there would be a number of innocent deaths. So, if they wanted to make their situation even worse, to go right ahead."

"Well, the fertilizer part is true. Do you think it will work?"

"Yes, for as long as we need. Which is not very long. I've just left the trucks, they require another ten minutes, then they can begin to leave. But what I want to know is how they found our location?"

"I believe," said the Director, smiling at Mikhailov, "we have a spy in our midst. A call was made from the guard's desk in the cellars, next to the elevator." He walked over to the technician. "And we have pinpointed their location using their cell phone."

"I'm on the way. I'll be there in a few minutes, send me the details. Whoever it is, they nearly succeeded. The CIA were in no mood to believe the news from MI6 that they were making a mistake. Only a high-level intervention stopped the attack."

"Interesting. One moment." He covered the mouthpiece. "Grigor, it will soon be time to leave. Join me in the truck park, our helicopter will be here soon."

Mikhailov walked towards the door, then turned. "This is a great day. The chaos in Moscow will be written in history. Of course, they'll send out a jamming code to help stop the missile attacks, but it will be too late. Our provisional government will make sure of that, and make sure who gets the blame." He pulled open the door and marched away.

The Director sighed and lifted the phone. "I swear if he hadn't left, I'd have shot him myself."

"Written in history, is that what he said?"

The Director laughed. "There's always a willing fool. He thinks he's the customer. Besides, there are only two seats on the helicopter. Do what you have to do. The helicopter will be here soon. I'll see you in the truck park in ten minutes."

CHAPTER 24

The elevator pinged. Montrose and Kirsty stood just inside the door of the missile room, their weapons raised. They heard a trolley being pushed into the elevator and the doors closing.

Kirsty made to look around the door, but the Thompson swung around her shoulders and clattered off the wall. She grabbed it and pulled it over her head, holding it out to Montrose. "Take this." She peered out. "All clear. Let's get the hell out of here." She moved quickly past the elevator and turned into the corridor towards the computer room. "Clear."

He had just followed her around the corner when a voice from behind stopped them dead.

"Stand still! Hands in the air! I swear I'll shoot you in the back."

Montrose looked at Kirsty. The Thompson was heavy in his hands. He glanced down, and saw the breech was pulled back, ready to fire. He looked up. It was six feet to the end of the corridor and the turn to the mannequin room.

"One of you might make it, but the other will die. So, make a choice. Who gets to live?"

The voice moved closer.

"And who gets to die?" Closer now. "Get your hands high in the air. Or I'll choose."

They lifted their arms. Montrose held the Thompson by the butt and held it high.

"Turn around."

They both turned slowly.

"Linden," said Montrose. "You fucking traitor. You worthless piece of ..."

"Oh, please, spare me the B-movie dialogue. My presence here is testament to the MI6 pension scheme, nothing else. The Director of this operation has been very generous. I have always thought that it's never treason if someone bids a higher price. It's one of the founding principles of the USA, I believe, and very much in evidence these days." Linden shrugged. "Every man has his price. And every man has his worth. Yours is exactly one million dollars." He pointed his gun at Kirsty. "Yours is not."

"Oh aye," she said, "is that right?"

"Ah, my Scottish friend. It's nice to meet you before your untimely demise."

"Welsh, actually, but listen, arsehole, if we stand here gossiping, you'll be joining us."

"Ah, of course, your little chat on the phone. And just soon after, would you believe, I received a message from London. They said they were going to bomb a site in Germany. Well, you can imagine how shocked I was. But not to worry, I soon put them right, and told them it was 'fake news' from that terrorist Connor Montrose. I must say, your reputation precedes you. The CIA were very grateful. I'm sorry to say that the fireworks party has been cancelled."

Montrose looked down at the green det cord along the edge of the corridor. "You do know that…"

"Of course I know, you fucking idiot. I'm going to watch it happen from a helicopter. Should be an excellent view. There are warehouses full of nitrate fertilizer and diesel fuel above us, so it will be quite a show. And I don't want to miss it." He levelled his gun at Montrose. "I just know you're going to play the hero, so you first. Drop your weapon."

"That's the first big mistake you've made," said Kirsty.

His eyes flicked towards Montrose's hand holding the butt of the Thompson. "Drop your weapon, or I shoot her. Right now."

"Relax," said Montrose. He took the pistol from his pocket and let it drop to the ground.

"Now, kick it to me."

Montrose didn't move.

Linden tightened his grip on his gun and jabbed it at Kirsty. "Don't fuck around. Kick it."

"Okay." Montrose jabbed a foot forward and the gun slid down the corridor.

"Now you," said Linden and nodded to Kirsty. "I know what you've tucked in your jeans, and it's not just your pert little bottom. Turn around and pull it out. Slowly."

She turned, dropped a hand to the back of her jeans, then wiggled her bottom.

"Just fucking do it, bitch."

"Well, there's no need for that kind of language, you slimey inbred cockweasel."

"Drop it!"

290

Kirsty pulled the Welrod from her waistband and holding it gently, placed it on the ground.

"Kick it to me."

She pushed it a few feet in front of her.

"Nice try," said Linden, "but I'll blow your pretty face off before you can reach it." He turned to Montrose. "Now you. Drop it."

"Really?" Montrose held the Thompson vertically, the muzzle pointing towards the roof. "This is an old open-bolt automatic weapon. It's cocked and locked with a full mag. If I drop it on its butt, what do you think is going to happen?"

Linden's eyes widened. "You…"

"Do you feel lucky?" said Montrose. His fingers slackened on the butt.

Napier dialed the only number on the screen. It rang several times and he wondered if it would be answered.

"Speak," said Saitsev.

"You know, I'm sure that the powers that be are wide awake and have computers listening to every channel they can, just waiting for someone to say a special combination of buzzwords that sets off alarm bells. Knowing that, if I were to impart information over an unsecured line, using those words, then that would be a terrible thing."

"I'm sure it would."

"But if I was to express my concern for some holidaymakers, whom I couldn't track down, you know, a list of friends of a man who recently passed away in a Mediterranean resort, that would work, yeah?"

"I'm sure it would. Do you think I know of this man's friends?"

"I don't know. Let's call him Boris. But you see, there's a lot I don't know, because I have their names from dead Boris' phone list, and my systems won't let me find out anything about them. Totally locked down, and I think to myself, why would that be?"

There was a pause on the line. "That is very strange. I think I know the men you mean. These friends of… Boris. It's a bit unsettling that you can't find out about their welfare. I'm sure you are worried."

"Yes, I am. And I'm thinking to myself, perhaps you should be more worried. Seems to me that they are being looked after by some of my friends in New York. Which is kind of them, but I wonder why?"

"It is indeed a mystery. Do you think their American friends are concerned for their welfare? These friends of Boris?"

"I don't know. But I get the feeling that someone loves them, and I can think of only one reason why. Because there's a lot of lost luggage out there. You don't know where it is. I don't know where it is. But I think Boris' friends know where it is. Otherwise, why would their friends in New York be so concerned for their welfare?"

"That is a very interesting opinion. And I know that one of Boris' friends left for Germany. That puzzled me, but now it makes sense, if he was looking for his luggage. Do you suspect that they are not playing for the home team?"

"Well, if they were, you would know. And you would know where the lost luggage is."

"That is true. So, if they are not on my team, that leaves only one other option."

"I think it does." Napier glanced up as Faber shoved open the door. "Happy hunting." He cut the call.

Faber stood before the desk. "Sir, an airstrike was called. A place in Germany, near Dresden."

"An airstrike?" Napier slipped the cell phone into his pocket.

"Yes. Then they cancelled it minutes later. It's crazy. The order came from the top."

"Why didn't I know…?"

Two men loomed in the doorway. "Director Napier, we are here to relieve you of your duties, on the orders of Director Campbell. You will remain in this room until further notice. A military guard will be placed outside. You may not communicate with anyone unless permitted to do so." The man strode forward, lifted the desk phone and disconnected it. "You will also hand over any cell phones, sir."

"There's only one." He pulled out a phone. "My official CIA device." He placed it on the table.

The man picked it up and headed for the door. "Director Campbell said to inform you he will call you very shortly and that you are to be immediately available."

"Well, how's he going to do that? Telepathy?"

"I will return with the phone, sir." He turned to Faber. "Director Napier is to be left alone."

Napier shrugged.

Faber followed the two men out and closed the door.

CHAPTER 25

Montrose lifted the Thompson until the muzzle almost touched the stone roof of the corridor.

"Don't be stupid," said Linden.

A low rumbling suddenly increased in intensity and they felt the air vibrate around them as a bomber roared overhead.

Linden stood with his mouth open as the sound receded, then cracked a smile. "Really, the Americans are the most gullible people on the planet." He pointed his gun at Montrose. "Put it down. Slowly."

"Make your mind up, dickhead. I thought you wanted me to drop it?"

Montrose flicked his eyes towards Kirsty and he turned the Thompson slightly to conceal his thumb moving towards the safety catch.

Kirsty lifted the magazines looped around her neck and held them out in front of her, letting them swing in the air.

Linden flinched and stepped back. "I won't tell you again, Montrose. Lay it down, with the muzzle pointing towards you. Or I will shoot her in the guts and hand her over to the guards. And you, bitch, lay the magazines down."

"Oh, well," said Kirsty, turning to Montrose, "when you put it like that," she flicked her eyes towards the mannequin room, "how can a girl refuse? Why don't you talk to me like that, Connor? I find it so…" She swung the magazines in a tight loop around her hand as Montrose threw the butt of the Thompson to the ground. It slammed into the stone and a burst of fire spewed from the barrel of the Thompson, spraying into the roof, scattering shards of stone and hot metal around them.

Montrose lunged for the Welrod, pushing Kirsty down the corridor. "Cover!"

Linden threw himself to the ground and fired blind, but the bullet smacked into the spare magazines, wrenching them from Kirsty's grip as she rounded the corner.

Montrose grabbed the Welrod and saw Linden swing his gun towards him. He squeezed the trigger as Linden rolled to the side. The bullet spattered off the wall as Montrose turned and ran.

Just around the corner, he almost tripped over Kirsty as she lay on the ground, trying to untangle the det cord around her ankle. He grabbed her and the det cord and hauled her into the mannequin room.

Kirsty pulled the cord free from her legs. "Get me a gun!"

"Take this," he said, and handed her the Welrod. "Make sure he doesn't come through that door."

"Connor, we have to…"

He jerked a thumb to where the room stretched away before them, lined with empty cabinets and discarded mannequins. "Too far. And we're outgunned. We'll never make it." He grabbed the det cord and looped it in his hands. "Just make sure he doesn't come through that door."

Kirsty jammed herself against the wall and brought up the Welrod. "He's got a fucking machine gun." She watched Montrose run for the door to the firing range. "Connor, that's a dead end!"

"I know, just keep him busy." He switched off the light and the doorway fell into darkness.

She stared at the door to the corridor and brought up the Welrod, then saw the muzzle of the Thompson appear. A cabinet exploded in a cloud of glass and the muzzle disappeared. She heard Linden's voice.

"Pointless, Montrose. Brave, but absolutely pointless. You know how this is going to end."

"Yeah?" said Kirsty. "You telling fortunes now? Reading fucking tea leaves? You tell me, you piece of shit traitor, how's it going to end?"

"Sweetheart, I've got several of your magazines here. You've got a World War Two peashooter. Very handy for slotting a Nazi on the Paris Metro in a dark tunnel, but not what you'd call the best weapon for a firefight."

"You reckon? It only takes one round in your head and the game's over. And you stick your head in here and I'll slot you before you ever see my face. Remind me, does the Queen still hang traitors? You know, the Tower of London? A trip through Traitor's Gate?"

"Don't give me..." The muzzle of the Thompson appeared again at the edge of the door and gouts of fire spewed out just feet from her head. Cabinets shattered and mannequins jumped lifeless into the air as bullets sprayed across the room.

"Kirsty!"

She glanced behind her.

Montrose stuck his head around the door in the firing range. "In here. Now."

She edged back towards the doorway, the Welrod extended. A hand pulled her into darkness.

"Keep your head down. Follow the torch beam." He stuck his head out the door and groaned loudly. "Kirsty! Help me!" Then he turned and shone his phone down the range and pushed her forward.

They scrambled across the gritty cement floor and dropped behind a line of sandbags set under the 50 metre sign. "Give me your phone," he said. "Open the camera and set it to infra-red."

She pulled it out and set the camera and he lifted her hand to the edge of the sandbags, then pointed it towards the door. The screen was blank. Darkness settled around them.

A burst of fire came through the door and the screen lit up with tiny white dots. They could hear Linden.

"Bad choice. You're in a firing range. And a dead end. It looks like I'll get to practice on some live targets. What fun!" The screen lit up again with another burst, and the muzzle showed white as he entered the doorway and switched on the light.

The det cord jammed into the light socket above the door detonated in a blinding flash. The remaining lightbulb blinked weakly into life.

Montrose ran over to the body. The det cord had blown just above Linden's head and sheered his face from his skull. "Don't look. It's not a pretty sight."

Kirsty stepped past him. "Looks pretty good to me." She pushed aside smoldering scraps of flesh and cloth and tugged open Linden's jacket, checking the pockets. She pulled out a cell phone, but the screen was shattered and the casing cracked. "Shit. We're going to have to get out of the cellars before we call Pilgrim." She pulled the bloodied strap of the Thompson over what was left of Linden's head and loaded another magazine. "Time to go. I don't want to be here when the bombers get back."

The door opened. Napier watched the man enter the room, carrying a speakerphone. He connected it and left without saying a word. It began to ring and he watched it for a few moments, then hit a button. The screen on the wall flickered into life. He saw Campbell looking down at notes on his desk.

He started talking without looking up. "Napier, I'm going to give you one last chance."

Napier leaned back in the chair. "Shove it up your ass."

Campbell glared at the screen. "You don't seem to appreciate the gravity of your situation."

"Sure I do. I've had a gun pointed at me many times, and by better men than a desk jockey shitstain like you. Anyone ever point a gun at you? I don't think so. Though I bet you've had a few nasty paper cuts, eh?" Napier began to laugh.

"Director Napier, this operation…"

"Your operation, Campbell." He sat up and pointed a finger at the screen. "Your operation. I've been playing catch up from the start. You already knew all the contacts in Blokhin's phone. Big surprise to me, but not to you. Because you didn't get it from us. We tried to access the files before we gave you the names and you had already blocked them. Now, why would you do that? How could you possibly know?"

"Napier, there could be many…"

"Oh, fuck off. You must have crapped yourself when we found those names. Because the next thing I know is I'm off the operation and I've got goons in here taking away my phone and locking me in an office."

Campbell sighed. "I have no interest in your amateurish conspiracy theories. If I were in your precarious position, I would be…"

"You gonna kill me?"

"What?"

"You're gonna have to kill me. It's the only way to shut me up. You knew about Blokhin. You knew about his friends. It doesn't take much to work out that you knew it all. You are up to your neck in…" He heard the squeak of Campbell's chair as it was shoved back.

"Shut up! You stupid amateur! I warned you before, you take me on and I will crush you! And when I am finished you will be legendary throughout the CIA and beyond, as the idiot who was responsible for the deaths of thousands. So, how brave do you feel now?"

"Bring it on, shithead."

Campbell stared at the screen. "You really have to wise up, Napier. You think this is a personal conflict with me, but you are facing an oncoming train of pain. This is one of the most ambitious projects ever undertaken by the CIA. You're just a noisy cog in a huge machine, so it's time you got on board and do exactly as I say. I hold your reputation and career in the palm of my hand."

"Squeeze. See what happens."

"Napier, we are on the brink of controlling Moscow. Our friends are in position. We will have the Russian bear by the balls. Then you can do the squeezing. Any time you like. How do you think you would feel?"

"Nauseous, to be frank. I think you took that analogy a step too far."

Campbell shook his head. "Enough. Time for you to choose. You win or lose. And think of the prize. Once the Russian government falls, as it surely will, we will be ready to move. No government will be able to stand the diplomatic pressure that will come to bear. They will be seen as pariahs, murderers, fueled by hatred of the west, driven to sponsoring terror throughout the Middle East and Balkans."

"So, what's new? They've been doing that for seventy years."

"Not live on YouTube they haven't. The world has changed."

"And you'll let innocent…"

"Napier, you were once a soldier. We're at war with the Russians. We always have been. People die. A friend of mine told me this quote recently, from a great American, General Patton. He said, 'The object of war is not to die for your country, but to make the other bastard die for his.' We are going to make sure that happens."

"By letting innocent people die?"

"Napier, the whole world will be screaming at Moscow to release the missile software so that they can be stopped. And they will release the code. If they don't, then the new government will." He leaned forward. "We are so close, Napier. It's time for you to choose."

"How many?"

"What?" Campbell looked blankly at the screen. "How many what?"

"How many people have to die before they release the codes and work out a way to stop the missiles. How many?"

Campbell sat back. "I'm wasting my time."

"Got another question for you." Napier stood up and walked towards the screen. "We got a report stating where the missiles were located. A place in Germany. We were going to bomb it but the attack was called off. Why?"

Campbell shrugged and looked down at his notes. "False information. Someone panicking."

"Someone must have been pretty sure to load two fucking bombers and send them to drop their payload on a NATO country."

Campbell got up. "I have no time for this. Make a choice. You are in or out. In, you keep quiet and do what you're told. Out, and you'll go down in history as an incompetent responsible for thousands of deaths. Your choice, make your move."

Napier walked straight up to the screen. "Go fuck yourself."

The screen darkened. The door opened and a man entered and disconnected the phone.

Faber stood in the doorway.

"No visitors," said the man.

"Hey, I'm just bringing him a coffee." He held up a paper cup.

"Okay."

Napier sat behind the table.

Faber placed the cup on front of him.

"Sir, you need anything?"

Napier kept his voice low. "Go away." He watched the

man with the phone, standing in the doorway, trying to listen.

"Sir?" said Faber.

"Go away. I want you to go away, and be with someone who will be a witness to the fact that you were not with me in five minutes time. Clear?"

"Yes, sir."

Napier leaned back in the chair. *"Alea iacta est."*

"Sir?"

"It's what Julius Caesar said when he crossed the Rubicon river, and led his army into Rome. Such an act was treason. It means 'the die is cast'."

Faber said nothing.

"You're a good man. Go. Now."

Faber nodded and turned away.

Napier watched the door close and heard the key turn in the lock. He took out the phone from his pocket, held it in his hand for a moment, then chose the only number in the contact list. It was answered immediately. "Dimitri? We need to talk."

Saitsev cut the call. He looked up to the ceiling, clasped his hands behind his back, then began to breathe slowly. He closed his eyes.

"Sir? The team is in place. They have surrounded the dacha. Security has been suppressed. They are awaiting orders."

Saitsev didn't answer. He let his lungs empty, then slowly sucked in air. He knew he'd remember this moment. For good or for bad. When he spoke, it was almost a whisper. "Kill them all. God will know his own."

"Sir?"

He opened his eyes and turned to the table. "Kill them all. All the traitors. The spies, the money men, the pederasts, the gangsters and the generals. Clear the temple. Kill them all. No one in that *dacha* is to come out alive. No one."

The man spoke quietly into the phone and gave the order.

Saitsev closed his eyes again. "And the cargo plane?"

"Circling just outside the area, sir. They are being questioned by Dresden airport. So far, they have not responded. They have lined up their flight path as instructed."

"Understood."

"Sir, that flight path is taking them away from Dresden airport. Do they have another airstrip they can use?"

Saitsev didn't look at him. "No. They don't. Tell the pilots to unseal their orders."

CHAPTER 26

Branches whipped against his face and he brought up his arms to shield himself and charged into the road. He caught up with Kirsty as she grabbed the key of the Porsche and jumped into the driver's seat.

"Anything?" she said.

He brought up his cell phone. "Nothing. No signal."

"Get in." Kirsty fired up the Porsche and had the wheels spinning before he could close the door. She wrestled the steering wheel as the car's hood snaked from side to side, then straightened up when the tires bit into the tarmac. She floored the throttle, keeping it hard down and hauled back on the gear lever every time the engine hit the rev limiter, and each time the Porsche took a lurch forward.

Montrose held the phone in front of his face, aware of trees flashing close by his window. He glanced over at the speedometer. It registered over 200 kilometers per hour.

"Now?" Kirsty held her arms tight on the wheel.

"Not yet. They must have disabled all the cell masts. We need to get in range of..." The signal indicator flickered then showed five bars. He was just about to shout when the phone rang in his hand.

Kirsty stood on the brakes.

The phone flew out of his hand and into the footwell. Montrose was pinned against his seatbelt. Within seconds, the car had slid to a halt. He stared at the ringing phone. He looked at Kirsty.

"Answer it. I'll call Pilgrim and get the bombers back."

The ringing stopped. "Who the fuck was that? Nobody else has got this number." He undid the belt and reached down.

Kirsty ignored him and dialed her phone. "Mr. Pilgrim. Get the bombers back. Linden cancelled the bombing. He was a traitor. He's dead." She thumbed the loudspeaker.

"I'll try," said Pilgrim, "but even if they are in the air, and I assume they are, it may take ten or fifteen minutes."

"That's too long," said Kirsty. "They are ready to go. They might get some, but they're gonna need an army to shut down the whole of eastern Germany."

The phone rang in Montrose's hand. He pressed the loudspeaker button.

A voice came over the line. "Linden? Are you there?"

Montrose looked at Kirsty and grinned. "Linden? Oh, man," he said, "have I got bad news for you. You must be Linden's new boss, Mr. Director. The man who was going to top up his pension fund."

The voice became shrill. "Where is Linden?"

"He's in the cellars, with half his fucking head missing."

There was silence on the line. "Who…?"

They heard the rotors of an approaching helicopter and Kirsty got out of the car and stared down the road.

Montrose shoved open his door as a dark blue helicopter

flew low over their heads, following the road towards Rhiandorf. "He said he was going to take a little trip with you. Guess now you're on your own."

"Montrose?"

"Yeah. Let me guess. You're another member of my fan club."

Kirsty nudged him with her elbow and pointed to the sky. From the east, a cargo plane descended slowly, and below it two parachutes drifted towards the ground.

"You are the luckiest man alive, Montrose. But it won't last forever. I have directed my men to bring me your head. Literally, your head on my desk. It's only a matter of time. There is nowhere in the world you can hide."

"Whatever. I'm going to make one phone call and you and your crummy warehouses will be blown to shit."

Kirsty watched the parachutes drift below the tree line and out of sight. The cargo plane slipped lower in the sky.

"Too late, Montrose. By that time I'll be far away from here."

"You think so? That's some strategy, asshole. They'll find the missiles. They are going to close this whole country down, every road, every…"

"Who cares, you idiot! It only needs one missile to get out of here! And they are just about to leave. Really, I'm surrounded by imbeciles and amateurs. Strategy, you say? I have forgotten more about strategy that you will ever know."

Kirsty nudged Montrose and pointed to the cargo plane, then traced her finger through the sky and down the road to Rhiandorf. "He can't see it. He's below the tree line."

"I think I'll have your severed head delivered to me in an

ice bucket," said the Director. "Then I'll probably feed it to a stray dog. Anyway, I must go, I have work to do."

"I'll find you."

"You will die before you get anywhere near me…"

"I know where you are now." There was silence on the line. "I can hear a helicopter approaching through your phone. The one that just flew over our heads."

Kirsty stood with her mouth open, watching the cargo plane as it came lower. "That's Russian. Oh, my God. The wheels aren't down."

Montrose said nothing as it approached. It would be over their heads in seconds. He felt the phone slip in his hand and grabbed it tight. "Oh, man," he said. "You are so unbelievably fucked. And you can't see it."

"I have no more time for this nonsense. Goodbye, Montrose. We have to bring this operation to a conclusion, but it really has worked out rather well. Yours, on the other hand, has been a complete failure."

"Oh, yeah?" The roar of the cargo plane echoed around the forest. "I forgot. You're the master planner." The sound of the helicopter came down the line, its rotors slowing to a halt.

Kirsty pointed to the Porsche. "Get in!"

The Director laughed. *Let your plans be dark and impenetrable as night, and when you move, fall like a thunderbolt*. Do you know who said that? Sun Tzu, in T*he Art of War*, written over two and a half thousand years ago. I would recommend you study the classics, Montrose, but it's a bit late for you."

The cargo plane's screaming engines came closer and Montrose shouted into the phone. "Yeah? Well I got one for you. Mike Tyson. *Everyone has a plan 'till they get punched in the mouth*. Look up, asshole." He ran for the car, slamming the door shut as Kirsty hit the accelerator. He could hear the Director's screams just before they were drowned out by the noise of the jet engines, and a fireball blew past their windows, the shockwave slamming into the back of the car.

Kirsty held on tight, twisting the wheel to keep the Porsche in a straight line. A thick black cloud engulfed them before they emerged onto a clear stretch of road. She kept her foot down until the shadow filling her rear-view mirror faded away. She pulled the Porsche into the side and got out.

Montrose stood beside her. The forest was on fire and flames climbed high above the trees.

"I hope they're safe," she said.

He turned towards her.

"The bodies. The people. The soldiers and the children."

"Yeah. I hope so." He walked back to the Porsche. "We should go."

"I know."

She got in the car and pulled the door closed, then sat very still, her hands gripping the wheel. She stared into the distance.

Montrose got in beside her. "Which way? North to Poland? South to Bohemia?"

She reached over to the rear parcel shelf and grabbed the sunglasses, handed him a pair then slipped hers on. "Connor, have you ever seen *The Blues Brothers*?"

"The movie? John Belushi? Yeah."

She flexed her fingers on the wheel. "It's seven hundred miles to Monaco. We've got two fake credit cards, two fake IDs, three thousand Euros in cash, an eighty-year-old automatic weapon with three magazines and the quietest assassination pistol ever made."

Montrose could hear the roar of the forest burning behind him. He pulled the door closed.

"And there's a club full of pedophiles ready to reopen for business. I need a very sharp knife, four pounds of plastic explosive and a big bag of ball bearings."

He nodded. "Amazon?"

"No," said Kirsty. "Priti."

Montrose pushed on his sunglasses and pointed down the road. "Hit it."